Casting Lots

A Christian Novel by

James J. Stewart

ISBN: 978-0-9861334-4-2

Other books by James J. Stewart available at
Amazon.com and CreateSpace.com:

Gaardian Tales (Christian Fiction)
Life Before Conception
Starlight Adventures
The Still Small Voice
Stepping Beyond
The Gaardian Saga [The four above in one volume]

Other Christian Fiction
Tom's Town

Poetry and Inspiration
Faith and Yosemite [Christian poetry with pictures]
Faith Fuel
Lasting Love
Walking in Faith

Yosemite Picture Books
Ever-Changing Yosemite Valley
Faith and Yosemite [see above]
Portraits of El Capitan
Portraits of Half Dome
Starlight Over Yosemite

1.

It was Richard's eighteenth birthday. He was a prodigy at the piano, and he had taken his first lesson just after his fourth birthday. Typically, he practiced two hours a day. He was celebrating his natal day with a Sunday night dinner at his favorite restaurant with his girlfriend, his parents, and her parents. Lawson's Restaurant was right on the beach in La Jolla. His parents, Debby and Bob Donovan, always took him out to eat on his birthday. His older brother, Josh, was somewhere in the world with the CIA. Richard's girlfriend, Charlotte – "Char" – Hickman, was going to have her birthday in September. Char had an older sister, Abby, who was married and living in another state. Her parents, Joseph and Marie, really liked Richard.

Lawson's was unique in so many ways. There was a full moon that evening, and the roof had been retracted. Everyone could see the moon and stars coming out as the sun finally set. The Pacific Ocean's waves were crashing on the beach less than a dozen feet from the window beside their table. Lawson's served only prime rib. Customers decided how much prime rib they wanted, and then what veggies and other side dishes they wanted with their beef.

Char sat next to Richard, and they adored one another. They had started dating more than three years earlier, though they had known each other since they were children. She had practically deafened him over lunch as she screamed "Yes!" when he asked her to marry him that afternoon. They decided to announce it to their parents over dinner. Now was the time. Char quietly slipped her engagement ring on her finger on her lap, and then she nudged Richard. He cleared his throat. "This afternoon I asked Char to marry me, and she said yes." As their parents began congratulating them all at once, Char extended her left hand, showing off her half-carat solitaire.

She was not just smiling – she was glowing. "We've been talking all afternoon about when we want to have the ceremony. We're graduating in three weeks, and four days later Richard starts his European concert tour."

Richard nodded. "I did not want to start the tour without her, so I've asked her to join me and make it part of our honeymoon." Their parents' eyes got bigger. "About an hour ago I got a call from Jessie at Ticket Blogger. He has pulled some strings and gotten us a suite at the Amangani Hotel in Jackson Hole for the weekend after we have graduated."

Char smiled. "I talked to Pastor Barry today, and he says he'll do our ceremony at the church on Saturday morning after we graduate, but we have to squeeze in three sessions of pre-marital counseling between now and then."

Bob asked, "When will you fly to London? Will we see you off from here in San Diego?"

Richard smiled. "You will see us off from here in San Diego as we leave on our honeymoon. Ticket Blogger is paying our way to fly first class directly from Jackson Hole to London. We will arrive there on Monday, and after we get a night's rest at the hotel, I'll go over to the Royal Festival Hall to practice. I'll get ready on the piano that I'll be using that weekend with the London Philharmonic. First rehearsal will be Wednesday for the performances on the weekend. We'll have a two-day break, and then I'll do a recorded solo performance for the BBC. After that we will be off to Paris and Rome."

Marie smiled. "It sounds like my precious daughter is going to be even more of a concert groupie with her favorite prodigy!"

Char grinned. "Absolutely! From the very beginning, I've known that the piano will be Richard's mistress, but wherever we can find two pianos, we can play together for relaxation, just as we do now. I can't compete with his mistress, but we can sure have fun together!"

Richard shook his head. "Actually, I think Char is every bit as good as I am, only she doesn't do classical music, and she prefers the electronic keyboard."

Their waiter brought the salad cart, and as he fixed their salads for them, conversation ceased. They focused on getting the ingredients and dressings they wanted. The sun was well below the horizon as they held hands for a short prayer before they began eating. Joseph ordered a bottle of sparkling cider, and it was delivered just before the entrée cart arrived at their table. They were in no hurry, and their leisurely dinner continued to well past ten.

+ + +

Those final three weeks of high school were a whirlwind of activity for both. In addition to finals and graduation, Char and Richard worked the three wedding conferences into their schedule. When they took the Taylor-Johnson temperament profile, and they were not surprised to see how well they knew each other.

On Monday, they were invited to a party by some of their school friends, but they declined. When Char had talked to some of her friends, she found out that there were not going to be any adults present. She told Richard, and they decided that they were not ready to add their first hangovers to their schedule. When their church youth group announced a graduation party at their church, they readily agreed.

The prom needed some discussion. Friday night after dinner, they sat on a bench overlooking the ocean. The moon was waning, but it still seemed almost full. Char squeezed Richard's hand. "I've been thinking about the prom."

"So have I," he said, nodding. "I made most of our plans before we got engaged."

She smiled. "I want to spend the evening dancing with you, but do we really need to go out to dinner first?"

"Not if you don't want to."

She nodded. "None of our friends know that we're getting married the following weekend. Why don't you pick me up at 7:30? We'll go to the prom, and we'll go home. We have to be at the church early the next morning to go over the wedding ceremony with Rev. Hanna."

Richard nodded. "I'm glad that you're thinking this way. I'm doing additional practice to get ready for London. I could use the extra time before the wedding and our honeymoon. I'll pick you up at 7:30. I'll have a corsage for you. Do you want to pin it on your dress or wear it on your wrist?"

Char grinned. "I'll definitely have to wear it on my wrist. My dress is strapless."

He leaned over and kissed her. "I've never seen you in a strapless dress before. It ought to be a treat for my eyes." They kissed for a while, and then he took her home. At her door, he said, "I'll pick you up at 7:00 tomorrow for our youth group party. I'm going to wear denims and a jacket with that western sport shirt you gave me for my birthday. We should take our swimsuits."

Char smiled. "I think you'll look good in that shirt and denims. I'll be casual, and I'll bring my swimsuit, but I'm not sure what else I'll wear yet. I'll see you tomorrow." They kissed once again, and then she went inside.

Saturday evening's pool party for the church youth group included a few surprises. Most of the kids had not been there before because Jack and Cheryl Wyle had only joined the church two months earlier. In addition to a thirty by fifty-foot pool, there was a tennis court, and there were two regulation-size pool tables in a large room over the garage. The patio area had a huge gas-fired barbeque, along with a commercial refrigerator. There seemed to be unlimited hamburgers, hot dogs, and everything else needed to keep the kids well fed for the evening.

Two of the five original bedrooms in the house had been converted into a home theater with a huge screen and impressive sound system. Although a few of them watched a movie, most of them stayed by the pool.

About half of the forty or so kids there were seniors. There were also eight adults, though the majority of them stayed in generally in the background. When Richard and Char began saying good night, the rest of the kids decided they needed to go home as well. After profuse thanks expressed to the Wyles, the house became quiet around 1:00 AM Sunday morning.

Richard and Char had to rehearse with the church's praise team the next morning, so they both got only a little more than five hours sleep. With Richard doing extra practicing and Char getting ready for both the prom and the wedding, that entire week was one of little sleep.

+ + +

When Richard rang the doorbell on Friday night, Char's father answered the door. "Good evening, Richard." They shook hands. "Is that tux yours, or did you rent it?"

"Good evening, Mr. Hickman. It's mine."

"It's sharp. I like it."

Char came around the corner from a hallway. "Hi there, handsome!" She smiled.

It took a moment for Richard to find his voice. "Hi there, gorgeous!" He grinned. In his left hand was a small box. He held it out to her. "Here's the corsage I promised you." He helped her open it.

Marie Hickman came from the same direction as her daughter. "Good evening Richard. Let me help you two with that." She snapped the strap around Char's wrist. "It's beautiful, isn't it Char?"

"Yes, it is."

Richard was still smiling. "You look absolutely amazing in that dress! It's even nicer than the one you wore as homecoming queen!"

Char turned slightly pink. "Thank you."

Joe nodded his head towards the curb at the front of the house. "Did you rent that white limo?"

Richard grinned. "Absolutely! We'll have the same driver taking us to the airport after the wedding."

Smiling, Char said, "Awesome! Let's get going." She kissed her parents, as Richard hugged Marie and shook Joe's hand. Then they walked down the sidewalk to the waiting limousine.

When the driver closed their door, Richard said softly, "How am I going to keep my hands off of you until the wedding next weekend?"

Char smiled and nodded. "Looking at you, I can better understand now why so many couples make extravagant plans for the rest of the night after the dancing is over." She leaned over and kissed him on the cheek. "I'll be thinking about what you just said every moment, until right after our pastor pronounces us husband and wife."

It was several miles from Char's house to the prom. It was held in the ballroom of the Hilton Hotel in San Diego. As they walked into the lobby outside of the ballroom, they saw a few couples entering the lobby from the elevators. They had little time to talk about that though, as they began greeting the other couples. They went in as the band began to play.

After about an hour, the principal, Vernon Knopp, went to the microphone. "Good evening. We've heard several people asking for some classic-rock music. I know that Richard Donovan is here with his fiancé, Char Hickman. Richard, there's a Steinway grand backstage.

If they roll it out for you, could you do your thing that you do so well, if we have Char get on the electronic keyboard? How about it?"

There were applause and cheers. Richard looked at Char. She nodded, and they headed for the stage. After kicking things off with "Rock Around the Clock," they did some of the biggest hits of The Beatles, Elvis Presley, Michael Jackson, Madonna, Elton John, Led Zeppelin, Pink Floyd, and The Carpenters. After a little over an hour, Richard asked the band to continue playing "Close to You," while he and Char returned to the dance floor to dance. By the time Char was safe at home, and Richard had paid their driver, it was after 2:00 AM. Even after sleeping in up to almost 8:30 AM, Richard could hardly get out of bed for breakfast Saturday morning.

Sunday night was another first for Richard and Char. They returned to the same ballroom at the Hilton Hotel, only this time it was for a dinner concert to benefit Samaritan's Purse Disaster Relief. Richard and Char did not know how much the dinners were, because for them, their plates were free. The hotel wrote off the cost of the entire delicious dinner as a tax-deductable donation, and at Richard's request, they had brought in a Baldwin SD-10 concert grand piano for him to play.

For the first hour, Richard played music by J. S. Bach, Amadeus Mozart, Frederick Chopin, Ludwig van Beethoven, Johannes Brahms, Claude Debussy, George Gershwin, and Sergi Rachmaninoff. Then he went to a microphone. "As all of you know, this concert is a benefit for Samaritan's Purse. After a fifteen-minute intermission, this dinner and concert are going to take a very different turn. Some of you think you know what is going to happen. I assure you, it is going to be even more exciting." He looked at his watch. "Fourteen minutes from now, it will be best if you are back in your seats."

While the audience took a break, a stage crew moved the piano on its dolly to the left side of the stage, and music stands and chairs were arranged on the stage. Additionally, rolled out onto the stage was a platform containing a trap set, along with a xylophone, a vibraphone, and a two-tier electronic keyboard set. There were the sounds of other instruments coming from behind the stage curtain.

When Richard returned to the stage, he brought Char with him. Silence descended over the entire ballroom. "Ladies and gentlemen, this beautiful young lady is my fiancé, Char Hickman. She will be at the electronic keyboards for our second and final set of music this evening. As most of you know, California is blessed with some wonderful music schools. A year ago, Char and I sent letters to several of those schools, announcing this concert. We asked each of those schools to supply us with one or two faculty members to play their own instruments in a jam session." There were quiet murmurs in the audience. "On each of those music stands," Richard pointed, "there are cue sheets for several pieces in a variety of styles covering rock and roll, country, folk, and jazz. This is unrehearsed, so if this is disastrous, everyone can blame the new kids on the block – Char and I." He pointed at himself and gestured towards Char.

He smiled, as there was quiet laughter.

"Under your plates this evening, there are small yellow envelopes, labeled, 'Do not open until you are told to do so.' You may do so now or later, that is your choice. Inside is a list of all the musicians, and the eleven schools they represent, that will join us at this moment on the stage. If you please, welcome them now, and then we will begin." As the audience began to stand and applaud, the other musicians joined them on stage.

For the next eighty-eight minutes, the event was amazingly casual. The audience clapped, stomped their feet, and sang along. Some couples got up and danced beside their tables. According to reporters from the various media, no one in Southern California's entertainment industry had ever seen anything quite like it, or anything even remotely similar.

When it was over, people continued to mill around for more than two hours. They talked to several journalists from various media. Both Richard a Char had less than three hours of sleep before they had to get up and go to school the next day, but there were only four days until their graduation.

At the end of the week, as hundreds of people celebrated behind the stadium after the graduation ceremony, both families were silent with regard to their plans for Saturday morning's wedding. Char and Richard wanted to tell their friends about their plans. As they told each other repeatedly, however, "A secret is a secret is a secret." Their parents had other plans, nevertheless.

That night, while Char tossed and turned, Richard slept soundly.

"Dad, why do you and Mom like playing jazz together so much?"

"There are at least two reasons. First, your Mom and I love each other, and so we love doing things together."

"What's the other reason?"

"Someday you'll see how jazz lets us express our emotions musically so that we connect with others through the music."

"Am I going to be a keyboard player someday like you and Mom?"

"I don't know, son. If you enjoy making music for others, do it, but didn't you say wanted to be an astronomer?"

2.

The morning skies were clear and bright. Though everyone knew they were engaged, the wedding was supposedly a secret. Char had rented a wedding dress, and shortly after 8:00 AM, she went to the church with her Mom to get ready. The "Bride's Room" was the church library, just down the hall from the rear of the worship area. Pastor Barry Snow said he would do the ceremony at 9:00 AM. He met with Richard in his office at 8:30, where he put on tuxedo pants and a white dinner jacket. The office was behind the stage of the worship area, and Pastor Barry put on a CD recording of Arthur Rubenstein playing Chopin waltzes while they got ready.

Char did not think she needed a full hour to get ready, but Marie fussed over every detail of her look until just a minute or so before 9:00. There was a knock on the door, and Marie opened it to her husband. "Doesn't she look great, Joe?"

Her father's smile filled his face. "Wonderfully! Is my daughter ready?"

Char nodded. "Ready as I'll ever be, Dad!"

"Good. There's a little change in the ceremony."

"What's that?"

"Me!" Char's sister, Abby, came through the door.

"Abby! I thought you said that you and James couldn't make it!"

They hugged. "There's no way James and I could miss this!" Abby looked her sister up and down. "That's even better than my dress was! It's amazing!"

"Thanks!"

"Mom, you can go on in. After Dad gives Char away, he'll sit with you and James." Abby opened the door for her mother.

Marie kissed Char on the cheek and left the room. "Josh, Richard's older brother, is going to be best man instead of Mr. Donovan." Char's eyes grew wide. "He flew in late last night from who knows where. I'm going to be your matron of honor instead of Mom."

Char beamed. "I'm so glad you're here!"

"I am too."

There was another knock on the door, and Mrs. Snow came in. "Abby, it's time for you to start down the aisle. I'll bring your sister in a moment."

"Okay." Abby kissed Char on the cheek and left.

Char turned and looked at herself in a floor-to-ceiling mirror one more time. "This is turning out to be even more exciting than we planned."

The pastor's wife nodded. "Come on. I'll open the door into the worship area for you. When I do, just walk through and have your special day."

Char nodded, and they left the Bride's Room. She was quiet and calm as she went down the hallway. Mrs. Snow went ahead, and she had her hand on the door handle as Char approached and stopped. Mrs. Snow asked, "Ready?"

Char took a deep breath, let it out, and nodded.

As the door was opened, Char froze, her eyes grew wide, and she put her gloved hands over her mouth. The church was full of people who had silently snuck in while she and Richard were getting ready. Putting her hands down to her side, tears of joy cascaded over her smiling face as she started forward to the sounds of a Chopin Nocturne being played on the piano.

As she slowly walked down the aisle, she looked around. It was not just their church family. Their classmates from school were there, and many were standing because the seats were full. Some of her friends waved silently, and she grinned and waved back.

It was all recorded on video, set up by professional videographers who were friends of Richard's brother,

Josh. The front of the church was banked with red roses supplied by Abby and Josh.

For both Char and Richard, everything happened through a haze of joy, just as they had rehearsed with Pastor Barry. They heard him say, "I now pronounce you husband and wife. You may now kiss." The world around them seemed to disappear for a moment. Then he said, "I am pleased to now present to all of this church family and friends, Richard and Charlotte Donovan!" There were cheers along with the applause.

Arm in arm, they walked up the aisle, and everyone else followed. When they got to the recreation area down a long hallway, there was another surprise. Carl Hashinger, a member of the church and owner of Hashinger's Restaurant, had prepared a buffet of gourmet finger food, including a four-foot-tall muffin tree and decorative arrangements of fruit-kabobs.

Char had designed wedding announcements and arranged to have them printed a week earlier, not knowing the plans being made by her their parents. While Richard's brother arranged with his friends to edit the video and make video disks to go in the envelope with the announcements, Abby worked to make the announcements to go together with the video disks. The wedding disks would be duplicated and sent out the following week with the announcements while Richard and Char were in London.

Since their flight was shortly after 2:00 o'clock, and they had to go through airport security, it was about 10:30 when Char and Richard changed into their traveling clothes and ran through a shower of birdseed to their waiting white limo. Their families followed in their own cars to the airport to see them off. They said their good-byes in a frequent flier's club lounge.

+ + +

It was the first time that Char had flown first class. "I love this!" She leaned over and kissed Richard on the cheek. This feels sinfully luxurious!"

Richard looked at his bride. "It's good we can relax and be comfortable." He paused. "When Pastor Barry led me out to the front of the stage, it blew my mind to see those hundreds of people. Evidently, being so quiet to surprise us was a real adventure for them."

Char nodded. "When Mrs. Snow opened the door, and I saw all of those people, I think I was in shock for a moment! The whole ceremony turned into a dream-like experience. Seeing Abby and having her as my matron of honor was a surprise, but it did not occur to me that she was only the first surprise."

"Dad said that they got together with your parents and decided that we would probably always regret not having our friends at our wedding, so they pooled their resources. I think they're going to be friends as well as shirt-tail relatives."

Char looked at him. "I agree. On another subject, I've got a question."

Richard smiled. "Anything, my love."

She grinned. "Okay. Your camera is digital, and you don't have any film cameras. Why do you carry an old 35mm film canister in your pocket? I saw it when we were changing clothes."

He reached into his pocket and took it out. "You may think this is weird. Do you remember our ninth-grade church school teacher, Mr. Johnson?"

She nodded. "Yeah."

"Do you remember the lesson where he talked with us about the Biblical practice of casting lots, as a means of prophecy to determine God's will?"

Again, Char nodded. "I remember thinking of that lesson as seeing a little strange to me. I didn't understand how it was different from gambling."

"I didn't either, but it made me curious. I went to the Balboa Public Library on Mount Abernathy. Mrs. Bachman pointed me towards some books on everyday life in the Roman Empire. That got me started, and then I began researching the Internet." He opened up the film can and poured out two nickels on a cushion of cotton. "When you and I first started having lunch together in the seventh grade, I told you that I had started collecting coins."

She nodded. "I remember. Have you continued collecting them?"

Richard smiled. "Yes. These don't look particularly rare, but a collector knows that they are. This one," he handed her one, "is a 1955-D Jefferson. There're lots of them in circulation. In this case, though, look carefully. The 'D' is struck over an 'S,' and that makes it rare. In that condition, it's worth nearly twenty dollars. This one," he traded nickels with her, "is worth much more. It's a 1937-D Buffalo. There're lots of them out there, but look closely at this one. At the mint, when they were cleaning the dies, they did too much polishing in one area, and so the buffalo only has three legs. That one is worth more than three hundred."

She nodded. "That's interesting, but what has this to do with the Biblical practice of casting lots?"

"Nothing. Old coins just interest me. ... You may remember from Sunday School that the technical name for casting lots to determine God's will is cleromancy. Another name for it is sortition. In the Old Testament, the lots were carried by the priest in the breast-piece of his priestly garments, so they were small. They were probably made of stone. The Hebrew names for the lots were *Urim* and *Thummim*, and those names are derived from other words meaning blessing and curse or smooth and rough. Today's lots are called dice, and they are usually six-sided. Evidently, the sacred lots were two-sided, like coins, so I use these."

"You cast lots to determine God's will?"

Richard nodded. "For the really important things in life, yes. Does that weird you out?"

She nodded. "Kind of. This is a side of you that I never knew about. How is it different from gambling?"

Richard was serious. "That question was important to me, too. I've exchanged emails with several professors who teach the Bible, and I've read a number of books that I've gotten through the public library. Here's what I've come up with, based upon all of that, and so far it has consistently worked."

"Really?"

"Yes. First, when doing it, I always cast lots in an attitude of prayer and worship." Char nodded. "There are four possible outcomes with two coins, including heads-heads, tails-tails, heads-tails, and tails-heads."

Char nodded. "That makes sense, but how is this not gambling?"

"I'm getting to that. The Biblical lots were blessing versus curse, so I have translated that to yes versus no. If it is heads-heads, the answer is 'yes,' and if it is tails-tails, the answer is 'no.' If it is a mix of heads and tails, there is no answer, and that is vitally important."

"Why?"

"If there's no answer, it is just that, and I do not ask that question again for at least a week. On the other hand, if I do get an answer, I do follow up to be sure."

Again, Char nodded. "I understand now, but it still sounds like gambling. Can you give me an example?"

Richard smiled. "I'll give you the example of the most important question I've ever asked God."

"What?"

"Last Easter, I told Jesus that I loved you, and I asked Him if I should ask you to marry me. There was no answer." Char's mouth dropped open. "Hold on! Sunday after Sunday, I kept asking God the same question and got no answer. The Sunday before my birthday a month ago, I asked God the question, and the answer was heads-heads. I got excited. I asked Him if you would tour with me and sometimes play keyboard performances with me, and the answer was heads-heads. I asked Him if He would help me pick out a solitalre ring for you at Franzes, and the answer was heads-heads." Her eyes were getting bigger. "I asked Jesus if I should ask you over dinner that Friday, and the answer was heads-heads. I asked God if we would have children, and I got heads-heads. I asked Jesus if our marriage would last longer than those of our parents, and the answer was heads-heads. It sounds a lot less like gambling when you get heads-heads six times in a row, doesn't it?"

Char put her arms around Richard, and they kissed passionately. Richard looked into her eyes. "Since starting high school, I've been casting lots probably about once a month or so. From this day forwards, if I'm going to cast lots to determine God's will, I want you to join me in asking the questions."

Char nodded. "I'll pray about this." She reached up and pressed the call button, and a flight attendant was there a moment later. "How long until we land at Jackson Hole?"

He looked at his watch. "I expect we'll start making our final descent in about fifteen minutes or so. Can I get either of you something?"

They shook their heads. "No thank you."

Char unbuckled her seat belt. "I'm going to the rest room before we start our descent."

"Okay."

+ + +

Sunday morning, they awakened at 5:00 AM in the Bridal Suite of the Amangani Hotel in Jackson Hole. When Char opened her eyes, she saw her husband gazing at her. "Good morning, my love."

He smiled. "Good morning to you too, my beautiful bride. We didn't get much sleep last night. I think our bodies are under the impression that we're still in the Eastern Time zone."

She smiled. "Yes, it almost feels like we've slept in. It's Sunday. Where shall we go to church?"

Richard turned and pointed out through the glass doors leading to their balcony. "Those mountains are the Teton Range of Grand Teton National Park. There's a chapel just inside the Moose Junction entrance. Even if there's no scheduled worship service, we can still go in and pray."

She smiled and nodded. "Okay, but I want breakfast in bed first."

He grinned. "Great idea! You grab the phone and order for us, while I take care of nature calling."

As he got out of bed, she asked, "What shall I order?"

"Anything you want – just order enough for both of us." He walked rapidly around the corner into the bathroom.

Char picked up the phone, looked at the dial's index, and pressed '6' for room service. "Good morning to you too! This is Charlotte Hickman – NO! Charlotte Donovan. I'm in the bridal suite. ... Thank you. ... I'd like to order breakfast for two. Eggs over easy for each of us, along with one order each of bacon and sausage, two English muffins, preserves, and two large orange juices. ... No thank you. How long will it be before it is here? ... Thank you. Bye." Richard came around the corner, and she said, "Stop right there, Richard."

"What?"

"Turn around ... all the way around. Do it again. ... Thank you Lord! You've given me one fantastic husband!" They laughed. "Breakfast will be here in about fifteen minutes. What shall we do while we're waiting?"

Richard pulled the covers down. "I've got a few ideas, don't you?"

About twenty minutes later, there was a knock at the door. They put on their robes, and Richard answered the door. "Good morning! Come in!" The attendant brought in a cart, spread a cloth on their table, and spread the dishes out there. Richard added twenty percent to the bill and signed it. "Thank you!"

"Thank you, sir! Congratulations to you both."

Char smiled. "Thank you!" The attendant left.

Richard pointed. "Get back into bed, and I'll serve you."

"Okay." She got into bed and pulled up just the sheet.

Richard brought her a glass of juice and put it on her nightstand, and he put the other glass on his stand. He heaped preserves onto their English muffins on a plate, and put it in the middle of the bed. Then he took one plate of eggs, added bacon and sausage to it, and took it to his bride. Then he fixed one for himself and crawled into bed. He looked up at the ceiling. "Thank you, Lord, for my incredible bride. We will always stand on your promises. Thank you for this food. In Jesus' name, Amen."

"Amen! This looks good. I was just thinking a minute ago."

He swallowed some juice. "What?"

"When we decide to start a family, and I get pregnant, I hope we can plan things so that you can be there when I give birth."

"That's easy, at least I think so." He ate some bacon. "Once we know that you're pregnant and our due date, I'll block out four months either side of that date for family time, so I can take care of you and the baby."

Char smiled. "Take care of me? That sounds fun!"

They ate in silence for a while. When Richard finished the last of his juice, he said, "Before we get ready to go, let's take some time just to read the Bible and pray for a half-hour or so."

"Okay. When I was a little girl, I remember my Mom saying to me over, and over again, 'Those who pray together stay together.' I think that's good advice, don't you?"

"I do too." He got up, went to his suitcase, and brought back his Bible. He piled up some pillows against the headboard for them to lean against. Then he opened his Bible to 1 Samuel 14:36, where King Saul inquired of Urim and Thummim what sin came between his army and God, and he read it aloud through verse 46. "Do you remember when we studied this with Mr. Johnson? I felt uncomfortable with that passage when he first read it. Saul was not a faithful king, was he?"

"Yes. That passage still makes me uncomfortable." She took the Bible from him, and she turned to Acts 1:21, and she read aloud through verse 26. "When Mr. Johnson read that passage, and we talked about it, I felt more comfortable with the subject, but I still had no desire to cast lots to determine God's will."

"I didn't either. Have you ever heard of the Moravian Church?"

"Sure. They are Anabaptists, aren't they?

"Yeah. They cast lots to elect bishops, approve missionaries, select church sites, and at times decided on marriage by casting lots. They stopped doing it in the late nineteenth century."

"Really!"

"Yes. Do you remember how the church divided, east versus west, Orthodox versus Roman Catholic?"

"Sure."

"Well, the Eastern Orthodox Church still employs the casting of lots under certain circumstances to this day."

Char nodded. "I was awake last night for a little while, and I prayed about what you had said about casting lots yesterday. I'm still not sure I'm comfortable with it."

"I understand. Let's pray before we get up and get going."

"Okay."

"Mom, have you ever seen lava flow from a volcano?"

"No, we were never even close to lava flow."

"You and Dad knew about the volcano before it erupted, didn't you?"

"Yes."

"Were you scared?"

"Definitely, but I trust God with everything. He's more important than my fear."

3.

Richard and Char got to Chapel of the Transfiguration in time for their 10:00 AM service, and after everyone had left, they went up to the altar at the front. They gazed out through the window behind the altar at the Teton Range. Char prayed, "Lord. You know I'm not a risk-taker when it comes to my faith. My new husband has been taking risks of faith with casting lots for more than four years now. Lord, I confess, I'm more than a little scared, but I love and trust my new husband. I'm willing to try this, if you'll please be patient with me Lord." She turned to her husband. "Please take out those nickels."

"Okay." He poured out the little film canister onto the altar.

She picked them up. "Lord, will you bless us by letting us use lots to determine your will?" She dropped the coins on the altar.

Heads-heads.

"Will you please allow me to test this method of prophecy?"

Heads-heads.

"Will it rain today?"

Tails-Tails.

"Will there be an earthquake today?"

Heads-heads.

She swallowed hard. "Will the earthquake be between now and 3:00 o'clock?"

Heads-heads.

"Will there be major damage from the quake today?"

"Tails-tails."

She thought a moment. "Will there be thunderstorms tonight after midnight?"

Heads-heads.

"There's no rain, let alone lightning and thunder, in the weather forecast. I'm impressed, Lord. I'm ready to believe that you are really speaking to us right now. Will you please allow me to ask one more impertinent question?"

Heads-heads.

She swallowed. "When you are through giving us lightning and thunder this evening, will you show us something that both of us will know is from you?"

Heads-heads.

"I believe that we can stand on your promises, Lord."

"I join my wife in that belief, Lord. We give you praise, thanks, and glory in Jesus' name. Amen."

"Amen," said Char softly.

"AMEN!" The Priest for the chapel was standing behind them. "That's the first time in more than forty years in ministry that I've heard such truly bold praying from people who are not ordained clergy." They were now facing him. "May God richly bless you both and bless your marriage. Do I understand that you two are newlyweds?"

Richard nodded. "Yes. We're the Donovans. Her name is Charlotte, and mine is Richard."

She nodded. "People call me Char. I enjoyed your meditation this morning."

"Thank you. Where did you get married?"

She grinned. "Yesterday morning we got married at our church in La Jolla, California. It was supposed to be a small wedding, but when we walked in, our parents surprised us with a crowd of hundreds."

"Wonderful! That's an excellent beginning at making memories together. How long will you be in this area?"

Richard smiled. "We're leaving tomorrow morning. I will be playing the Grieg Piano Concerto with the London Philharmonic next Friday and Saturday evenings. I'll also be doing a solo concert for the BBC while we are in London."

"Wonderful! Is this your first trip to Europe? You look very young."

Char laughed. "We just graduated from high school last Friday! Yes! This is our first trip out of the country."

"And your name is Richard Donovan?"

"Yes."

"Will the concert be recorded?"

"Yes. The Saturday evening concert will be both recorded and broadcast live over the BBC."

"I shall watch for that album on Amazon. Enjoy your trip to the Tetons. I've enjoyed meeting you!"

"We've enjoyed meeting you as well."

As they left the chapel, the sky was completely devoid of any clouds except for a few wisps above the Grand Teton. Leaving Moose Junction, they went north until they got to the turnoff for Signal Mountain.

Char pointed. "Let's go up there!"

"Okay." He turned, and they headed up a steep and sometimes narrow switchback road. At the first turnout, the view was very nice, but at the top, they could see in almost all directions. They got out of their rental car, and Richard grabbed his camera to take more pictures. He took some with Char in them, and she took some with him in them. Richard pointed. "That's Jackson Lake, I think, and that little one over there is Jenny Lake."

"I love it up here!"

The ground began to shake. They held hands and sat down on the ground. There were several larger jolts, and countless small ones. They looked at each other, and they said together, "Amen!" She looked at her watch. "Two forty-five! All that God does, God does well!"

Richard nodded. When they felt as though the quake had subsided, they made their way to the car. When they were down off the mountain, they headed towards Jackson Lake, and after lunch at Signal Mountain

Lodge, they drove all over the park taking pictures of one another in various places.

That evening, when they got back to their hotel, they explored the entire lower floor. In a large hall, they found a Steinway grand, and Richard tried it out, playing a Brahms Prelude in E Major. Then they went to the dining room. Char had roast duck, and Richard had a porterhouse steak. With food and tea in them, they headed back to their room to relax.

It was after eleven, but neither of them was sleepy, so they turned on the news on a large flat-screen television while lying on their king-size bed. The weather forecast called for clear and cool that night, and increasing cloudiness the next day. They made out for a while, and then went back to watching the news. Snuggled together, they both dozed off for a while.

At 12:55, their room was lit up with a flash of light, and with a simultaneous clap of thunder. They were both awake and on their feet without thinking about it. They went to their patio door and slid it open. There was another flash and a clap of thunder as the power went off and torrential rains began coming down. A few seconds later, the lights came back on, and there were thunder, lightning, and rain for more than thirty minutes.

Suddenly, everything was quiet. There was no sound whatsoever, even from nearby traffic. They heard a faint sound of wind, and then the clouds parted rapidly and disappeared. In their place was a full moon. Richard pointed. "It's a full moon. When I was in grade school, I used to play a bunch of old pop tunes associated with the moon."

The moon seemed to be getting brighter, and then a halo appeared all around the moon. "Nice!" said Char.

"Yeah, nice!"

A second halo appeared around the first. "Wow Lord! That's terrific!" Char murmured. Then a third halo appeared and became a rainbow, surrounding the first two. Char got down on her knees. "Thank you, Jesus. Thank you!"

Richard knelt down beside her. "Thank you, Lord, for giving us the eyes to perceive your will. Thank you for giving us the faith to believe in what you reveal to us, and thank you for the courage you've given to both of us to trust in your ability to achieve all that you reveal."

Together, they said, "Amen!"

Holding hands, they got up. Char spoke first. "Now I share your trust in God to speak through casting lots. I somehow think that our lives together may become like a wild ride."

Richard grinned. "I'm game, especially since you're with me."

+ + +

After getting through airport security the next morning, they stopped to get some breakfast at a fast-food restaurant. Char had a breakfast wrap with an orange juice. Richard also had juice, but he put an order of bacon between two potato cakes. Char took a bite of his created 'sandwich.' She chewed and swallowed. "Wow! That's much better than I thought it would be. I'll have to try that again sometime!" As she returned to her breakfast wrap, Richard finished his creation, and went back to get what he needed for another 'sandwich.' Char took a bite of that one too, and she winked.

As he finished, he leaned back in his chair. "Our flight into JFK is on time, but we're going to be delayed several hours because of equipment difficulty. What would you like to do?"

She nodded and swallowed the last of her wrap. "It seems to me we've got two choices – either exploring the airport or taking a taxi into town."

He nodded. He took the juice cup, and he wiped it out with his napkin. Reaching into his pocket, he got out the film canister and put the nickels into the cup. "Lord, will you speak to us regarding what we should do while waiting at JFK?" He put one hand over the top of the cup, shook it, and dumped it on the table.

Heads-tails.

Char blinked. "Okay, so we go with the flow."

"I was wrong to try that. We weren't in an attitude of worship." Richard put the nickels back in the canister. He looked at his watch. "They should be loading in about ten minutes. Maybe we should head for the gate."

Char nodded. "Sounds like a plan."

They began walking. As they approached the gate, they heard a page: "Donovan, party of two, please come to the service desk at Gate 9." They started walking more rapidly, and they went directly to the gate desk.

An attendant looked up. "May I help you?"

"Yes," said Richard, "We're the Donovans."

"Just a moment. ... Yes. Your flight from JFK to London has been changed. You no longer have a layover. I'll print out your new tickets here. Let me see your old ones." As they got out their tickets, she continued to type. She reached out and got their tickets. "Thank you. Your new flight is closer than the old one in distance, but you will board your flight to London about thirty minutes after you arrive at JFK. The gates aren't far apart, so I suggest that you do your best to get something to eat before you get on board." She looked at them as she handed them their tickets. "I have a suggestion."

"What's that?" asked Char.

"Most of the time, first-class passengers like you want to get on board first, and you will still have that opportunity if you want it. I suggest that instead you plan to board near the end of the line, so that you have time to get something decent to eat. You'll be boarding at Gate 34, and there's a place called 'The Hooligans' across from Gate 32. They serve good food. You have your tickets, so you can go ahead and get on board."

"Thank you," they said almost simultaneously.

They went down the gangway, and they got settled into their seats. Richard looked at her. "Remind me to thank Jessie at Ticket Blogger for this."

Sitting in their seats, Char looked out their window. "Okay. I can see now why God didn't answer us back at breakfast."

Richard nodded. "Right. I was just thinking about something. When we were at that benefit dinner before we graduated, Arnold Bettis, the head of the music department at UC San Diego came over and spoke to me. You were in a conversation with someone else at the time, and I forgot to tell you about it."

"What did he say?"

"He said that if I want to earn a music degree there, he could arrange for me to be there as an artist-in-residence while earning my degree. You could work on a degree too. What do you think?"

"Let's pray about it, and we'll ask the Lord about it when we're ready."

Richard nodded. "As you like to say, 'Sounds like a plan.'"

When they arrived at the gate at JFK, they were about ten minutes ahead of schedule. It was not hard to find "The Hooligans," and both were hungry enough to eat heartily and at leisure. As they approached their gate, the flight was still loading, and they got on immediately.

Their flight to London was uneventful. A passenger in coach sent a message to Richard, asking him by way of the flight attendant if he was going to perform at Royal Festival Hall. The attendant handed Richard an autograph book, and Richard signed it.

Char said, "Is that your first?"

He grinned. "Outside of Mervin and Elle at school, I guess it is."

"Merve asked for your autograph?

He nodded. "Last month. He knew that being first violinist in our orchestra was fine, but as a college freshman, he'll be a small fish in a big pond until he establishes himself. He said I won't go through that, so he said he wanted my autograph now, while it is cheap!"

Char grinned. "That's Merve! What about Elle?"

He shook his head. "Don't you remember what she said in the eighth grade to me? You were standing next to her. She announced that one day I would be her husband, and if not, she would at least have my autograph. What did she say to you at the reception on Saturday morning?"

Char rolled her eyes. "She told me that if I got tired of you just to let her know, so she can take you off of my hands! I told her, 'Sorry, girl, no Cocoa Puffs, you're just coo-coo.'"

Richard laughed. "She is a little nut, isn't she? Whoever I hire to screen fan mail will have to be told about her."

She rolled her eyes again. "Fan mail? I suppose that's going to be part of our life together. I hope you don't get much hate mail."

He nodded. "If I do, I suppose I should not be surprised. Right now, if you'll hand me my briefcase, I'll do some review of the Chopin and Liszt I'm doing next weekend."

+ + +

When they walked in the door of the London Savoy, the staff was amazingly attentive. They had been sent pictures of Richard and Char, so they were greeted by name and treated like royalty. Richard was told that they had prepared two practice rooms for him, with one equipped with a Steinway, and the other equipped with a Bösendorfer. Richard was intrigued because he had never had the opportunity to play a Bösendorfer. Yamaha had bought the company in 2008, but the pianos were unchanged.

They were taken to a Luxury King River View room, overlooking the River Thames. Char felt almost overwhelmed. Two staff members were there to help her unpack their belongings while Richard went downstairs to examine the pianos. He kissed her on the cheek before going down to look at the pianos and try them.

The hotel manager, Lawrence Abbott, escorted Richard into the first rehearsal hall. As Richard walked up to the Steinway, he said, "This is a fully restored concert grand about a half-century old. I think you'll find the action was well-adjusted and even, and it should be perfectly tuned. If it is not, please tell me."

Richard sat down, adjusted the bench, and began playing "Consolation" by Franz Liszt. "Mr. Abbott, it is indeed well tuned, and the restoration is excellent. I may come back to this to do some practicing. Meanwhile, may I please see the Bösendorfer? I would like to try playing some Bach on it."

"Certainly – please follow me this way."

They walked out of that rehearsal hall, down a corridor, and into another hall, which was much larger. In the center was the Bösendorfer piano. Richard smiled. "This is the Model 290 Imperial, isn't it?"

"Yes, Mr. Donovan, it is. Are you familiar with it?"

"Only by its reputation. It is a delightful surprise to have the opportunity to sit down here, even if I don't use it as my practice piano." He sat, adjusted the bench, and began playing some Bach. Both Richard and the hotel manager became lost in the sound as he played the entire piece.

Lawrence Abbot cleared his throat. "Mr. Donovan, I have been the manager of this hotel for nearly thirty years. In all this time, I have never heard anyone take advantage of this instrument's capabilities the way you do. You are an amazing talent, sir."

"Thank you. You are very kind. This is an amazing instrument. It far exceeds my expectations. With your permission, I would like to use this as my practice piano while I am here this week. Will it be available all week? I hope so!"

"Yes sir."

"Please call me Richard."

"Thank you, Richard. I will see to it that it is always available to you this week. Do you wish to practice now, or do you wish to return later?"

"My wife and I are both quite tired due to our flight from New York. We need to get some rest. She may also want to practice on the other piano later."

"Very well. Whenever either of you need access to either hall, just dial 43698 on a house phone." He handed Richard a card with the number written on it."

Richard nodded. "Thank you, Mr. Abbot. This is truly an amazing instrument. Thank you again."

"You're quite welcome."

They walked out of the rehearsal hall, which Mr. Abbot locked. At the elevators, they parted company, with Richard going upstairs. As he walked into their room, Char was standing by a huge window, looking out over the river. She turned and smiled.

Richard walked up to her, hugged her, and kissed her. "How are we doing? Are we all moved in?"

She nodded. "Fine, ... and yes, we're moved in. ... It's beautiful here, isn't it?"

He looked out over the water. "Yes, it is, and so are you."

"Thank you, kind sir." She did a mock courtesy.

He smiled. After we get some rest, I'll take you downstairs. You simply have to see and hear the Bösendorfer I'll be practicing on. It's amazing!"

"Really! I've never heard you talk about a piano that way before."

He nodded. "That's because there is no other piano like this one. In the early twentieth century, this model was created so that a piano could accurately play some of Bach's organ music. It has 97 keys instead of the usual 88. The extras are all in the bass."

"Really! Does that make it larger?"

Richard laughed. "Much larger! It has the largest sounding board and largest harp of any piano made. Playing it is like playing a small orchestra. Debussy and Ravel wrote some music just for this piano. If I had one, I'd definitely learn those works and record them." He yawned. "Right now, though, let's get some rest – maybe even some sleep before dinner. My first orchestral rehearsal isn't until Wednesday morning, so I'll have all day tomorrow to practice."

Char kissed him. "Okay." She hugged him. "Let's get some sleep." She went to a phone by the bed and dialed zero. "Hello. This is Mrs. Donovan. We are going to get some rest, so we do not wish to be disturbed until," she looked at her watch, "until 6:00 PM. Thank you." She hung up and turned off the light. They slept soundly.

"Dad, one of our pianos doesn't look like other pianos."

"That's right, son. It's wider because it has additional low note keys."

"You like playing it together with Mom?"

"Yes. It's lots of fun."

4.

Tuesday began well enough, and it got even better. After Monday night's dinner, they had gone upstairs, taken a shower together, and settled in for the night. They awakened at 6:00 in the morning feeling refreshed but not particularly energized. After a leisurely breakfast in the hotel dining room, Richard took Char to see and hear the Bösendorfer piano that he was going to use for practice. After playing Bach's *Passacaglia in C minor* as he had for the hotel manager, he cut loose and did some country, jazz, and Broadway show tunes.

Char couldn't stop smiling. "You were right! This is an amazing piano. Maybe after you make your first million we can get one for our den!"

Richard laughed. "We'd have to get a big house for it first!" He looked at his watch. "I should get over to Royal Festival Hall and start practicing. The first rehearsal is tomorrow morning. I want to get used to that instrument. I'll probably come back to this piano this evening after we have dinner." He stood up and kissed her. "Have the Concierge help you arrange some sight-seeing, and try these pianos for yourself. I'm sure I'll be back by 5:00, okay?"

Char hugged him, and then they started walking out of the hall. "Can I come to rehearsal tomorrow morning?"

He smiled. "Of course. Meanwhile, I'll see you this evening. If you have any problems, you've met Mr. Abbot, the General Manager. Also, I told him that you might want to practice on the other piano."

She nodded. "Right. Bye!" As he headed towards the hotel entrance, she turned and went to the elevators. After telling the operator which floor, she looked around at the inside of the lift and lightly touched the wall.

"This is your floor, Mrs. Donovan. Have a pleasant day."

"Thank you." Char walked to her room and inserted her key. Stepping inside, she stopped, took a deep breath, and smiled. There was a soft knock on the door behind her, and she opened to the bellhop.

"Here's a package for you Mrs. Donovan." He handed her a small rectangular box. It was addressed to the two of them. She opened her purse and gave him a pound note tip. He said "Thank you, Mrs. Donovan," and he was quickly gone.

Closing the door, she took the package to a table and opened it. Inside were a note, and a plastic film zip bag. She read the note.

Dear Richard and Charlotte (Char),

I've met all kinds of people here in the Tetons. Only one other time have I witnessed anyone at the chapel altar casting lots. I was very impressed with the two of you. It took me several hours to get an address for you. With this note, I am sending you three quarters. It is easier to abandon thoughts of gambling when you use three or more coins. I remembered your questions at the altar when I noticed the earthquake in the afternoon and the thunderstorm after midnight. Amen! You might like to know that the quake you felt was the beginning of a swarm that is continuing. It might be in the London paper. BTW, I'm not a coin collector, but these three are among the oldest I've found lying around on the chapel floor. Use them with joy, and may God bless you both!

John

Char opened the tiny zipped plastic bag and poured out the quarters onto the bed. They looked old. Two of them had a seated Liberty. One was 1870 CC, and the other was 1873 CC. The third quarter was dated 1916, and it had a standing Liberty. Char liked that one the best. Returning the coins to the bag, she opened her purse. She stopped. She looked at the coins, put them in the bag, and then she stuffed the bag into her bra. Closing her purse, she considered calling the concierge and went to the bedside phone. It had a flashing red light. She picked up the receiver and pressed zero. "Hello, this is Char Donovan, do we have a message?"

"Yes, Mrs. Donovan, it is a voice mail. I will play it for you, and it will be saved until you tell us to delete it, or when you check out. Here is your message."

> *Hi! This is Robin Martin! I graduated from La Jolla High when you two finished your sophomore year. I've been singing at Milan's La Scala Opera ever since. I'm in London, visiting with friends. If either of you is interested in joining me for some sight-seeing, just leave a message for me at the Royal Opera House. I'll be there all morning today. Bye!*

Char looked at her watch. She hung up and pressed zero again. "Hello, would you please put through a call for me to Robin Martin at the Royal Opera House? ... That's right, Robin Martin. ... Thank you." When she hung up, she went to the window and gazed down at the River Thames, where hundreds of people were milling about.

The phone rang. She walked to the bed, sat down, and picked up the phone. "Hello? ... Yes please! ... Hi, Robin! This is a nice surprise!"

On the phone, Robin sounded effervescent. "Hi Char! It's good to hear your voice!"

"It's good to hear you, too. So you've got friends there at the Royal Opera House?"

"Yes! I've sung with two of them both in Milan and in Rome. I heard from Elle that you and Richard had gotten married. Where's Richard?"

"He's practicing at the Royal Festival Hall. His first rehearsal with the London Philharmonic is tomorrow. He's getting used to the piano. He'll do most of his other practicing on a Bösendorfer here at the Savoy."

"A Bösendorfer! Is it one of the big ones with the extended keyboard?"

"Yeah, it's incredible."

"I heard one in Rome when I was there last summer. How about I take you out to lunch today, and we can catch up with each other. I'll show you some of the sights."

"That sounds great! Richard won't be back here until about 5:00."

"Good! I'll get you back there before 4:30. There is a lot to see. I'll come to your room at about 11:30, okay?"

"Great! See you at 11:30."

She hung up, and then she pressed zero again. "Front desk please. ... Thank you. ... Hello. This is Mrs. Richard Donovan. I have a friend coming to meet me for lunch at 11:30. Her name is Robin Martin. ... Yes, the soprano from Milan. ... Yes. Will you please have someone escort her directly to my room when she arrives? Thank you."

Opening her purse, she took out a few pound notes and put them in a drawer of a table near the door. Then she went to the bathroom to change clothes, pick out some walking shoes, choose a coat for the cold and damp, and fix her hair. She was picking out a scarf when there was a knock at the door. She looked at her watch. It said 11:32.

Going to the door, she took a pound note out of the drawer and opened the door. "Robin!" They hugged, and

Char handed the bellhop the note. He did a little bow and was gone. "You look great! How are you?" Char closed the door.

"I'm great! Have you seen today's paper?"

"No, why?"

"There's a big picture of Richard on the first page of the second section."

"Really!" Char reached for a tasseled cord near the door and pulled down. "Just a moment, I'll get one." There was a knock at the door, and she opened it again. A tall man in uniform was standing there. "Good morning, David. I understand that there's a picture of my husband in today's paper. Would you please see if you can secure a copy for me?"

"Yes, Mrs. Donovan." He turned and walked away.

Char smiled at her friend. "The Philharmonic has gone all out. This suite includes the services of a butler on call."

Robin laughed. "Really! Give me the tour! That looks out on the River Thames, right?" She walked over to the window. There was a knock on the door, and when Char answered, David handed her that day's issue of the *London Times*. As she looked through the sections, Robin looked over her shoulder, and she pointed. "There it is! There's Richard!"

Char smiled. "Wow. I think that was taken at the benefit concert at the Hilton in San Diego."

"When was that?"

"It was the Monday before we graduated. It turned out to be quite an event when faculty from eleven music schools joined us onstage to jam."

"Whoa! Really?"

"Yeah. It was recorded. Leave me your address before you leave, and I'll send you a disk."

For the next four hours, the two old friends did their catching up, had lunch, and did some shopping.

+ + +

Richard rehearsed most of the morning at a Steinway concert grand piano on the stage at Royal Festival Hall. Shortly before noon, a distinguished-looking Asian man came down the aisle and introduced himself. "You must be Richard Donovan. I am Akira Eng."

Richard stood up to shake his hand. "I'm pleased to meet you at last. We've spoken on the phone, of course."

"Yes, of course. How do you like this Steinway?"

Richard nodded. "It's quite good. The action is just as even as the one at the Savoy, although over there I've decided to practice on their Bösendorfer Imperial. It is magnificent. I love its rich sonorous sound, though the action is not quite equal to the action of this Steinway."

Akira nodded. "I'm glad you're comfortable with this. It will be tuned once more on Friday afternoon before the first performance. ... speaking of which, my colleagues in the music world are still talking about the benefit concert you put on a week ago."

Richard's eyes got bigger, and his mouth dropped open for a moment. "You heard about it here in London?"

"Oh, definitely yes. Word got out that both James Strang and Raymond Endo had performed for the first time in years in that ensemble during the second half. I've been asked to inquire of you if it was recorded."

Richard smiled and nodded. "Yes, it was. In that ballroom environment, the acoustics were favorable to what we did. In hindsight, the risk Char and I took was frightening."

"Char is your bride?"

Richard grinned. "Yes! We got married this past Saturday morning. At the benefit for Samaritan's Purse, I did all classical solos for nearly an hour. Then, during a brief intermission, chairs and stands were brought out for the larger ensemble. The stands contained only cue sheets for jamming – no music. In addition to the piano, we brought out a two-tier electronic keyboard for Char, along with a trap set, a xylophone, and a vibraphone. The other instrumentalists brought up their own guitars, banjos, electric guitars, a clarinet, a trumpet, a trombone, and two bass guitars."

"Really! What did you play? You say you were scared?"

"Char and I were definitely scared, sir. It could have been disastrous, since, not only had we not rehearsed, but also this kind of thing had never been attempted before, as far as we knew. The ensemble was entirely made up of music professors from eleven music schools in Southern California."

Akira Eng pulled up a chair, and Richard sat down again. He was intensely interested. "So tell me about what happened next. I've only heard bits and pieces from newscasts and on the Internet, from people who recorded parts of this on their cell phones."

"About a year ago, Char and I sent letters to several music schools, announcing the concert. We asked that each of the schools supply us with one or two faculty members to play their own instruments in a jam session. On each of the music stands, there were cue sheets for pieces reflecting famous hits from rock and roll, country, folk, and jazz. We started by taking the folk tune, "This Land Is Your Land," just as it is commonly played as a folk song. It was fun. Then I asked the drummer from Cal-State Long Beach to give us a Country Rock beat, and we did it in that style. After some applause, I started doing the song as jazz on the piano. The drummer picked up on it, followed by xylophone and vibraphone. The guitar and banjo players stood down for that, but the clarinet and brass with the rest of us got people on their feet."

The director nodded. "I understand that it went on longer than you expected."

Richard smiled. "Yes. For almost ninety minutes, we played both casually and fervently. Some couples got up and danced beside their tables."

The director again nodded. "I have asked you about this because there has been a change – at least tentatively – in the schedule."

"A change?"

"Yes, but it requires your permission and that of your bride."

Richard was now serious. "Go on."

"This is a bit complicated, but potentially great fun. As it happens, Wembley Stadium, our stadium where we have football – soccer to you Americans – it has a break in its schedule this weekend. If you agree – and only if you and your bride, Charlotte, say yes –, there will be a concert shell set up on the field. There are musicians all over England that I can call upon to do a jam session like the one you did in San Diego."

Richard was stunned. Silently, he looked up at the rows of lights up near the ceiling. "Mr. Eng...."

"Please call me Akira."

"Okay. Akira, are you a religious man?"

The old Asian smiled. "I used to be a Buddhist, but my wife introduced me to Jesus, and we both attend Holy Trinity Brompton here in London whenever we can."

Richard nodded. "My wife and I are also Christians. Before I can say yes, she and I need to talk about it and pray about it. May I call you this evening to give you our answer?"

Akira nodded. "Of course, but I will call you at your room at the Savoy. ... As a matter of fact, could I come there this evening to hear you play on that Bösendorfer?"

Richard beamed. "That is an excellent idea. Shall we meet at about 8:00 PM? I'll ask Mr. Abbot, the hotel manager, to have you escorted to that hall."

"Excellent." The director stood up, and Richard stood up to bid him farewell." I will let you return to your practicing now, and I will see you at 8:00 PM."

Richard nodded and shook his hand. "I will see you then, sir."

The director ambled off, and Richard sat down again at the piano. For the next two hours, Richard polished his performance of the first movement of the Grieg Piano Concerto. After taking a break for a snack, he finished the afternoon working on the other two movements.

He caught a taxi back to the Savoy, and he immediately went to their room. As he walked in, he stopped short. Sitting in a chair across from Char was someone he'd not seen in two years. "Robin! What are you doing here?" He strode across the room and gave her a hug as she stood up.

"I'm visiting friends here for a few days. While you've been practicing all day, Char and I have had lunch and gone shopping."

"That's great." As Char stood up to greet him, he gave her a hug and a kiss. "Hi, beautiful!"

"Hi, handsome."

Robin smiled. "I know that the two of you have things to talk about, so I'll be going back to my hotel. I'll see you tomorrow, Char."

Richard held up a hand. "Will you join us for dinner tomorrow?"

"I'd love to!"

Char gave her a hug. "See you tomorrow morning. Just come straight up."

"Okay. Bye you two!" She waved, opened the door, and was gone.

Richard opened his arms, and they held each other for a few minutes. "There's something that Akira Eng, the conductor, has asked us to do, and I told him we would talk about it and pray about it."

They sat down in chairs by the big window. Char nodded. "What's up?"

Richard smiled. "While we've been graduating and on our honeymoon, news of our benefit concert last week has been flashing all over the music world."

Her eyes got bigger. "Really!"

"Right. So far, I'm scheduled to do the Grieg Concerto on Friday and Saturday evening, and I'm scheduled to do the live BBC concert on Monday evening."

"Right. That's the schedule you're contracted for."

He nodded. "Right. The new opportunity is simply something almost as fantastic as that benefit concert. If you and I agree to it, they will set up an acoustic bowl on the soccer field at Wembly Stadium. There are musicians all over Britain, according to Akira, who will jump at the chance to jam with us. If we agree, it will happen Saturday afternoon."

Char's mouth was hanging open, and she shut it. "Wow." She swallowed. "Wow. Will you have the energy to do the Grieg Saturday night if you jam for a couple of hours in the afternoon?"

Richard nodded. "I've been thinking about that. I think if I don't play in every piece that afternoon, I'll have energy for the evening."

"Okay. Before we pray about, I think we should cast lots for it too, and that brings me to this." She extended the note from the chapel priest.

Richard read it over quickly, and then he went back over it again. "I didn't realize that the priest was there and listening most of the time."

"I didn't either." She reached under her shirt and got the coins out in their little plastic bag. "Here are the quarters. What he said about using three coins instead of two sort of makes sense."

He looked at each of the quarters very carefully. "Even though he sent these to us as a gift, we should offer to pay him."

"Why?"

"All three of them are both old and rare, worth several hundred dollars, perhaps more than a thousand."

Char raised her eyebrows. "Are you sure?"

He nodded and held one up. "I tried to buy one of these two years ago at an estate auction, but I was out-bid. Let's kneel on the bed."

They got up on the bed, and Char put the quarters in front of them. He said, "Let's pray silently before we begin asking God questions."

She nodded, and they prayed silently for several minutes. Then Richard picked up the quarters, cleared his throat, and said, "Heavenly father, will you speak to us through these quarters this afternoon?" He tossed the up into the air about a foot.

Heads-heads-heads.

Char quietly asked, "Lord, will it please you if we do this extra concert?" She gathered and tossed the coins.

Heads-heads-heads.

Richard picked them up. "Will you guide me and give me extra strength to do all of this?"

Heads-heads-heads.

Char picked up the coins. "Will you please help us choose the songs you want us to use?"

Heads-heads-heads.

Richard started to straighten up, but Char reached for the coins again. "Lord, will you please forgive another question, one that may seem impertinent?"

Heads-heads-heads.

She gathered the coins. "Lord God, will that earthquake swarm in Wyoming turn into a major event before we can get back to the United States?" She tossed the coins a little higher.

Tails-tails-tails.

Richard gathered the coins and looked upward a moment before asking, "Heavenly father, will the Yellowstone Caldera start to become a volcano on the afternoon after we get back to the United States?"

Heads-heads-heads.

Richard lowered his head down to the surface of the bed, and Char did the same. Quietly, he asked, "Precious Lord, will this result in a nuclear winter?"

Heads-heads-heads.

Char had a sharp intake of breath. She picked up the coins. "Will you give us the words to say when they need to be spoken, wherever we are?"

Heads-heads-heads.

Richard gathered the coins. "I have just two more questions, heavenly father. Please forgive us, and be patient with us. First, will the nuclear winter last more than seven years?"

Tails-tails-tails.

Finally Lord, thank you for using us. My final question is simply this: Will the nuclear winter last more than six years?"

Heads-heads-heads.

Richard's voice cracked. "Amen, Lord. All that you do, you do well."

Char was crying. "Yes, Lord, you are faithful. We trust you, and we love you. Amen, Lord."

Richard murmured. "Millions of people will starve, and millions will die."

"Yes."

They held each other and cried until it was time to get their dinner. Afterward, they went from the dining room directly to the practice room containing the Bösendorfer Imperial piano. Akira Eng arrived promptly at 8:00 PM to hear Richard play it, and they had an enjoyable evening talking about music from their different perspectives.

Shortly after 10:00 PM, Akira left, and Richard and Char went back to their room. It was after 11:00 when they turned off their light. Both of them slept soundly, and Char dreamed.

> "Mom, how long was the sky dark after the volcano erupted?"
>
> "The clouds did not start going away until the seventh year."
>
> "Wow!"

5.

Neither Richard nor Char spoke to Robin the next day of what they had learned, and they did not say anything else to anyone either, with one exception. Richard got high praise for all that he did that weekend and on into Tuesday. Each evening, when they read the Bible and prayed together, they talked about not only the concerts but also the coming disaster. They cast lots to try to learn more, but all they got was a mixture of heads and tails. God was not revealing any more to them yet.

On Wednesday, as they rode the high-speed train through The Chunnel under the English Channel, they read an extensive article on his BBC solo performance the evening before. A reporter named Abby Rather had interviewed him after his performance. She recalled something he had said at the impromptu concert at Wembly Stadium on Saturday afternoon.

"Mr. Donovan, after playing some blues numbers, you said something to the effect that you believed a nuclear winter is coming. Would you enlarge upon that?"

He nodded. "It had nothing to do with the music except that I believe that we will have many reasons to sing the blues when that nuclear winter comes."

"So you believe we are headed for nuclear war?"

"No, it will be a natural disaster. A volcano will unexpectedly form in North America. The volcanic ash will create the nuclear winter."

The article went on to say Richard had no further elaboration to offer. Then the article continued and talked more about his music in general, and that concert in particular.

Char looked up from the paper, and she looked at Richard. "Did you feel uncomfortable with her questions?"

He shook his head. "Praise God, no. Since we had prayed it through, I felt like God was guiding me and answering our prayers for that."

"In Paris, you're not doing the Grieg again, are you?"

"No, and I'm glad. My last couple of hours at the Bösendorfer, I did a change of pace and began practicing for this weekend's performance of Sergi Prokofiev's Concerto Number Three."

"I like that. Are you mostly ready for it?"

"There're some lines I want to polish, and there're some things to work out with the orchestra in Paris, but there's plenty of time to work on it. Speaking of which," he reached into his briefcase and brought out some music, "I think I'll use part of this train ride for review."

"Okay." Char picked up a magazine.

* * *

Their stay in Paris was very similar to their time in London, but they enjoyed the French food and wine more. Richard performed the Prokofiev on Friday evening, Saturday afternoon, and Saturday evening.

When they got back to their hotel on Saturday evening, they prayed and cast lots to decide where they would worship. Church after church they cast lots for got *tails-tails-tails*, until they found one that got them *heads-heads-heads*. It was amazing. As they walked in the door, they heard someone cry out, "Char! Richard!"

Looking across the foyer, they saw Jack and Cheryl Wyle. Richard glowed with excitement. "Mr. & Mrs. Wyle! We didn't expect to see you here!"

They all shook hands. Cheryl looked at Char. "We never expected to see you this morning, but we saw Richard on stage last night at the concert."

Char was excited. "What brings you to Paris?"

Jack smiled. "My company is opening a new office not far from here. We distribute cameras from Europe to stores in the United States, and having an office here will help us, in many ways. I'm glad we got to see you last night again, Richard. Your talent is amazing!"

"Thank you."

The pastor approached. "Are you the Richard Donovan that put on that impromptu concert at Wembly last week? I'm Pastor Harold."

Richard nodded and smiled. "Yes sir. This is my bride, Char, and she was at the electronic keyboard in that concert."

The pastor shook both their hands. "Would you two like to do some good-old-fashioned praise music with our praise team this morning?"

Richard shook his head. "That would not be fair to them, because they have practiced and know what they intend to do. We won't interfere with that."

Char was also shaking her head. "I agree. Richard and I are here to worship."

The pastor nodded, and he pointed. "Here comes our praise team leader. Bob, this is Richard and Char Donovan. You were telling me about them yesterday."

Bob shook their hands. "I'm so glad to meet you! Has Pastor Harold asked you to join us?"

Richard nodded. "Yes, but we declined. It would not be fair to those of you who have rehearsed and planned the worship."

"Okay. ... I have a thought. Pastor, didn't you say that you wanted to close worship with singing that old hymn, "Victory in Jesus?" He nodded. "How about not doing it straight, as written, and just put up the slides and let Richard and Char lead us in their own style?"

Pastor Harold nodded. "It's okay with me, but Richard? Char?"

They looked at each other. Richard shrugged, but Char nodded and said, "Okay, but you can expect us to improvise and jazz it up."

The Pastor and music director smiled. "However the spirit moves you," said Pastor Harold.

The worship service rocked, and the people praised God.

+ + +

When Char and Richard landed in Rome, it was as though they stepped into another world. A limousine rapidly drove them to the Waldorf Astoria, which was both classic and romantic. Robin came down from Milan to greet them at the Airport and helped them get settled at the hotel.

As Robin was saying good-bye, Robin stopped her. "Wait, Robin. There's something I've been meaning to ask you. I heard that you married a wealthy Italian vintner. You have not mentioned him. Did you get a divorce already?"

Robin shook her head. "No, not at all. I love him, and he loves me, but before he married me, he married his vineyard that had been passed down to him. Richard is married to his music, but it works for the two of you differently than for my Sal and me. You are often part of his music. I love wine, but I'm not a wine expert, and I'm not interested in the grapes, the pressing, or any of the things that go into making and selling wine. It's not me."

Richard shook his head. "With all of that, do you still have a good marriage?"

"Oh, yes, but I try not to think about it, because I don't want to be lonely. Once the grapes are harvested, and the wine is in the kegs, he and I will travel together and enjoy the rest of the world. He will get reports once a week from the cellars, and later, once the wine is in the bottles, he and I travel once again while the vines are cleaned. After that, the process starts over. When he and I are together, it is magic. The rest of the time, we don't see each other. This next season will be different because I am pregnant."

"Congratulations!"

"Thanks Char. Once Geno and I are parents, I will be there all the time raising the kids while he tends the vineyards. When we travel, we will take the kids along. I know that kind of life would not work for you and Richard, but it does for us. Besides, I have my operatic career and my fans. I seldom feel lonely. He hears me sing every time the company puts on another opera. I love this life!" She paused and picked up her purse. "I've got to go now. I'm going on holiday to Athens while I can still travel. Bye you two!"

"God be with you," said Richard, smiling.

"Thank you, my friend! Bye!" Char had a tear running down her cheek.

Richard turned towards her and took her in his arms. "I have just the one performance on Friday, and then we're headed home. We're supposed to touch down at JFK on Saturday morning. I hope God gives us at least a glimpse of what awaits us when the nuclear winter begins."

Char nodded. "I hope so too, but I'm sure God will provide what we need."

Richard smiled. "We can be sure of that. That call I got a short time ago was from Luca Ricci. He asked me if I could do the Grieg instead of the Beethoven, and I reluctantly said okay. We'll rehearse on Wednesday and Thursday."

"Good. The bellhop told me that channels 101 through 189 are American stations by satellite feed. After dinner, let's watch some television, or maybe a movie. We've not done that since we left the states."

He nodded. That sounds really good. It's almost time for dinner, so let's get ready."

She nodded. "It won't take long to get ready. I was told as we came through the lobby that dress for dinner is casual."

He smiled. "Excellent. I'll be happy for not having to wear a tie."

"I can wear a pantsuit!"

"Are you going to wear the green one?"

"Right. Why do you ask?"

He grinned. "I'm trying to think ahead towards later!"

She winked. They quickly got ready, and they went out the door less than thirty minutes later.

In the dining room, they were seated a small booth. The waiter spoke nearly flawless English. "How would you like to begin your Cena or dinner?"

Richard looked up from the menu. "Bring us a bottle of your best Spumante. What do you suggest for my wife's aperitivo?"

"How about a nice quiche?"

Char nodded. "Good. Do you have a prawn cocktail or something similar for my husband?"

"Yes, indeed! I will be back with your order momentarily."

Richard smiled. "Because of vocal music, we know Latin pronunciations fairly well, don't we?"

Char nodded. "Looking at the menu, I don't think I need any primo, but I'd like the lamb as secondo, with the waiter's choice of contorno."

Richard grinned. "Very good! I think you've got those pronunciations down pretty well!"

Their waiter returned with the wine. "Have you thought about what you want for primo?"

Char shook her head. "We don't need primo, but we'd like the lamb secondo, along with any contorno that you think are best."

The waiter nodded. "I will bring your aperitivo next, and when you have finished those, I will bring the lamb. How do you like the Spumante?"

Richard smiled. "We are young Americans, so we have not had much experience with wines, but I like it."

The waiter nodded. "Very good. I will be right back with your aperitivo."

By the time Char and Richard had finished their Cena, including Dolce and Caffè, they were so full of food they could hardly walk. As they got on the elevator, Richard said, "If breakfast is that big, we'll have to sleep until noon!"

Char laughed. "I don't think I could eat another bite until tomorrow noon! That Spumante was wonderful. I'm a little light headed."

Richard grinned. "That's all right. I don't mind getting you ready for bed!" Char stuck her tongue out at him and then smiled.

When they turned out the lights in the bedroom, both were asleep almost immediately. In the night, however, Richard had a dream. Suddenly awake, he sat up, got out of bed, and went to his laptop on the desk. When the software beeped, Char woke up too. "Hey! What's going on?"

"I had a dream. If it's from the Lord, Yellowstone Caldera will start erupting as the super volcano that it is while we are in the air after we leave New York. Our plane will shift its route southward but still land in Los Angeles. I'm sending Dad an email to keep an eye on the flight numbers to see if our flight lands in Los Angeles or San Diego."

Char watched over his shoulder. "You're telling them why."

"Yes." He continued to type rapidly, and then he sent it. "What was the name of that man we talked to at the benefit that was from UBS Cable News?"

She thought a minute. "Do you mean the guy who approached us just before we got back into the limo?"

"Yeah."

"No, but I remember the woman who was his anchor partner – Andrea Power."

Richard turned to looking at her. "Did you know her before that night?"

"Yeah. She's actually a second cousin of mine. Growing up, I sometimes played at her house up in Santa Monica. She's about nine years older than me, but we know each other pretty well."

"Is she a Christian?"

"Definitely. Why do you ask?"

"What do you think about telling her our story in terms of how we've learned to cast lots, and then tell her what we know about Yellowstone?"

Char was thoughtful. "Even if she believes everything I tell her, it will be risky for her to take it to either her boss or her partner."

"Then if you tell her, after that also tell her that you understand the risk she's taking if she breaks the story. Do you have her email address?"

"I can do better than that. I can call her." She walked towards the phone.

"It's about 3:00 AM here, so it is early evening on the West Coast."

Char picked up the phone, and in less than five minutes, she was talking with her cousin. At first, Andrea said that it was less than thirty minutes until she had airtime, but Char was amazingly persuasive. She condensed what they knew into a little over five minutes. Then Char said, "Andrea, tell me honestly. Do you believe what I just told you?"

"Strange as it seems, I believe you, Char. If I put this story in front of my boss, it might send my career into the stratosphere, or it could send me into the crapper. I need to get off the phone so that I can type it up and give it to him."

"Okay, Andrea. Thank you."

"I'll talk to you soon. Bye."

"Bye." Char hung up. "She believes me. With God's help, God will use her to save a lot of lives."

"I agree. I can't sleep now. We know too much. Let's get ready for bed, and then we'll worship and pray."

"Right."

They had dreamless sleep.

6.

The taxi dropped them off at Leonardo da Vinci Fiumicino Airport two hours before their flight. They had purposely eaten a good-sized meal at the hotel before they checked out. After they got through security, and they were seated at the gate, Richard composed a detailed text message covering all that they knew. Then he handed his laptop to Char. "Read this, and tell me if I have left anything out."

Char read it through, and then she went back over it. "I think you should say that there will be six full years with no sunshine in the northern hemisphere, with only a little clear sky south of the equator. Additionally, can you put a little more emphasis on starvation and possible looting?"

Richard nodded and took his laptop back. He seemed to type even more rapidly than he played the piano.

When he handed it back to her, and she read it again. "Good. I think that covers it. Now, who are you going to send it to?" She handed it back to him.

"I've got both our address books on here. I'll send it to everyone in my address book – how about yours?"

"Okay, but put my name with yours in the signature area."

He nodded. "Right." He typed rapidly for a moment. "Do you have any final thoughts?" His hand was poised over the 'Enter' key.

Char looked into Richard's eyes. "Let God be glorified! Do it!"

He hit the enter key.

It would be many hours before they began to realize what they accomplished with that e-mail. His address book reflected his newfound fame, including addresses in the media, in universities, and in government offices.

His brother's email, monitored by the CIA, picked it up, and it generated a flurry of activity. Her address book included contacts through her father's business and various industries. It was the Internet equivalent of stirring up an anthill.

Less than an hour later, their plane took off, bound for New York's John F. Kennedy International Airport. During their nine-hour flight, they read, talked, and prayed, but mostly they slept. Both got up and walked the length of the plane a few times. Three people recognized Richard, and he signed autographs.

Since they were in first class, they were among the first to get off the plane and go up the gangway into JFK airport. As they came through the door, a man and a woman approached them, showing FBI badges. "Richard and Charlotte Donovan, we're with the FBI, would you please come with us? We'll take care of getting your baggage through customs, and we'll see to it that you're on your next flight on time. Meanwhile, there're some people that want to talk with the two of you." The woman led the way, and the man followed Richard.

They went down several corridors, and as they came through a doorway, Richard's brother, Josh stood up. "Hi, Richard! Hi, Char!" Did you have a good flight?" He shook Richard's hand and gave Char a hug.

Richard cocked his head to one side. "Are you here because of that email I sent a few hours ago?"

"Yeah, and more."

Char shook her head. "Why, Josh?"

You sent it addressed to everyone in your address books, but you didn't use blind carbon copy."

Char burst out laughing. "I'm sorry to laugh, but that means everybody saw who got the email as well as the email itself."

Josh smiled. "Yeah. The addresses alone took up four pages. I work for the CIA, as you know, and it took us a few hours just to go through all the addresses and identify them. All those governmental and industrial addresses, as well as celebrity addresses, sent up red flags like confetti. It made our whole agency scramble!"

Richard chuckled, and then he saw another man standing there who they did not know. "Who's this, Josh?"

He smiled. "I'm sorry. This is Reginald Curry, the U.S. Secretary of the Interior. Mr. Curry, this is my brother, Richard Donovan, and his wife Charlotte. Most people call her Char."

They shook hands, and then Reginald Curry spoke. "Please sit down for a moment." They sat down around a table there in the room. "As your brother said, that email caused quite a stir, to say the least. As a prophecy, it did not read like the stuff we often read in the tabloids. It was so detailed. It was very convincing. But then God above nailed it."

Char raised her eyebrows. "God nailed it?"

The secretary chuckled. "I'm a Christian, just as you are, though I probably don't go to church as often as you two do." He paused. "When you sent that email, it was time-stamped, hours, minutes, seconds, just as all emails are – or at least should be." He paused, scratched his head, and then smiled. "At the very moment you sent those emails out onto the Internet, there was a jolt of an earthquake measuring 7.8 on the Richter scale in Yellowstone. It was in addition to the quake swarm that was and still is going on under the area. That jolt got our attention, and according to your timeline, the main eruption should begin in about..." he looked at his watch, "...two hours."

The Secretary of the Interior stood up, and the others stood up with him. "I just wanted to meet you today, so I can tell President Williams that I did so. I'm not sure, but you may hear from him soon. Everything may begin to change drastically in two hours. Now, the FBI will get you on your plane. The pilot has been told in confidence what is about to happen, and he will be routed a little further south than usual. The flight plan still takes you into Los Angeles, but he may have to divert to San Diego, which would be better for you anyway. It was nice to meet you two. ... Now, go!"

"Thank you, sir," they said almost together.

The two FBI agents walked them to their plane and stood on the gangway until the plane's door was closed. Richard and Char settled into their seats, and soon the plane was being pushed away from the gate. She stared out the window. "With you staring out the window that way, I'm wondering what's so interesting out there."

"What?"

"What's so interesting out there?"

"Nothing, I guess. I was just thinking – when you were using those nickels with worship before we graduated, how often did you get a mix of heads and tails?"

He was thoughtful. "I guess not very often, but I wasn't keeping track. Why do you ask?"

Char turned to looking at him and spoke quietly. "Our anniversary comes up next week. We've been married almost a month. We've worshiped together every day since the day after our wedding, and we've cast lots in worship nearly every day. When we do so, we never do it less than half-dozen times, except when God doesn't answer – and we sometimes use them even more."

Richard was thoughtful, and then his mouth dropped open. He closed it. He also spoke quietly. "I'm in awe." He paused. "By now, a lot of people know that we cast lots as part of our worship. There're going to be those who call it just gambling, and there're those who will label what we do as evil. There might even be a few who accuse us of causing the Yellowstone Caldera to erupt."

"Whoa! May God protect us! We have to trust Him. He's led us down this path, so we have to surrender all of this to Jesus. God has given us a gift, and we have to be good stewards of our gift."

Richard nodded, and quietly he said, "Amen." He took Char's hand and closed his eyes. "Lord, we are yours, now and always. Amen."

"Amen."

The plane's public address system crackled to life. "Ladies and gentlemen, may I have your attention please. Our captain has informed us that there is bad weather throughout the northern Rocky Mountains. So air-traffic control is shifting our route further south. This could take ten to fifteen minutes longer, but he will try to make up the time. Those of you with connecting flights out of Los Angeles will still be able to get to those flights. Thank you."

In Los Angeles, the flight arrival and departure displays said that their flight from JFK was arriving at Gate B18. When Richard's parents checked with the airline, they were told that their son and daughter-in-law would arrive at Gate C-5, so they waited at the security checkpoint near that concourse. They didn't even look at the display.

Meanwhile, hundreds from the media were waiting near the security checkpoint at the other concourse. By the time a plane from Miami arrived at Gate B18, Richard, Char, and his parents were on their way back to La Jolla. Debby Donovan spoke animatedly. "Your Dad and I have been getting calls from your realtor almost every day."

Char smiled. "Has he found anything for us?"

Debby nodded. "He found quite a few places that were down in the valley, but you two wanted to be in the mountains. He has found you two houses at Lake Arrowhead. When your pay came from London, the bank called him and told him that they would take care of all the financial arrangements, whichever house you pick.

One of the houses is available immediately, and the other one will be ready for occupancy in two weeks."

Bob spoke up. "Your Mom and I talked about letting you stay with us temporarily, but we got a call from the Hilton where you did the benefit concert. They have a suite waiting for you if you want it." He paused. "You know what's going on at Yellowstone, don't you?"

Richard looked at Char, and she nodded. She said, "Yes, Dad, we do. What was the last news you heard?"

"They're calling it a super-volcano. They're estimating that the final mountain could be twenty thousand feet or higher. That's just media speculation, of course."

Richard shook his head. "That's not the worst of it. We're headed for a nuclear winter that will last more than six years."

Debby turned to facing him. "What do you mean a nuclear winter?"

"The volcanic ash from the volcano is being shot into the air to elevations of a hundred thousand feet and more. That will cause what can be described as an anti-greenhouse effect. Cooler temperatures worldwide will mean year-round winter conditions, losses of crops, and widespread starvation all over the Earth. Millions of people may die over the next six years."

Char's cell phone rang. She looked at the screen. "It says 'Potus.' I don't know a Potus, do you, Richard?"

He gestured for her to give him the phone. "Hello. ... Yes, I'll hold. ... Yes, sir, this is Richard Donovan. ... Yes. ... No, sir, not until tomorrow morning. It will be best to meet with the whole cabinet... no, sir, we have to pray first. ... No, sir. With all due respect, Mr. President, we know more about it than you do. ..." Char's eyes got huge. "No sir. ... No, sir. ... We can be at the main gate at 8:00 AM. ... Very well, sir, 5:00 A.M. As you wish, sir. We will see you tomorrow." Richard hung up. "What you saw on the screen was the acronym for 'President of the United States,' P-O-T-U-S. He wants us to be in

Washington tomorrow morning. I guess the Hilton shuttle can take us to Coronado Island. We need to be there at 0500. A Navy jet will fly us into DC. You heard the rest of the conversation."

Quietly, Char said, "Did he want us to go right now?"

"Yeah, but you heard me refuse. You and I have a lot of praying to do tonight."

"That is for sure!" She turned to his parents in the front seat. "Mom, Dad, we'll have to tell you more about our first tour after we get back from Washington. In the next week or so, you had better be sure that your house is weather tight and as insulated as you can make it."

+ + +

At the gate on Coronado Island, there was a jeep waiting for them, and it led the Hilton Hotel shuttle across to the runway. The military-version Gulfstream was waiting, and it took off immediately. They had prayed through the night, and now they were confident, though both were somewhat scared.

When they landed in Washington, the sky was dark with clouds, and a cold wind was blowing. Their car was escorted by a motorcycle with flashing lights but no siren, and they quickly found themselves at the entrance to the White House. Security was quick but thorough, then they were led deeper inside by a Marine.

They were escorted to a substantial room nearly filled by a huge oblong table. People were already seated around it, but President Williams was not there. Seated next to Richard was Reginald Curry, Secretary of the Department of the Interior, who they had met at JFK Airport when they returned from Rome. He greeted them warmly, "Richard, Charlotte, it is good to see you. I hope you were able to get some rest last night."

They shook their heads, and Richard said, "No, sir, we did not sleep."

Mr. Curry then introduced them to everyone at the table, which took several minutes. After introducing the woman on Char's right, who was Postmaster General, a moment later President Everett Williams entered and sat down. "Good morning, everyone."

There was a chorus of "Good morning, Mr. President."

He looked at Char and Richard. I assume you are the Donovans." They nodded. "Welcome. Since the two of you provided the warning for the disaster that is beginning to unfold, we are all here to listen to what you may have to say, though that email was surprisingly detailed. Please add to what it said as you think appropriate. The floor is yours."

Richard nodded. "Thank you Mr. President, his eyes scanned everyone around the table, "and thank you everyone for listening to us. We are both eighteen years old, and we graduated about a month ago from high school in La Jolla, California. The morning after our graduation, we got married, and for the last few weeks, we have been on a concert tour in Europe. I am a pianist, and Char is gifted using electronic keyboards." He looked at Char.

"He has told you that because we wish to acknowledge at the beginning that we know we are very young, and we have no political expertise. We are still growing, both spiritually and in other ways. Most of what we have to say will sound incredible, if not impossible." She looked at Richard.

"On the first flight of our honeymoon, I told Char about my ongoing interest in casting lots as a means of prophecy. We had both heard a Bible teacher tell us about the Biblical practice when we were in the ninth grade. I still carry a little film canister with two nickels in it. With it, I was on an exploring adventure of sorts. Char was very skeptical, but in Chapel of the Transfiguration in Grand Teton National Park, we tried it for the first time as a couple. The results stunningly convinced us that God was speaking to us in this way, and every day ever since we have been worshiping with each other with the inclusion of casting lots. It will not be helpful for you to hear all the details of the last few weeks." He looked at Char.

"Let us summarize for you what Biblical casting lots is about this way." She reached into her pocket and brought out coins. "Here are three pennies. Most of you have gambled at one time or another, so you know a little about gambling and odds. In a moment, I hope it will be clear to you that what we do is not gambling. If I drop these three pennies on the table," (she does so), "the odds are rather small that all three will come up heads or all three come up tails. Do you all understand that?" Everyone around the table nodded. "If you understand those odds to be small, what are the odds that someone could do that six times in a row, and all three of them come up heads?"

Several people smiled. The President murmured, "That would be almost bizarre."

Richard nodded. "We agree. During the last few weeks, when we worshiped, we asked God questions, where all heads meant yes and all tails meant no." There were murmurs around the table. "Please don't jump to conclusions. We agreed at the beginning that, when we first cast the coins in worship, if the result is a mixture of heads and tails, God is not talking to us. That means we stop." There was more murmuring around the table.

Robin smiled. "As incredible as this sounds, we will tell you something that is mathematically virtually impossible. Since the day after our wedding, we have cast lots in worship every day. In each instance except for one, we have cast lots at least six times. We have done it as many as fourteen times. In that one exception, it came up a mixture of heads and tails. Otherwise, every time we have cast lots as part of worship, the result has either been all heads or all tails."

There was total silence. More quietly, she said, "Every time, the prophetic result was fulfilled up through yesterday. Some of what we learned last night in worship may not be fulfilled for seven years."

President Williams' eyes bore into them. "Please explain that."

Richard nodded. "A nuclear winter is beginning. It is the reverse of the so-called greenhouse effect. Clouds will cover most of the Earth for the next six-and-a-half years, and our planet will cool significantly, like a minor ice age. The crops of traditional farming will fail. Starvation will be rampant. Millions of people will die. The clouds will not significantly scatter until seven years from now."

The President asked, "Do you expect us to believe all of this?"

Char shook her head. "One of the things we know is that many will not believe us until it is too late. Politicians who try to profit from this disaster, either politically or financially, will be assigned to the ash heap of history. If God reveals things to us regarding individuals, we will declare whatever God reveals. Frankly, the two of us are cynical regarding our government."

"Has God revealed anything to you about me?"

Richard looked at him. "Mr. President, if you want to hear it, we will tell you, but you will not like it."

The President looked around the table. "Tell me."

Char looked at him. "If we tell you here, in front of your cabinet, will you still see to it that we get back home safely?"

The President nodded solemnly. "These are my witnesses."

Richard nodded. "Very well, Mr. President, we will tell you simply this: If you totally abandon your partisan ways, you will succeed in getting a favorable spot in history. If you do anything, however, for partisan reasons, for either political or financial gain, you will be mostly forgotten by history."

The President cocked his head. "Do you have any personal suggestions – either of you – that might help in this crisis?"

Char nodded. "This is not from the Lord, but from me, based upon what I've learned from one of my history teachers and from my father. ... Our biggest problems will be food supplies and looting. I think martial law would only make things worse. Local law enforcement will need all the help it can get, though. As for food supplies, the government stockpiles will run out quickly, but you can use the military to set up greenhouses for growing hydroponics crops."

Richard nodded. "This reverse greenhouse effect caused by the volcanic ash will render many environmental regulations moot, and some will be destructive to our population. That agency needs to relax their enforcement of regulations meant to forestall the so-called greenhouse effect. This nuclear winter renders all arguments regarding the greenhouse gases to be moot for at least several years. Electric supplies and various fuel supplies must be maintained, regardless of environmental concerns. Power will be needed not just for normal heating and light. It will also be needed to help with the greenhouse crops. Beyond all this, Char and I will continue to pray, even as I continue to perform as concert venues become available."

Char nodded again. "We'd like to go home now, Mr. President."

Reginald Curry said, "Excuse me, Mr. President, but if you'll permit me, I'll see to it that they get home."

"Thank you, Mr. Curry, but that won't be necessary. General Oswald, as Chairman of the Joint Chiefs, you got them here. It's up to you to get them home. They are to have twenty-four-seven security, but have that security stay in the background as much as possible. If they need assistance in getting into their new home now that their honeymoon is officially over, see to that too. The San Diego Hilton cannot keep them free forever. They're going to be looking at houses the next few days."

"Yes, Mr. President, I'll take care of it. Char? Richard? Please come with me."

As they left the conference room, there was vigorous discussion. As they flew south and west back to San Diego, they both slept soundly.

> "Dad, after you and Mom got married, did you sleep here that night?"

> "No, son, we did a concert tour in Europe for our honeymoon."

> "Did you come back here when you got home?"

> "No. We lived in a hotel until we moved in here."

> "Was this the first house you looked at?"

> "No, we looked at several houses, but God helped us find this one."

7.

It was the middle of July, but at Lake Arrowhead, there was more than a foot of snow on the ground. Soon, the lake was expected to freeze over completely. The first house they looked at was not what either of them liked. Now in the second house, they stood in the living room, looking out over the lake. Their realtor, Ricky Hanson was encouraging. "This has over thirty-five hundred square feet, and it has everything you said you wanted. The seller has lowered the price because he wants to live closer to the ocean."

Richard nodded as he stepped back from the window and looked around again. "This 'great room' is big enough for having a couple of pianos. What do you think, Char?"

"It's what I pictured us as wanting in so many ways, and we can afford it, but this is an important decision. We have to pray about this. Using Ontario as our airport would be so much better than LAX, with fewer crowds. I'm having second thoughts about the area though, Richard."

"Okay." He turned to the realtor. "Ricky, we'll go back to San Diego and pray about it. We like it, but we're a couple that prays about most decisions, particularly major ones."

"I understand."

"We will probably call you tomorrow morning after breakfast, okay?"

"Okay." They zipped up their coats, and went back to their cars. "I'll look forward to your call. Have a safe drive back down south to San Diego."

They waved, and the two cars headed down the mountain. Richard was curious. "What are your second thoughts, lover? Is it the house, the area, or what?" He glanced over at her.

"It's not the house. It's almost exactly what I pictured in my mind when we told Ricky what we wanted. I've always loved Arrowhead, and I love Big Bear practically as much. I think we should make a list of general locations and cast lots for where we should live. Somehow, I think it may be important to our future."

He nodded. "If we're going to consider locations, I would start with Arrowhead at the top, followed by Big Bear. Where else comes to mind?"

"If we're thinking in terms of airport access, those are the two best places in the Inland Empire area. I wouldn't want to fight the traffic in Orange County. What about the Long Beach area?"

"Really? I thought you wanted to be in the mountains. That's on the ocean. We might as well be in San Diego."

Char shook her head. "The Long Beach Airport is small but very nice. If you perform regularly with the Los Angeles Philharmonic, Long Beach would be considerably closer."

Richard shook his head and smiled. "Charlotte Hickman Donovan, there are so many orchestras in so many cities. I doubt that we'll be in Los Angeles as often as you think."

She leaned over and kissed him on the cheek. "You're right! I was thinking too provincially. Still, there're two places in that area that would be worth considering."

"Name them."

"I'm thinking of Signal Hill and Rolling Hills."

"I know where Signal Hill is – it's just south of the Long Beach Airport. Where's Rolling Hills?"

"They're north and slightly west of San Pedro, in the Palos Verdes Hills. It's a short distance from the Long Beach Freeway, giving us accesses not only to the Long Beach Airport, but, by freeway, the rest of Southern California."

Richard nodded. "It sounds decent. Are there any other areas you think we should pray about?"

Char was thoughtful. "The only other area I can think of is north and east of the Burbank Airport."

Richard shook his head. "I'm not real fond of the Bob Hope Airport, though it is small. Those hills can get blistering hot and smoggy in the summer."

Char nodded. "Okay. Since we plan to have kids, let's try to avoid the smoggier areas. Didn't you sign a contract with Fogg Talent Management?"

"Yes. A woman named Bobbi is our new manager. Why?"

"Why don't I give her a call, and see if she has any suggestions?"

"Go for it."

The call lasted more than a half hour, keeping them well occupied as they drove into the greater San Diego area. As they pulled into the Hilton's valet parking, they were ready for dinner.

They got on an elevator, and pushed the button for their floor. Char looked up at Richard. "I think before we change our clothes and go to dinner that we should have some worship and cast lots."

"That's a good idea. Dinner can wait for a while, although I must admit I'm hungry."

In their room, after shedding their jackets and shoes, they knelt on the bed. They thanked God for the day and for their safe travel to and from Arrowhead. They also prayed for President Williams and his cabinet. Char asked, "Heavenly Father, will you please speak to us regarding where we should live?"

Heads-heads-heads.

Richard asked, "Lord, do you want us to live in that beautiful house we saw at Lake Arrowhead?

Tails-tails-tails.

Char prayed, "Lord, is it your will that we find a house in Rolling Hills, above San Pedro and the Palos Verdes Peninsula?"

Tails-tails-tails.

Char cleared her throat. "Father, is it your will that we live in the Big Bear Lake area?"

Tails-tails-tails.

Richard put his head down on the bedspread. "Father, the other place we have considered is Signal Hill. Is there a house there that you want us to have?" He rose up and tossed the quarters.

Heads-heads-heads.

"Okay. Will you please guide us to the house you want us to have?"

Heads-heads-heads.

"Forgive me Lord, but I'd like to ask one more question. Is this house important to both our future and the future of others?"

Heads-heads-heads.

"Amen! Thank you Lord!"

"Yes, thank you Lord! Amen!" Char hugged her husband and kissed him. "Honey, why don't you call Ricky while I start getting ready for dinner?"

"Okay." He took out his smart phone and pushed numbers. "Ricky? This is Richard."

"Richard? I thought I wasn't going to hear from you until tomorrow morning. Have you decided to take that house at Arrowhead?"

"No, I'm sorry Ricky. It's fantastic, but after serious prayer we know where we'll find the house we both need and want. It's on Signal Hill, not far from your Long Beach office."

"I'm in Long Beach now. Let me get to my computer." There was a long pause. "I've got two houses for sale on Signal Hill ... no, wait! One just was listed a minute ago. ... Let me look at the features. ... Okay. ... The new one is forty-two hundred square feet. It's about the same price as the Arrowhead listing. ... Yes! This might be the one for you. How soon do you want to see it?"

"How about tomorrow? We can fly into the Long Beach Airport, and you can show us all three if necessary. It could be either in the morning or the afternoon."

"I'm free in the morning. What time shall I pick you up?"

"As I recall, there's a daily flight out of San Diego into Long Beach leaving here at about ... just a minute, let me get to my computer." Richard paused. "Hang on a moment, let me tell Char." He called out, "Char, how about we fly into Long Beach tomorrow morning?"

He heard her voice from the bathroom. "What time?"

"We'd leave here about 7:00 to fly out at 8:30."

"That's fine. Does Ricky have something?"

"Yes! A new listing."

"I'm okay with looking at whatever he's gotten."

Richard turned back to his phone and clicked a URL on his computer. "Okay, Ricky. Char and I will fly out of San Diego at 8:35 and land in Long Beach just after 9:00."

"Is it that little commuter airline, Fast-Flight?"

"Right. See you tomorrow morning." He hung up.

+ + +

The flight to Long Beach was somewhat bumpy. After landing, they walked quickly to Ricky's car. "You take shotgun. I'll get in the back seat." Richard held the front door for Char, and then opened the rear door and got in. Ricky's car was large, roomy, and warm. A few snowflakes were drifting down.

Ricky put the car in gear, and they headed out on Donald Douglas Drive to Lakewood Boulevard, where he turned right. "The first house I'm going to show you is the new listing I mentioned. I think it was listed probably five minutes before you called. I remember its being built after the condominium complex burned down last year. On the same half-acre of land that the high-rise condos sat is this house." He turned left on Willow.

A few minutes later, Richard shifted forward. "Did you say that there was a fire?"

Ricky turned south on Redondo Avenue. "Yeah. There was a condominium high-rise there at the top of Signal Hill. They were very expensive and had panoramic views of this part of the county. The fire gutted the whole place, and it was razed. Insurance did not cover it all, and people walked away from it. The property was auctioned off, and this house was built." He turned right on Hill Street.

Moments later, they were approaching the top of the hill. Char asked, "How far above the ocean are we up here?"

"The hill's top is a little over three hundred fifty feet above sea level. It's not high, but there are days when you are above the smog or fog, and you can't see the houses below you very well. Here we are." He pulled into the driveway of a triple garage, and they got out.

Richard stretched. "That cold wind cuts right through us, doesn't it, Char?"

"It does. Let's get inside quickly, Ricky."

"Okay. He led them up a curving sidewalk through a well-landscaped yard. "Even with this cold weather, so far the plants are doing okay. There's an irrigation system on a timer that's keeping everything watered." He opened the front door, which was beautifully paneled dark wood and heavy. "This is a wood-clad steel door, so it provides decent security. I turned off the security system about a half-hour ago."

Char and Richard walked into the entry hall. There was a large spiral staircase on their right going both up and down. They hung their coats on a natural wood coat rack there in the hall. There was also a shoe rack. Opening large sliding doors, they walked into a huge room. Ricky said, "Just like the house at Arrowhead, this one is centered on a great room. This one seems larger because the ceiling is so much higher with the cathedral ceiling. It's a little longer too."

Char was smiling. "I like it. It has a nice feel."

Richard went to the windows, which faced three directions, and walked most of the perimeter of the room. He clapped his hands a couple of times. "It has nice acoustics. It's pretty live, but we would need to put in drapes for privacy anyway. That would deaden things a bit. What's through there?" Richard pointed.

"That leads to the kitchen. There's a mud room just inside the back door to the left. On the right is a breakfast nook. Then, under the upstairs bedrooms are a home theater, a storage room, and a half bath." He pointed.

Char headed for the doorway, and Richard followed. Ricky snapped on a light switch, and the kitchen lit up. Char was impressed. "This is terrific – stainless steel built-ins, stone counter tops, the works. It's nice and large, too. I like it."

Richard nodded and smiled. "Let's see the home theater." He walked on ahead and in. "This is very nice. Is the owner leaving the equipment behind, Ricky?"

"Yes. Mr. Eng says it does not fit into his new home over in Malibu."

Richard turned to Ricky. "Did you say his name is Eng? Is his first-name Akira?"

Ricky looked at the listing in his notebook. "Yes! Do you know him?"

Richard grinned. "Definitely! He's the maestro of the London Philharmonic in Great Britain. We met him last month when I performed with him."

Char smiled. "It's a small world! Let's see the bedrooms. I assume they are upstairs."

"Yes. Come this way." Ricky led them up the spiral staircase. "There's another staircase, a straight one, at the other end of the hall. It's for emergencies, and it's designed to be fire resistant for twenty minutes." He led them into the master bedroom, which was very substantial. He then showed them two walk-in closets and a sizeable contemporary bathroom. After showing them two other slightly smaller bedrooms and a roomy bathroom in the hall, he led them back downstairs. "What do you think?"

Char pointed downward from the entry hall. "What is downstairs?"

Ricky grinned. "That's a surprise I didn't tell you about. Come on." He led them down an extension of the spiral staircase. When they reached the bottom, they were facing a sliding glass door, dark on the other side. The realtor reached for a switch, and the lights illuminated a swimming pool and hot tub. "Surprise!"

"Whoa!" Charlotte grinned, and so did Richard. "Upstairs was not humid, and I didn't smell chlorine, so this never occurred to me! This is all totally underground, isn't it? There're no windows!"

"Right," said Ricky. "Through those slotted doors is a room under the kitchen that houses the pool equipment water heater, a geothermal heating and cooling system for both the house and pools, and an emergency generator. The generator kicks on within a few seconds if there's a power failure, and it turns back off automatically when power is restored. It runs on natural gas." Ricky punched in a code on an eye-level touch-pad, and the sliding doors opened. They went in. Inside, it was warmer and humid.

Richard looked around. "I see that the walls are tiled. That's nice. I don't smell any chlorine."

"That's because, just like with many indoor hot tubs, bacteria and viruses are treated with fluorine. It has little or no noticeable odor. Fluorine can't be used in outdoor pools because it breaks down in sunlight. ... Now that you've seen it all, what do you think?"

Richard glanced at Char, who was still smiling. "We both like it, but we need to see the other two houses. Then we'll pray about it."

+ + +

The other two houses were both smaller and older, but one of them had an observatory in the attic, equipped with a retractable roof and a post for mounting a telescope. When Char asked Ricky if the first house had an attic, he said that there was one above the kitchen.

After having lunch at The Four Fiddlers, they returned to the airport for the flight back to La Jolla. As they were about to say their good-byes, Richard had a parting comment. "As before, our bank is ready to take care of the financing on whatever house we choose. When we're prepared for our choice, we'll call the bank, and the bank will call you. That's because one or both of us might be on the road. If necessary, you know our lawyer, Jane Stark. She's empowered to purchase the house we choose."

Ricky nodded. "I remember. Have a safe flight, you two!"

After saying their farewells, they went out to the plane. On the short return flight, they talked about the features of all three houses. Both liked the house on the northeast side of Signal Hill because they knew they could see both the lights of Southern California at night and see planes taking off and landing at the airport. The other two houses faced southwest, and they had views of Catalina Island when there was no fog or smog to obscure it. All three houses had either sunrise or sunset views. Char was not sure about having a pool in the house when they had children.

When they were worshiping and casting lots, they wanted to be sure that they got God's choice, so they cast lots for the two houses at Lake Arrowhead, as well for the three on Signal Hill. Tails-tails-tails came up for all the houses except one, and it got heads-heads-heads. They said 'amen' with no further question in their minds.

"Mom, why don't we keep the cross on our roof anymore?"

"We have a neighbor who is not a Christian, and he filed a complaint."

"I like having the cross up there when I'm sleeping, Mom."

"I do too, honey, but now we keep it in the box in the closet. I don't know why our neighbor is still complaining, but he is."

"I know why, Mom."

"Okay, why is he complaining?"

"Whenever I wake up in the middle of the night, I take it out of the box, put it up there, and plug it in. When my alarm goes off, I go up and take it down."

8.

Early in the morning in early September, Char glanced at the caller ID as she picked up the phone on the nightstand of their bed. "Good morning, General Oswald. It's good to hear from you."

"Good morning. Is your husband handy?"

"No, sir, Richard is downstairs practicing and can't be disturbed."

"My staff and I have been scratching our heads, trying to figure out where to set up greenhouses for hydroponics crops. The trouble is, even in the southern states, snow is going to get pretty heavy, and most greenhouses aren't built strong enough to support the weight of massive snow. The idea that you and Richard offered us just does not seem practical. Do you honestly think we should go ahead on that basis anyway?"

"No, sir. We have cast lots for this, and I've been expecting to hear from you. If you do a survey of government properties that include underground installations, many of them are no longer used. They can easily be turned into moderate climate crop-growing facilities that don't need to be heated very much. You will only need to install lighting for plant growth. Don't forget, you need to notify your counterparts in friendly nations on that. Cooperation is the key when it comes to alleviating wide-spread starvation."

"When the word gets out we've got food, there may be a large migration from Latin America northward."

"Yes, sir. Our borders need more controls, northern as well as southern."

"Has God given you any particular word regarding food distribution to Canada?"

"No sir."

"Word we have from Brazil is that they are quickly getting organized to cooperate with other countries feed the rest of their continent."

"That's good to hear."

"I'll call you again in a week or two to see if you have any further helpful word."

"Thank you, General Oswald. We will expect your call. Good-bye." She hung up.

Cinching up the tie on her bathrobe, Char left the bedroom and went downstairs. She walked across the great room towards Richard, who was practicing silently on their digital Yamaha keyboard, using headphones.

He looked up, stopped playing, noted something on his music, and hung his headphones around his neck, smiling. "Hi, beautiful. What's up?"

Char leaned down and gave him a lingering kiss. "Good morning, again! We just got the call we expected from General Oswald. I told him what the Lord had revealed to us about underground agriculture. I also told him to pass the word to our country's political friends as you and I discussed. I also mentioned border security, but he did not indicate he knew of any particular problems. Shall I call your brother? If we do, I hope the general won't think we're going around him."

Richard shook his head. "My impression of that man is that he's both brilliant and practical. I don't think he'd get angry if he got word from the CIA. I can take a break to call him, if you'd rather."

She shook her head. "You keep practicing. I promised to keep distractions for you to a minimum today. When we break for lunch, I'll fill you in."

"Thanks." He winked. "I love you." She grinned. He put his phones back over his ears and resumed playing the keyboard.

In the kitchen, Char brewed a cup of Earl Grey tea, and then she went back upstairs. In the smaller bedroom they used part-time as an office, she sat down and dialed Josh's cell phone. "Hey, Char, how's the weather up there?"

"Cold and dark, Josh. Yours?"

"The same. What's up today with you and Richard?"

"Richard's practicing, and I'm taking care of business, although I've not even had any breakfast yet."

"I just finished an early lunch. Are you calling only to rattle my ear, or have you got something else on your mind?"

"Both. I like chatting with you, Josh, but before I go further, have you and Francine set a date yet?"

He chuckled. "We're trying to set up a date to have our wedding in that glass chapel a few miles from you."

"Are you talking about Wayfarer's Chapel in Rancho Palos Verdes?"

"Yeah. We're having a hard time coordinating a date."

"Richard and I know that chapel very well. It's a small venue for weddings, but it is uniquely beautiful."

"Right. That's why we like it. I only have a little time, Char. What else is on your mind?"

"I had an expected call from General Oswald this morning."

"The Chairman of the Joint Chiefs of Staff? What did he say?"

"It's what he didn't say that bothered me. Has the CIA told him about the Mexican cartel that plans to take over food distribution?"

"How did you ... no, never mind. I'm still getting used to you and my brother being prophets."

"So does the general know?"

"I don't know, but I'll pass the word along. I'll tell my boss that you asked. That usually gets things started. I have to go. Say hi to Richard for me."

"Okay. Bye." She hung up. Thoughtful, she looked up at the ceiling a moment. Getting up from the desk, she went to the bedroom and quickly got dressed. After brushing her hair, she went downstairs.

She stopped near Richard and his keyboard. At first, he was so totally absorbed in the music, he did not see her. Then he looked up, stopped, and lifted one earpiece on an ear. "What's up?"

"I'm fixing some breakfast. Would you like something?"

He smiled. "No thanks, I ate earlier." He lowered the earpiece back onto his ear and resumed playing.

Char fixed herself a decent-sized breakfast, heating up some pre-cooked sausages, and toasting a couple of frozen waffles. She put her plate on a tray, along with a large glass of orange juice, and took it to the far side of the great room, next to the windows. As she ate, she thought about the phone calls at first, and then she simply relaxed and enjoyed watching snow falling in big flakes onto Long Beach. In the distance, Catalina Island was completely white, looking like a giant iceberg.

Finished with her breakfast, Char went to the kitchen and put the dishes in the dishwasher. Then she went upstairs to their master bathroom. It took her only a few minutes to brush her teeth and wash her face. Then she went back to her desk in the office bedroom. Sitting down, she touched another number she knew well. "Good morning, Bobbi, this is Char Donovan."

"Good morning, Char. Is Richard going to be ready for Friday night?"

"He'll be ready. He always is. Since this performance is local, we'll drive our own car. As I understand it, the Philharmonic comes to Long Beach about five times a year. Is that correct?"

"Correct. I'm coming with my husband to this one, because I have a particular love for the Tchaikovsky First."

"I love it too. Richard's been asked to do it in Moscow next spring. I've marked my calendar tentatively, so let me know as soon as it is definite."

"We should know for certain by the end of this week. Snow doesn't bother the Russians. They've been dealing with long, hard winters for centuries, haven't they?"

Char laughed. "Isn't that the truth? You'll notify the State Department when the date is set?"

"I'll take care of it, Char. Some of our other artists have to reschedule performances. Flights in the northeastern U.S. and Western Europe are being canceled. Volcanic ash is making air travel impossible. The ash is spreading a little wider each day of course."

Char made more notes on her laptop. "It will get worse before it gets better."

"Right. I have another date to ask you about. It's short notice."

"Shoot."

"In Tokyo, there's a Bach festival in January. In addition to Bach's St. Matthew Passion performed by the Philadelphia Orchestra with the Münchener Bach-Chor from Munich, the German Chorus wants to perform a Bach motet accompanied by piano, but they have not decided *which* motet yet. They are asking Richard to do that accompaniment, and the sponsor wants him to do a selection of his favorites of keyboard works by J. S. Bach also. They're offering an interesting and unusual incentive to get Richard to say yes on this short notice."

Char was typing rapidly on her laptop. "What's the incentive?"

"The piano for the event will be a Bösendorfer Model 290 Imperial. As his fee, they will let Richard keep the piano after the performance. Of course, they will pay all expenses for both of you, and they will pay for shipping the Bösendorfer to your home."

Char stopped typing. "Wow! That's an amazing offer. What is the date they need us, and how soon do you need to know?" She started typing furiously again while she listened.

"The performances will be January five and six, and you will need to be there on the first for rehearsals. They need to know the day-after tomorrow."

Char gulped. "You're right. That's short notice all right! Let me look at our calendar." She clicked on a symbol on her taskbar and scrolled the calendar to January. "The first two weeks of January are clear right now. Richard and I will discuss it and get back to you."

"Okay. Let me know as quickly as you can. Bye!"

"Bye!" Char hung up. When she stood up, the phone rang, and she sat back down. "Hello?"

"Char, this is Bobbi, again. Something slipped my mind, and I had to call you back. We got a strange request from Sony, the company that is sponsoring the Bach festival."

"Did you say *strange*?"

"Yes. Richard can do the Bach festival without doing this, but this add-on just seems weird to me. Maybe it won't to you."

"Go on."

"Evidently, you and Richard did a benefit concert just before you got married, and you did an impromptu jam session in London in the early summer. It was before I connected with you through the agency. I've only heard a few snippets of comments about those two concerts."

Char laughed. "At the San Diego Hilton ballroom, the benefit concert began with Richard doing classical selections. Then, after an intermission, he and I hosted a jam session. We added a two-tier electronic keyboard set for me, along with a trap set, a xylophone, and a vibraphone. Other instrumentalists brought up their own guitars, banjos, electric guitars, a clarinet, a trumpet, a trombone, and two bass guitars, played by music professors from eleven music schools in Southern California. On each of the music stands, there were cue sheets for rock, country, folk, and jazz. The CD of the concert was published by Samaritan's Purse two weeks ago. You can get the disks online. In London, the impromptu jam session was with British musicians who joined us in Wembly Stadium. It was crazy! They recorded it, but we've not heard about a CD yet."

Bobbi laughed. "That explains a lot."

"How so? Forgive me if that sounds Japanese!"

"Right. ... Anyway, Sony wants you and Richard to host a jam session in Tokyo Dome. If you agree, they'll bring in musicians from all over Southeast Asia, New Zealand, and Australia. I think they want to outdo the British! The night before, they will want all the musicians to get together and do some planning and improvising."

Char laughed. "I'll pass this on to Richard with the rest of what you've told me. I'll get back to you tomorrow." Bye!"

"Bye!"

Char stood up and looked at her watch. It was 11:45. She went back downstairs, keeping to one side so as not to disturb Richard, and went into the kitchen. It took a little over twenty minutes for her to heat up some previously baked chicken and baked beans. She also tossed a salad and got out some chips.

As the aromas of the reheated food reached Richard's nostrils, he stopped abruptly and joined Char in the kitchen. She was pouring coffee, and she looked up. "Are you hungry?"

"You bet!" He put his arms around her and kissed her cheek. "I've pretty much got the Tchaikovsky First polished, so it's just a matter of rehearsing with the orchestra in the afternoon before the concert. What've you been up to? Did you talk to Josh?"

Char smiled. "Your brother knows how to make things happen at the CIA. It wouldn't surprise me if he got a promotion soon."

Richard nodded, closed his eyes, and looked up. "Thank you, Father, for this food and this day, for Char, and for the love you've put in our hearts for each other. Amen." He took a bite of chicken and chewed. "It wouldn't surprise me either, but I think he likes field work, so he may resist getting a promotion for a while."

"I've been talking to Bobbi. ... There's the possibility of a last-minute engagement. How'd you like for us to get a free Bösendorfer Imperial?"

Richard put his forkful of beans back on his plate. "What? Are you kidding me? We can get an absolutely free Bösendorfer Imperial?"

Char grinned. "Well, I have to admit, it would not be *absolutely* free. You'd have to work for it."

Richard was smiling with her. "Tell me what I have to do, and whatever it is – within reason, of course – I'll do it. Where is it? Do I have to carry it up Signal Hill on my back?"

Char laughed. "It won't be quite that bad, I promise."

"Go on."

"Sony Corporation is sponsoring a Bach Festival in Tokyo in January. The Philadelphia Orchestra is flying there, and they'll be joined by the Münchener Bach-Chor from Munich to perform Bach's St. Matthew Passion. The Chorus wants you to accompany them in the performance of one of Bach's motets, and Sony wants you to play some of your favorite Bach keyboard selections, all on the Bösendorfer. Our calendar is free, but we have to let Bobbi know by the day-after tomorrow. I was thinking that you could do some of that Bach organ music that has been transcribed just for the extended keyboard of that piano. I told Bobbi we'd pray about it and hung up, but she called back a few minutes later."

Richard swallowed and took a sip of coffee. "Why'd she call back?"

Char nodded and swallowed. "Bobbi said that she had forgotten to tell me about an unusual request from Sony. I don't know whether a CD of the Samaritan's Benefit got over there, or whether a Sony executive heard about our jamming in Wembly Stadium. It doesn't matter. Sony wants us to do a special jamming performance in Tokyo Dome. They will bring in well-known musicians from Southeast Asia, Australia, and New Zealand. This time, they want the musicians to get together beforehand to plan the performance and do some rehearsing. If we do it, I think that'd be a good idea."

Richard stopped eating. "I'd be willing to do it for Sony, in gratitude for the Bösendorfer. Tokyo Dome means performance in the round with what probably will be terrible acoustics."

"We can request that Sony be responsible for making the acoustics worthwhile." She put down her coffee cup.

"That's a good point. They've the resources to make it happen. It won't hurt to ask."

Richard nodded. "I'm going to get back to practicing. We'll pray about it before we go to sleep tonight, okay?"

Char smiled. "Okay. Tomorrow morning, shall we play for a while before we get up?"

Richard grinned. "You don't have to ask me that twice! ... Come join me at the piano for a moment." In the great room, he moved the adjustable piano bench to the left about a foot. "Let's do some four hands jazz. Do you want to stand, or pull up a chair?"

"I'll stand. What shall we do?"

"Let's jam 'When the Saints Go Marching In.'"

It was great fun for both for about ten minutes. As she returned upstairs, he went back to practicing. When they turned off the light that night, they both slept soundly.

"Mom, did you and Dad go back to Tokyo after the clouds went away?"

"Yes we did. That's when we learned about the churches that formed after we left."

"Were you surprised?"

"No, dear. All that God does, God does well."

+ + +

When they landed in Tokyo on New Years' Day, the airport was surprisingly quiet. Sony reserved a suite for them at the Conrad Tokyo. Going straight to their suite, they decided to take a four-hour nap before having dinner at one of the restaurants, *Kazahana*. They spent time in Bible study and worship after dinner before they retired for the night.

Early the next morning, Richard started rehearsing on the Bösendorfer piano, with Char listening in the audience seating. The German Chorus began to arrive three hours later. They had chosen *Jesu meine Freude* as the motet they would sing. There had been many emails exchanged between Richard and the director long before either of them had left their respective countries for Japan. Since it was written to be sung *a capella*, Richard had created accompaniment that did more than double the choral parts. In essence, he 'jammed' with "theme and variations" style. The director, who spoke fluent Japanese, German, and English, would introduce the motet by explaining to the audience what he had asked Richard to do.

After going through the roughly twenty-minute motet the first time, everyone in the chorus gathered around the piano, expressing their pleasure in German. Richard listened politely, smiling, not understand a word. The director interrupted with a sharp word, speaking to them in German. They smiled, and some of them chuckled. Herr Schmitt explained, "They did not realize that you don't speak German. Some of them speak English, and they will probably want to speak with you after the performance tomorrow night."

Richard nodded. "Overall, is the accompaniment what you wanted?"

"Oh, yes, Richard, I am more than pleased with what you have developed. The members of the chorus are amazed. Did you write out the accompaniment?"

Richard smiled. "In a way, a way I did. I played it on an electronic keyboard hooked up to a computer, and software generated the music. I have attached an ISBN number and copyright to it, and it is available as print-on-demand with Amazon."

"Excellent! I will share that with our audience tomorrow evening." He looked at his watch. "Let's go through it again one more time, then everyone can get something to eat. When we return this afternoon, we will begin rehearsing Bach's Passion with the orchestra. Have you been told the order of the program?"

Richard nodded. "I begin the evening with Bach selections on this Bösendorfer for about an hour. Then your chorale joins me on stage to do the motet. After a twenty-minute intermission will be Bach's Passion."

Herr Schmitt smiled. "We shall have two long but beautiful evenings, thanks to Sony, don't you think?"

"Absolutely beautiful, Herr Schmitt."

The director called the chorus back to the risers, and they rehearsed the motet once more. All were then very ready to have lunch. Richard and Char went back to the hotel. The taxi made slow progress through the snowy streets. When they saw a Japanese storefront for a Hard-Rock Café, they got out of the taxi and went in. It was a happy mixture of American and Japanese flavors.

When Richard and Char got to their room, there was a message waiting, and he picked up the receiver. "Good afternoon. This is Richard Donovan. I see that we have a message."

"Yes, Mr. Donovan. A limousine will come for you and your wife at 1400 today, and at 7:00 AM tomorrow morning, to take you to Tokyo Bowl. Breakfast will be served there tomorrow morning. That is the only message."

"Thank you very much." He hung up and turned to Char. "A limo will pick us up at 1400 this afternoon, and at 0700 tomorrow to take us to Tokyo Bowl. We'll have breakfast tomorrow there, whatever that means!"

Char grinned. "Richard Donovan! Don't you like Japanese food?"

He shook his head. "I've never had a Japanese breakfast. We had an American breakfast here at the hotel this morning, but I have no idea what that will mean at Tokyo Bowl." He looked at his watch. "That limo will be here in less than a half hour. Who knows when we'll be back?"

"Dad? Why didn't you play the Bach-Busoni piece as your encore?"

"Son, that piece can only be played on a Bösendorfer like the one we have at home."

"So, why did you choose that Chopin thing instead?"

"Your Mom likes it."

9.

After just the first rehearsal that afternoon, they knew that the Sunday afternoon jam session would be a hit. Friday evening's performance was special in many ways from Richard's point of view. The Bösendorfer piano's unique sounding board and harp produced rich harmonics that he knew were carrying clearly to the seats in the back of the large auditorium. The acoustics were amazing. The audience was blessedly silent as the German Chorus sang as he played, and they were thunderous with their applause at the end of each selection. The baroque keyboard pieces, which were originally written for pipe organ, had the sound of a small orchestra on the Bösendorfer Imperial.

When Richard finished playing Bach's *Passacaglia in C minor,* he stood up to take a bow. The audience's response began with nice applause, but it grew and grew, until all were on their feet. After taking three bows, he returned to the keyboard. The audience sat down, and all became quiet again. Richard shrugged and rotated his shoulders, closed his eyes, and tipped his face upward into the lights. Tipping his head back down and looking at the keyboard, he began the Bach-Busoni *Chromatische Fantasie und Fuge.* When he finished, faster than he had ever heard it played (let alone played it himself), the audience practically jumped to its feet, and the applause included whistles. Richard took two bows, and with his final bow, he waved and left the stage.

Char came backstage, and she wrapped her arms around him. "What inspired you to play the Bach-Busoni as an encore – and so fast?"

Richard shook his head. "I don't know. You know I planned that little a-minor fugue for an encore, but it must have been the Holy Spirit. I suddenly felt a fire inside of me, and hardly without thinking about it, I plunged into that Bach-Busoni." He lowered his voice and spoke into her ear. "I didn't know it could be played that fast."

Char looked at him and smiled. "All that God does, dear, God does well."

"Amen."

After the intermission, they took their seats in the front row for the *St. Matthew Passion*. By the end, they both had tears running down their cheeks as they smiled and applauded. It was, as Herr Schmitt had predicted, a long and beautiful evening.

When they got back to their room at the Conrad Tokyo, they read the Bible together and worshiped briefly. Then they practically fell into bed, exhausted, and it was not jet lag. Before they turned off the light, Char looked at him. "Richard, I've got to say that this concert tonight was different, and it was not just the Bösendorfer alone. Yes, as you played I felt like I was almost inside of the instrument. In addition, just like any other time we've actually performed together, I felt like I was playing with you. I can't explain it."

Richard nodded. "Maybe you can also picture something else. When I sat on that stool this evening, I felt like the Lord was within me, playing with me, and giving me power. When sound returned from my touching the keys, it was as if my hands were part of the instrument. I can't explain that either. This has been a very special day. Let's get some sleep." He switched off the light.

Their wake-up call caught them by surprise. They moved quickly to get ready. The breakfast at the Dome was a surprise as well. The grill that had been set up to serve American breakfasts was as popular as the Japanese food because of the musicians from New Zealand and Australia.

After over an hour of eating, introducing themselves, and conversing, Richard looked at his watch, and he raised his voice. "Let's get out on the field, everyone. We need to figure out how we're going to accomplish this concert. I'm glad all of you can speak some English!" There was some laughter. Everyone but the meal service attendants made their way onto the field.

Sitting at a Yamaha concert grand acoustic piano, Richard spoke into the boom microphone in front of him. "The sound system is installed and functioning. There are engineers and technicians up there," he pointed to one of the sky boxes, "and they are going to be adjusting the sound of each of our instruments in order to make everything acoustically pleasing." He waved at the skybox. "Good luck up there!"

A female voice boomed over them. "Thank oo."

Richard continued. "At our first rehearsal, those of you who don't have instruments in concert c had to improvise from the cue sheets. Trumpeters and clarinetists, are your cue sheets in order?" They waved and nodded. "Good. As you know, among us are major name recording artists and Sony's featured artists, who are going to sing along with us, taking turns. They will not necessarily be singing in their usual genre. They were not with us for the first rehearsal, but they are now. Welcome, everyone." There was polite applause from all the instrumentalists, and the singers applauded the band.

"All right, we'll begin with the Rock song that launched the genre in my estimation, 'Rock Around the Clock.' Let's first do it as traditional rock, then add a country flavor, and finally do it a third time with a jazz trumpet lead." So the rehearsal began. There were several bouts with feedback as they adjusted the sound system, but other than those glitches, the entire rehearsal was both hard work and great fun.

At a few minutes before twelve, Richard stopped. "All right, are there any charts we need to go over again for anyone?" Everyone shook their heads. The drummer waved. "Yes, Arnie?"

"I see you've got some old Protestant hymns slated for country-rock style."

Richard nodded. "I was saving the stuff that Char and I would lead off until last. Listen carefully, now, and it will be a lot easier than it looks because they're all set up in a similar way. Singers, the verses are solos that you take turns on. The choruses are everyone together except for the ending. At the end of each song, first, we do a vocally dominant chorus like the previous choruses, then we do an instrumental chorus without the voices, and then we all rock out in the final chorus. It's rather detailed on the cue sheets. Does everyone understand?" There were nods. "Okay. We'll start off by doing 'Victory in Jesus.'" He paused. "Everyone ready? ... Arnie, just as it says on the cue sheet, click us off at 152 beats a minute."

After the click-off, they rocked through the song. At the end, Richard said, "These five old songs work better with a little more country and a little less rock!" There was laughter.

Kelly, one of the singers was still panting a little. "Richard, I've sung that song since I was a little girl, but I've never sung it that way before. That was FUN!"

"Good. Char, any reflections?"

She nodded. "Arnie, can you give us a sample of a beat that's a little more country?"

After a moment, he did about four bars. Arnie asked, "Like that?"

Char shook her head. "Please forgive me, but let me give you an electronic sample from a benefit concert we did at the beginning of last summer." Putting a thumb drive into her keyboard, "Victory in Jesus" from the benefit suddenly came through the sound system. She played a full verse and chorus, and then stopped it. Most of them applauded. "In addition to Richard on the piano, and with me on the electronic keyboard, the other instrumentalists in that concert were all music professors from schools in California. Here in Tokyo, we don't have to do it exactly like that, but it ought to have the same flavor, don't you think so, Richard?"

"Absolutely. All five of these songs are a little different, but they can have the same flavor. Arnie, you're nodding your head, so I know you get it. How about it, the rest of you?" The others either nodded or waved. "Good. Let's try it again. Arnie, click us off."

The second time through, it was amazingly better. Richard knew they had it. After trying each of the other four songs once, Richard had to ask a question. "We can either do these five as a set, or we can intersperse them throughout the program. What do you think? Those who think we should do them as a set, raise their hand." No one raised their hand. "Okay, then they'll be interspersed. Tomorrow afternoon, remember to pace yourselves. It's easy for the singers, because they're not singing every song. Instrumentalists don't try to play every song – that includes Arnie, and the other percussionists. You five need to get together and talk about what songs you want to skip. We've done every song at least once by now, which is more than Char and I have done in previous jam sessions. It is definitely going to be fun. Everyone, be here tomorrow afternoon, ready to come onto the field, by 0100. We'll see each other then."

As Char and Richard walked back to the limo that would take them back to the hotel, Kelly approached them. "Char, I want to ask you about that recording you played. Is it commercially available?"

Char nodded. "A disk has been available for about a month, now. It's simply called 'The Samaritan's Purse Benefit Concert.'"

"Where was it made?"

"It was made at the San Diego Hilton ballroom. The disk is selections from that evening. If you want a copy of the entire evening's concert, you can donate to Samaritan's Purse, and they will send you a set of DVDs. Unknown to us at the time, the hotel had its cameras zoomed in on us. They took no profit from it and paid for the creation of the DVD set."

Kelly nodded. "Cool! Thanks! I contact Samaritan's Purse. See you tomorrow."

Char and Richard climbed into the limo and relaxed. As the limo began to negotiate the fog and traffic, Char murmured, "There may be other things that God has in store for us this evening and tomorrow."

Richard smiled. "I wouldn't be surprised. Right now, I'm tired, but I'm not hungry."

She shook her head. "I'm not really hungry, either. We had a good breakfast. Let's skip lunch and have an early dinner in our room."

"That's a good idea." He put his arm around her, and she snuggled up to him. They rode the rest of the way in silence. At the hotel, a few stopped them for autographs, but they soon could get to the elevators and went up to their suite.

Inside, on a table near the window, was an English-language newspaper. Char picked it up, and leafed through it until she got to the entertainment section. She sat down and read the review. "Richard, I think you should send an email to our clipping service, to make sure that they get a copy of this. It's a terrific review. Some guy from the San Francisco Chronicle was there last night and wrote this review."

Richard came over and looked over her shoulder. "That's by Bob Constantine. I met him at the benefit. So he wrote us a good review?"

"Yeah, he seems to be one of the better writers I've seen lately. This is thoughtful and well written." She looked up at Richard. "The message light on our phone is flashing. Do you want to get it?"

"Yeah." He went over to the bed's nightstand and picked up the receiver. "This is Richard Donovan. Do you have a message for me?" He paused for almost a minute. "Thank you. Please answer them saying that J & J Movers is an excellent choice. Thank you." He hung up. "Sony is shipping our new piano to Long Beach airport, and J & J Movers will hold it until we're home to let them install it."

Char smiled. "That's a dream come true and an answered prayer."

He nodded. "It sure is. I'm going to take a nap until we order dinner, okay?"

Char put the paper down. "I'll join you. We've a full evening ahead, and tomorrow will be, well, I don't know. In any case, it will be hard work for both of us. Did you know when you're speaking on that microphone at the piano over at the dome, the musicians all hear you in English, but the audience hears you in Japanese?"

"Yeah, and the words to our songs are going to be in both English and Japanese on the giant screens."

Char lay down beside him. "It's sure going to be interesting!"

+ + +

The Saturday evening performances were easily equal to those of the previous night. Back at their hotel, they asked the kitchen to deliver their breakfast at 0800 and left a wake-up call for 0730. The next morning, they managed to worship and cast lots before getting into their limo, to take them to the Dome.

They were on the stage, inspecting every detail, and checking the chord sheets on every stand. Richard looked up, and he saw several of the instrumentalists walking towards the stage. He called out, "Good morning! We did not expect to see any of you before noon!"

Arnie grinned. "I guess we're like you two. No matter what the venue or the occasion, we want everything to be as perfect as possible. Besides, the weather is great inside this dome!" He grinned again.

Richard smiled. "They're going to start letting in spectators at noon. Security will be tight to keep spectators off of the field and everything running smoothly." Richard went back to work, and the time flew by. At noon, he went to his mike at the piano, and he asked that the sound system be mute until 12:45.

At noon, they warmed up with 'Rock Around the Clock' followed by 'When the Saints Go Marching In.' At 0100, Char and Richard passed the word to gather around the piano. Richard said, "Char and I are Christians. I don't know what religious preferences any of you have. I have always prayed before every performance. If that's not something you appreciate, I simply ask that you at least stand there in silence. He closed his eyes and tipped his head upward. "Heavenly Father, you gave us the talent we have, and you've provided this opportunity to share our gifts with thousands of others." Warmth began to spread over all of them. "Please guide us and empower us even beyond our talents and our preparations I ask by the name of Jesus. Amen."

The prayer was answered. As they began with "Rock Around the Clock," energy flowed through them that none of them anticipated. By the time they did the jazz trumpet version, Richard was bouncing on the piano bench, and others were practically dancing in place.

So it went. Richard had planned for two hours of music, but with all the audience feedback coming from all around them in the dome, after three hours, they were not even beginning to get tired. After the first hour, Richard told fifty-five thousand people about the benefit concert in San Diego. At the end of the second hour, Char told them about the impromptu concert in

London's Wembly Stadium. She joked that she thought Sony was trying to outdo the British, and she got a great laugh.

After three hours, Richard announced a short break again, and began to share. "My wife and I are eighteen years of age, and we count it a extreme privilege to be here in Tokyo Dome, performing with these great musicians." There was about thirty seconds of applause and cheers. "Thank you. Speaking on behalf of all the musicians on this stage, I wish to thank the Japanese people for their gracious hospitality. This performance is nearing its end, but before we close, my wife, Char, and I would like to share something with this audience which is not generally known to the public."

A hush descended upon the stadium under the dome as Char came and sat down beside Richard. Char spoke on Richard's mike. "On the second day of our honeymoon this past June, we stood in a little chapel in Grand Teton National Park, in the state of Wyoming, in the United States of America. We tried something together that we considered unique. As students of the Bible, we had heard about an approach to prophecy using the casting of lots."

Richard continued. "Most of you are not Christians, so we are sure that what we are telling you sounds very strange. We believe that there is a God who created our entire universe. We also believe He has given us a gift. We certainly do not deserve it, and we definitely do not know why." Richard stopped to let the translator catch up. "Just over thirty kilometers from where we first cast lots together, there is now a volcano, and it is continuing to grow. When historians look back on these current days, they will have authentic records to show that, for reasons we honestly don't begin to understand, Char and I knew that the Yellowstone Caldera was going to erupt, and we reported it to our country's government agencies." He paused for the translator. "All of you know why it has been snowing here these past few months. Less than twenty-four hours after the super-volcano began to erupt, we had the privilege of meeting with the President of the United States and with his governing cabinet. We could only tell the President what the casting of lots had revealed to us." Richard cleared his throat.

Tears were running down Char's face. "Evidently, the media have not been told all the details that Richard and I supplied to our government. There have been a lot of theories expressed on the Internet and elsewhere regarding this environmental disaster and the reverse greenhouse effect." She wiped her eyes.

Richard winked at her, and gestured, so she went back to the electronic keyboard as he continued. "Based upon our Christian faith and our casting lots, these dark clouds will start breaking up in a permanent way during March of the seventh year. Let's focus upon that, ladies and gentlemen. This disaster will be mostly behind us in seven years. There will be suffering between now and then, but we will rise out of the ashes and have a fresh and clean world." He paused.

"Our last song has been translated into many languages. It dates back to the ugly slave-trading days prior to the twentieth century. Those of us here on the stage are glad you came, and we thank you. Now, ladies and gentlemen, let's do 'Amazing Grace.'" He nodded at the xylophone player, who played through the melody. Then the drums started a syncopated pattern at a faster pace. As the other instruments came in, they moved on to folk, country and blues versions. As they finished, every musician was emotional to the point of tears.

Afterwards, as their limo began making its way through the traffic, fog, and snow, they told her to take them somewhere they could get really good steaks. They were taken to a small but very nice restaurant that had booths where they could have privacy. After Richard ordered a Porterhouse steak, medium rare, and Char had ordered a Kansas City Strip steak, medium, the waiter left, and they were alone.

Char spoke quietly. "This morning's paper says Mount Yellowstone is taller than Mount Whitney. We'll never know exactly, probably, but it seems about twenty thousand people have died thus far because of it. There are beginning to be food shortages."

Richard nodded. "It will get much worse before it gets better. Here in Japan, they import a large percentage of their food. Jonathan, one of our guitar players at the dome, is from New Zealand. He says that their government is taking steps rapidly to ensure an independent and reliable food supply. They are cutting back on how much tourism they will allow during this time."

A police officer approached their table. "Excuse me, please. Please forgive the interruption to your meal. You are Richard and Charlotte Donovan, are you not?"

They nodded. "There is no cause for alarm. You should know that your statement near the end of your concert this afternoon has created a sizeable stir. Many in the media are clamoring to reach you to interview you. I need to know your wishes. Do you wish to meet with representatives of the media and answer questions?"

They shook their heads. Richard was emphatic. "We are not interested in having publicity. We are simply artists who enjoy entertaining. We must get to the airport tomorrow morning for our flight back to Los Angeles."

The police officer bowed. "We will provide you with an escort to the airport, and we will take you past the airline terminal directly to your plane." He bowed again. "Please enjoy your dinner." He was quickly gone.

Char smiled. "Wow. We expected a stir. The Lord is watching over us."

"Mom, have you ever been in a submarine?"

"Yes."

"Was it cramped?"

"No, it was comfortable enough."

"Was the food good?"

"It was okay. We got tired of drinking submarine coffee, though."

10.

At 6:00 AM, the phone rang. Richard picked up the receiver. "Hello?"

"Mr. Donovan, this is the front desk. We care to call to see if you are sufficiently awake to receive a visitor. It is a police officer. He says he met you last evening at a restaurant."

Richard shook himself awake. "The policeman? Sending him up please."

"Thank you, sir." The connection went.

Char rubbed her eyes. "Was that about a policeman?"

"Yeah, the one we met last evening at the restaurant. He's on his way up."

"I'll let you see him. I'm going to go take a shower."

Richard crawled out of bed and put on his robe. Going to the bathroom with Char, he ran a comb through his hair. Just then, they heard a knock at the door. Char closed the bathroom door behind him as he went to answer.

As he opened the door, the police officer bowed. "Good morning, Mr. Donovan, please forgive my calling on you at this early hour, but it was necessary."

Richard tipped his body forward slightly. "Please come in, sir."

"Thank you, Mr. Donovan, but that will not be necessary. Last evening, I told you that I would see to your safe travel to the airport, but now I must withdraw that arrangement. Flights between Japan and countries north of the equator have been canceled due to extreme weather conditions. Your United States Navy is sending a car for you, and it will be here at 0800. Other arrangements have been made for you and your wife, but I do not know the details. Again, please forgive my early call upon you and Mrs. Donovan. I wish you a safe journey!"

Richard said, "Thank you," as the police officer bowed, turned, and walked away. Richard closed the door. He looked at his watch, and walked to the bathroom. As he came in, Char was turning off the shower. "The police will not be escorting us to the airport because flights from here to the U.S. have been canceled due to extreme weather conditions."

"As we expected."

"Yes. He said that someone from the U. S. Navy would come to the hotel at 0800. He said other arrangements have been made." The phone rang. "I'll get it." Richard went back out to the phone by the bed and picked up the receiver. "Hello?"

"Mr. Donovan, this is Lieutenant Anderson from United States Fleet Activities Yokosuka. I am the leader of the detail that will escort you, your wife, and your belongings to transportation that has been arranged for you by Admiral Patton. My detail and I should be there at your room at 0750."

Richard looked up at the ceiling. "Since we cannot fly, Lieutenant, what kind of boat will we be on, Lieutenant?"

"I am not at liberty to say, Mr. Donovan. Can you and your wife be ready at 0750, sir?"

"Yes, lieutenant."

"Thank you, sir. The two of you will be served breakfast in the Officers' Mess when you reach the base. I will see you later. Good-bye."

"Good-bye." As he hung up, Richard turned, and Char was standing at the bathroom door.

She walked towards him and gave him a hug. "Good morning, my darling. What was that about?"

"A Lieutenant Anderson of the U.S. Navy will be here at 0750 with a detail to escort us and our belongings to our Navy base at Tokyo harbor. We will have breakfast on the base."

Char kissed him and then grinned. "If we're having a truly American breakfast, I want ham, eggs, and pancakes. I have enjoyed our visit to Japan this week, and the food here at the hotel has been very good, but I'm ready for something a little more ordinary."

Richard kissed her again. "Ham, eggs, and pancakes sound great to me too." He headed into the bathroom to shave and shower.

Promptly at 0750, there was a knock on their door, and they were ready. Lieutenant Anderson and two ensigns carried everything for them downstairs and quickly loaded their belongings into waiting large SUV. Richard and Char went to the front desk. As they approached, the woman at the desk said, "Everything has been paid, Mr. & Mrs. Donovan. Please enjoy your journey home."

Char smiled. "We know that, but we would like to express personally our thanks for the hospitality here at Conrad Tokyo."

She smiled and nodded her head. "You are quite welcome. I personally attended both your Friday evening and Sunday afternoon concerts. They were both memorable and enjoyable, thank you."

Richard nodded. "You are welcome. Did Sony Corporation provide a sufficient gratuity to the hotel staff, for all of those who served us?"

Again, she smiled and nodded her head. "Sony arranged for each of us who had the pleasure of serving you to have a generous gratuity. Thank you for asking."

Richard and Char did a shallow bow together. "Then we bid you farewell, and in our Christian tradition, we say, God bless you!" Their bow was acknowledged.

Once they were in the SUV, it moved rather swiftly through the traffic. The wind and snow created blizzard conditions. At the base's gate, they were waved through and taken to the Officers' Mess and into a small dining room.

Admiral Patton was their host. After they introduced themselves, they took their seats and placed their orders.

The admiral was very friendly. "Here in private, please call me Jack. I have been looking forward to meeting you since late last night when I got a call from the Joint Chiefs. I understand that you know General Oswald."

Richard nodded and swallowed. "We first met him last summer when we were flown to Washington to meet with the President."

Char smiled. "Last night, when we were worshiping, we came to know that we were not going to be flying. That same weather that has grounded commercial air traffic is probably not a major challenge to your larger ships, is it?"

The admiral swallowed some coffee. "It can be challenging, but our personnel are trained for it. That won't be a concern for you, however. There isn't any weather under the surface of the ocean." He smiled.

Char's eyes got big. "We're going by submarine?"

The admiral nodded. "A submarine named the Thomas Jefferson was decommissioned in 1985. This new one has the same name, but publicly it does not exist yet. After you get to San Pedro, we ask that you not mention the name of the sub or any of its unique features for at least six or seven years."

Richard nodded. "We can keep mum."

Admiral Patton smiled. "Good. General Oswald told me you that you can. Your special cargo was put on board early this morning."

Richard's face was blank for a moment. Then his eyes got bigger. "Are you talking about the piano?"

The admiral chuckled. "Yes. The truck's driver and helpers from Sony were so paranoid when they brought it to the base. The case was significantly bigger than a piano, and it was covered with caution stickers. After the Sony crew left, my Seabees uncrated it from the Sony packaging and created another crate that is far safer and fits considerably more easily into the cargo bay of the Jefferson. You won't be able to play it until you get it home, but it is very safe. Do you always carry your own piano with you when you travel?"

Char laughed. "No, sir! That piano is our payment for doing three concerts in Tokyo. The concerts were arranged at the last minute, and Sony offered the unusual payment in gratitude for our perceived inconvenience. We were more than happy to accept."

The admiral nodded. "I suppose it is a Steinway."

Richard shook his head. "No, sir, it is a Bösendorfer Imperial. There's only a few made each year, and it has extra keys at the lower end of the keyboard."

"Interesting! Is that the piano you played this past weekend? It has an amazing sound."

Char nodded. "Yes, sir. I'm curious about the musicians from Philadelphia and from Munich."

The admiral swallowed the last of the coffee in his cup. "There's not room for that many on a submarine. All of them are going aboard one of our nuclear-powered carriers, and they are having breakfast there as we speak. It will take them longer to get to the states, and there will undoubtedly be some seasickness, but they will get there safely. In a few minutes, I'll introduce you two to the Captain of the Jefferson, a man named Steven Lyman. You'll be in an officer's cabin for the voyage. I'm sorry, but there are only single bunks. They're comfortable, though. Submarines almost never take passengers. For the duration of this nuclear winter, however, I'm sure we'll be making more exceptions." He got up, and so did they. "Submarines are normally very quiet, but this one's more so. In spite of when I try to listen with my trained ears, I can't hear the engines. ...

Come with me. That SUV you came in on is waiting for us."

+ + +

Their cabin was less than a quarter of the size of their hotel room, but it was comfortable. The officer's mess was a few paces away and it did not take them long to learn how to use the toilet and shower controls. They were also told about the meaning of the signal lights above their door, along with the chime and buzzer signals. Char started reading a book on her laptop. Richard studied music on his. They both lost track of time until Richard glanced at the clock. "It's almost noon. Do you want to get something to eat?"

Char looked up. "After that big breakfast? ... I suppose I could go for a salad, if they have one – something light."

When they walked into the Officers' Mess, there was a cook standing at a window. "Hi, kids. What will it be for you?"

"Are you serving lunch?" Char smiled.

"Today's selection for all meals is on the wall to your left. We fix breakfast, lunch, and dinner 24/7. Just so you know, all fruits and veggies are canned."

Richard nodded. "I'll have a cheeseburger, fries, and a root beer."

"Hot and cold beverages are to your right. You'll have your cheeseburger and fries in less than five minutes. Do you want the works on it?"

"Everything but mayo. Char, if you get a burger, we can both get onions."

"Good! Make it two, sir!"

"I'm not a sir. Just call me Shorty. Pick out a table and I'll bring your meals when they're ready. I'm not busy."

They were hungrier than they thought, and they both ate ravenously. They topped off their lunches with ice cream. Since there were no days and nights, they had to keep track of time through the clock in their cabin. Much of the ship was off-limits to them, but they explored what they could.

Finally, they awakened one "morning" because the ship seemed to be slightly rocking. After morning worship and their usual routines, they went to the officers' mess. Shorty was on duty. "Good morning, Richard, Char. I wasn't sure you'd be stopping for breakfast before heading out. We docked at San Pedro about two hours ago."

"Really!"

"Fantastic!" Char smiled. "It's been nice getting to know you, Shorty. Can you rustle up some eggs and pancakes before we go?"

"Sure! Eggs as usual for both of you?"

They nodded, and soon they were eating. They were almost done when Captain Lyman came in and poured himself a cup of coffee. "Mind if I join you?"

"No problem."

"As Shorty probably has told you, we're in San Pedro. There's no rush, but a brown SUV will be waiting for you in about thirty minutes. J & J piano movers and installers pulled up on the dock about ten minutes ago. They said they would appreciate it if you went straight to your house so that they can place your piano where you want it."

"Terrific!" Richard smiled. "We have not been home since Christmas, so we're looking forward to enjoying home life before a tour starts in March. Where's home for you, Captain?"

He smiled. "For me, and for most of my crew, home is on Coronado Island in San Diego. I understand that you two are from La Jolla?"

Char nodded. "Yes, we are. How long has it been since you've seen your family, Captain?"

"I'll have dinner with my wife here on base this evening. She's driving up today. I last saw her three weeks ago. After you two depart from us, we'll be under water for two months. Then all of us will get thirty days' leave. Where will your tour take you?"

Richard took a breath. "It's like this: We'll be traveling by Amtrak to twelve cities in thirty-four days. We'll go up the west coast from here via three stops to Seattle. Then we go south to Lake Tahoe. We turn east going all the way to Boston, with stops along the way. We'll then go south to Orlando, then work our way across the South back to our home."

The captain nodded. "My wife and I enjoy traveling by train, but until now, we've flown to most places. If I could bring my wife along, I think she just might like traveling the world here on the Jefferson." He stood up. "I'll see you off when you're ready to leave."

"Okay." Richard nodded.

Char swallowed one more gulp of juice. "We've lived out of these suitcases long enough! Let's get home!"

"I agree."

Fifteen minutes later, their SUV transport was going up the Long Beach Freeway. Their driver had been briefed on her route, so she got off at Willow and turned east to Cherry before turning south. A few thousand yards later, they were at the top of the hill at their home. While two ensigns brought in their luggage and took it upstairs for them, Richard turned on the heat, and Char headed to the kitchen. After Richard gave the driver and the two ensigns fifty dollars each, they drove off.

The J & J truck drove up just as the SUV disappeared. Both the driver and the assistant got out. "Mr. Donovan?" asked the driver. Richard nodded. "I'm Gary Lelake, and this is Tom Sudengae. We'd like to come in first to see where we're going with your Bösendorfer. I last delivered one of these Imperials about seven months ago. We like to plan ahead with the un-crating and setup."

Richard nodded. "Sure. Come this way. I'm glad the snow has stopped at the moment, and up here we're above the fog – at least for now."

"Yeah." They followed Richard inside. Gary pointed. Is that a Yamaha AvantGrand?"

"Yes. We want to nest it together with the Bösendorfer. We want the Bösendorfer on the left so that the open lid will face the front of the room."

"Okay. Tom, let's get the Yamaha clear out of the way while we set up the Bösendorfer. Even if we have to move the Yamaha, more than once, it won't affect the tuning. Besides, it's lighter."

Tom nodded. "Right."

It took them more than twenty minutes to move the Yamaha and other furniture out of the way, and then to get the Bösendorfer crate to the middle of the room. The Seabees had built an excellent crate and marked it to show where the keyboard end and top were. The movers removed five of the six sides of the crate and set them aside. The rest seemed fast and easy. The entire job took just over an hour. Richard gave both Tom and Gary hundred-dollar bills, thanking them as they left.

Richard went into the kitchen. "Do I smell green tea?"

Char nodded. "I fixed a whole carafe full. I don't think I'll be able to drink another cup of coffee for at least a month!"

Richard laughed. "Shorty is a pretty good cook, but drinking that submarine coffee was like drinking mud! I'm with you on drinking tea for a while."

She smiled. "In Tokyo, I learned really to appreciate and enjoy a well-brewed cup of green tea. We have two coffee makers that were wedding presents, and I'm dedicating one to tea only."

"Do we have food in the house?"

Char smiled. "When I got the tea out of the rotating pantry, it was full in all three segments of each shelf. I looked in the fridge, and there were fresh veggies in the drawers. The freezer has plenty of meat and other stuff. Did you ask someone to shop for us while we were gone?"

"No. I wonder how we got fresh vegetables." There was a knock at the back door. "I'll get it." As he opened the back door, they could hear the rumble of a truck engine.

An man stood there in coveralls. "Hello, sir. I'm sorry to bother you. As we were picking up your trash, we noticed the empty crate, and we're taking it too. With the crate was this wooden box and it rattles." He pointed to a medium-sized flat box leaning against a nearby tree.

Richard scowled. "That thing? I don't know what it is. Just leave it there. I'll keep it for now and look at it later. Thank you."

"You're welcome, sir." He walked back to his truck, got in, and drove off.

Richard went inside, went to the counter, and poured himself a large mug of tea and drank a couple of swallows. "There was a wooden box among the crate debris, and I had the trash man leave it. I'll look at it later. What day is today?"

"Tuesday. Why do you ask?"

"There's a number on a card over the kitchen phone for Daniel Fitzceri. Bobbi, recommended him as a piano tuner. Call him, use her as a reference, and see how soon he can get over here to do a tuning. I'm going to go in and try out the Bösendorfer. It's probably badly out of tune due to the move."

"Okay." She went to the wall phone and punched in the number while Richard went to his 'new' piano.

Sitting down, he adjusted the bench and then played a couple of chords. He scowled. He did a chromatic scale, with his hands two octaves apart. As he heard tonal clashes, he grimaced.

Char walked into the great room. "How is it?"

Richard rolled his eyes. "Listen to this." He did the chromatic scale again.

"Eeww! That almost hurts my ears! You probably expected it though, didn't you?"

"Yeah – but I was hopeful. Moving an acoustic piano, even a few inches, risks putting it out of tune."

"You don't want to practice on it until after it's tuned, right?"

Richard shook his head. "Nope. I'll use the Yamaha for now, but not today. Let's check the fluorine level in the pool and maybe take a swim. Tomorrow's another day." Richard and Char slept well that night.

"Dad, I've heard you play with an orchestra many times. Have you ever played for a choir?"

"Yes. I played for a choir in Tokyo, once."

"Have you ever played with both a choir and an orchestra?"

"Twice."

"What was it like?"

"Son, words can't describe it. Those were the best experiences of my life apart from the births of you and your sister."

11.

Taking his last swallow of Earl Grey tea, Richard stood at the sink in the kitchen and looked out the window. He recognized the box leaning against the tree. Rinsing his cup out, he set it on the sink and went to the back door. The indoor-outdoor thermometer by the door jam said thirty degrees. Unlocking the door, he opened it, made a dash for the box, and ran back with it into the house. Locking the door again, he took the box into the kitchen and put it on the counter.

"What's that?" Char was sitting at the breakfast table finishing her tea.

"I don't know. It's the box I told you about last evening. It's not heavy. I need a screwdriver."

"There're a couple of screwdrivers in the mud room cabinet by the back door." As Richard went to get it, she continued, "I called J & J early this morning and talked to Tom, the delivery guy. He said there was a filler box in the crate, but that they left it with the trash."

Richard started working on the screws on one end of the box. "Since it was in the crate, it came from Japan, where the Seabees packed it up. Call Yokosuka Navy Base. See if you can get one of the Seabees that crated the piano.... Whoa! What's this?"

As he pulled the contents out, Char's eyes got bigger. "That looks like a cross! It looks like it's at least a couple of feet tall!" She got up and helped him get the bubble wrap off, which she put it in the trash compactor.

He looked into the box. "There's more!" He reached deep inside, and he brought out two smaller packages wrapped in bubble wrap. He unwrapped them while Char stood the cross up on the counter. Beside it, Richard put two battery packs and a power supply with cords. "Tip the cross, Char, I think these batteries go in the bottom."

Tipping the cross, she pointed. "There!" Richard put the batteries into the sockets in the base, and the cross lit up. Char smiled. "Wow! It's plain and simple, but it's kind of pretty."

He plugged the power supply into an outlet at the counter, and a small green light indicated that it was getting power. At the base of the other cord, there was a small yellow light. When he plugged the connector on that cord into a socket on the base of the cross, and the yellow light turned green.

They both stepped back to look at it. Char turned off the kitchen light. "It's not super bright."

Richard shook his head. "No." He looked up at the ceiling and closed his eyes. Char closed her eyes too for about a minute, but she opened them again when Richard spoke. "I think I know what to do with this. While you put in that call to the Seabees, I'm going to take this upstairs." He unplugged the cross.

As Richard left the kitchen with the cross, Char picked up the phone and called Washington. "Hello? General Oswald please. This is Char Donovan." She sat down on one of the kitchen chairs and waited. It took nearly five minutes.

"Hello Char! How are things on your little hill?"

"Dim with fog in the daytime and starless black at night. How about you?"

"It's the same nearly all over now. What can I do for you?"

"We've got a couple of mysteries, General."

"Shoot."

"When we came home from Japan, our rotating pantry was fuller than when we left, our freezer was full of meat, and the fridge had fresh vegetables."

"Fresh vegetables are beginning to get delivered from our underground hydroponics farms."

"There was no indication that anyone had been in the house, General. I know that you arranged for security cameras to monitor the exterior of our house. I'd appreciate it if you'd find out who has been here."

"I'll have the recordings checked, and from this day forwards you'll get a daily email on outside activity on your property, okay?"

"Thank you. As for the other mystery, I need to the Seabees at Yokosuka Navy Base. There was a box inside our crate that had nothing to do with the piano and had no Sony labels."

"What was in it?"

"It's an illuminated cross about a meter high."

"Really! A bonus, huh?"

"Whoever provided it, we want to thank them."

"That's understandable. I'll have the officer in charge of the Yokosuka Seabees call you within the next few hours, okay?"

"Thank you, General. Is Mount Yellowstone still growing?"

"No, not very much. It's still putting out some ash, but for the last three weeks, there's been no lava flow, and no more major eruptions. The survey this past Friday said that it was now just over twenty-one thousand feet."

"Wow. We just got home yesterday, so we've not caught up on the news. If we have any more prophecies for you, we'll call you immediately."

"Good. From this day forwards, always use my direct line. You don't need to go through the Pentagon switchboard."

"Thank you. God bless you."

"God bless you and Richard, too."

The connection ended. Char rinsed her breakfast dishes and put them in the dishwasher. Then she headed towards the stairs. As she started up, Richard was coming down, wearing his jacket. "It is beautiful! We're all set."

She smiled. "All set for what?"

He opened the closet door near their front entrance. "Put on a coat, we're going outside. I want to see how it looks." He unlocked the door and helped her to zip her coat.

"The cross?" Char was puzzled as she put on her coat.

"Yeah." He opened the front door for her. "When I was praying in the kitchen, I remembered how Ricky, our realtor, told us that part of the attic roof was retractable." He led her out to the end of the driveway, turned, and pointed. "It's now installed there, on the peak of our roof."

Char nodded. "It doesn't seem to glow much now, but I suppose in the pitch black of night, it will show when there's no fog."

Richard nodded.

"So long as we've got our coats on, show me how you got up there and what you did."

They went back inside, went upstairs, and went to the rear bedroom. A door led to drop-down attic stairs in a long and narrow closet. "Let me go first. I'll turn on the attic light and open the roof." Flipping a switch, the attic light came on.

Char closed the door behind her and started up. At the top, she looked around. "I didn't know the attic was finished off! This is nice."

"Yeah. Make sure your jacket is zipped to the top, it's kind of breezy up here when we open the roof." He pressed a rocker switch, and part of the roof slid back near a raised area with some steps at the end of the attic. "I think that Akira Eng may have wanted to have a telescope up here. This platform is big enough for an amateur observatory." Char nodded as he pointed. "There's a little flat spot right there at the peak of the roof. It's just big enough for the base of the cross, and it was easy to screw some clips into the frame to anchor it. Then I fished the power cord through that little groove on the edge of the sliding roof panel. ... Let's close the roof. Some snow is coming in." They ducked down, and he pushed the rocker switch for the roof to close. Richard pointed. "Right there you can see the power supply sitting on a rafter. I ran the power cord down the stud and plugged it into the outlet. I imagine that's for a telescope's clock drive, if we get one someday."

"It's very nice." She hugged him. "This is a big attic. It's easy to see that it's well insulated. We could turn it into a loft sleeping area. What do you think?"

He winked at her. "Our kids could play up here, when they're old enough."

She grinned. "Yeah! Maybe one of our kids will become an astronomer." They headed back down the stairs. As she opened the door into the bedroom, Char could hear the phone ringing, so she sprinted for the front bedroom office. "Hello?"

"Hello, Mrs. Donovan?"

"Yes."

"This is Lieutenant Howard Smith calling from Yokosuka Navy Base in Tokyo."

"Hello! We've been expecting your call. Are you one of the Seabees that designed and built that special crate for our piano?"

"Yes. I was responsible. Did the piano arrive in California okay?"

"Yes, it was fine. I'm calling about an extra wooden box inside the crate."

"I don't understand. There was no extra box that I'm aware of."

"When you opened the Sony crate, what did you have to do?"

"The piano was wrapped in moving blankets, and the legs and pedals were wrapped in bubble wrap. We created individual padded boxes for each of the legs and for the pedals. The crate we put on the Jefferson contained a padded box for the piano body, padded boxes for each of the three legs, and a padded box for the pedals. There was a gap when the crate was full, so we made an open wooden frame to fill the space."

"Was the frame about three feet by two feet by eight inches?"

"That sounds about right."

"Lieutenant, when the piano movers opened the crate, there was a box that size that looked just like the other boxes." She paused to look up at the ceiling. "It contained something personal for us, but we don't know how it got there. That's why I put in a call. Don't worry about it lieutenant. Thank you for calling. Bye."

"Good bye, Mrs. Donovan."

She hung up, and as she turned, Richard was in the doorway. "It sounds like our cross is still a mystery."

"It is surely that." The phone rang, and she picked it up. "Hello?"

"This is Captain Randall. I'm responsible for your security. I sent you an email, but I'm calling to confirm that we have no record of anyone coming or going from your house while you were gone. We are increasing your monitoring. The details will be in the email. Do you have any questions?"

"No, Captain."

They hung up. Richard asked, "The security?"

"Yes. No one came or left while we were in Japan."

+ + +

The second week of March, Char was at the Long Beach Mall doing some shopping, when she was approached by a man. "Do you live in that big house on the top of Signal Hill, the one with the nice piano?"

Char felt uneasy. "Yes. We're musicians."

"I'm John Jones from Heaven-Sent Insurance. Since you're out of town so much, we think your house needs some protection. For just $500 a month, we can guarantee the security of everything and everyone on your property."

Char forced a smile. "No, thank you, we feel that we are adequately secure." She swallowed. "My husband and I are doing just fine, thank you."

"I think you need this protection." There was a menace in his voice. "You wouldn't want anything to happen to you or your husband, would you?" He stepped a little closer.

"Is there a problem here?" A mall security officer approached.

"We'll see each other again." The man rapidly strode off.

"Thank you." Char smiled.

"That's why we're around, Mrs. Donovan."

Char cocked her head. "Do I know you?"

He smiled. "No. I'm part of your security team supplied by General Oswald. I'll file an incident report while you drive home. Do you have further shopping to do?"

She shook her head. "No."

"If you're headed home, we'll keep an eye out until you're safe inside."

"Thank you." Char strode purposefully out of the mall to her car, and drove directly home. When she went in the kitchen door, she could hear Richard practicing. She went upstairs.

Two days later, she was standing in the great room, drinking some hot chocolate, when a black SUV pulled into their driveway. Four men got out, carrying weapons. The driver got about three steps up the driveway before they found themselves surrounded and outgunned by a platoon of Marines. The driver started to raise his gun, and in less than ten seconds, all four men were dead.

Hearing the shooting, Richard left the piano, came, and stood beside her. "Trouble?"

Char shook her head. "It was all over so quickly! I guess those criminals did not know what they were facing when they drove up." As a tow truck appeared to haul the SUV away, along with a couple of ambulances. A captain walked up their sidewalk.

Richard went to the door. "We appreciate your looking out for us."

"That's our assignment, Mr. Donovan. What time are the two of you leaving for the train station tomorrow?"

Richard glanced beyond the captain to see the yard being cleaned up after the scuffle. "We'll be leaving in the morning. An SUV is supposed to pick us up at 0700."

"Good. There should be no problem, but you'll have an escort anyway. It's General Oswald's orders. This little sideshow will be part of what the media will cover tomorrow. Two of Mexico's cartels started to move in with some re-enforcements two weeks ago. Since you have security clearance, I can tell you that by tomorrow morning things will be very different in Southern California. Local and state law enforcement, coordinating with the FBI, and marines like us are doing some spring-cleaning tonight. ... If I don't see you tomorrow, have a good tour."

"Thanks," they said almost together. The captain turned and left.

Later, while Richard and Char were at the counter in the kitchen eating dinner, the phone rang. Richard took the call there in the kitchen. "Hello?"

"Hi Richard, this is Bobbi."

"Hi, Bobbi, what's up?" He winked at Char.

"I'm sorry to call you so late. I hope I'm not interrupting anything."

"We're finishing dinner. If you get to the point, I can get to my dessert with the most beautiful woman in the world."

"Right, okay. Richard, when you're up in Seattle, would you and Char like to do a worship and praise music event?"

"Where would it be?"

"Just before Yellowstone, a new sports dome was completed. It's got seating for up to eighty thousand. Area churches have booked it for Easter Sunday. You'd rehearse Saturday afternoon. You and Char would lead it, and there will be about thirty other musicians."

"How would this impact our schedule?"

"You're doing the Beethoven *Concerto Number Five* and the *Choral Fantasy* on Friday and Saturday evenings, but Sunday is open."

"We'll call you back in an hour, Bobbi." He hung up. "There's a new dome venue in Seattle that seats eighty thousand. Seattle's churches want to hold worship there Easter Sunday morning. We're being asked to lead a praise team of thirty or so musicians. I'll be doing the *Beethoven* on Friday and Saturday night, but the rest of the weekend is clear for this. What do you think?"

Char nodded. "You're doing the Beethoven in Benaroya Hall. If we do it, ... No. Let's pray about this and cast lots. What if there's something bigger going on here that we don't see?"

"I agree." They quickly put things away and put their dishes in the dishwasher. Then they went upstairs and knelt at the foot of their bed. Richard took the quarters in his hand. "Heavenly father, all the praise and glory directed at us belong to you. You have made us who we are, and you have guided us faithfully in our journey together. You know what we are being asked to do. Will you please speak to us through the casting of lots?" He tossed the quarters.

Heads-heads-heads.

Char picked them up. "Father, Seattle's churches want to use the city's new sports facility to hold worship there as they celebrate the resurrection of your Son, Jesus. Is this according to your guidance and your will for them?" She tossed the quarters.

Heads-heads-heads.

Richard picked up the coins. "Father is it part of your plans for us that we should lead the praise team in Seattle on Easter?" He threw.

Heads-heads-heads.

Char picked up the quarters. "Heavenly Father, do you want us to share our witness there during that worship service as we did in Tokyo?"

Tails-tails-tails.

Richard picked up the coins. "Will you guide us to speak of our faith to individuals and small groups while we are in Seattle? He tossed them.

Heads-heads-heads.

Char picked them up. "Heavenly Father, will you please use us throughout our concert tour by train that we begin tomorrow? She tossed them.

Heads-heads-heads.

Richard picked them up again. "Please forgive us for asking one more question. Will you use the friendships and connections we make on this train tour in the places where you will use us in the future?" He tossed the coins a final time.

Heads-heads-heads.

"Thank you, heavenly father, for using us for your name's sake and for your glory. The glory is all yours, and all that we share with our audiences comes from you. We praise you and thank you in Jesus' name. Amen"

"Amen." Char stood up. "Let's finish packing!" That night, Char had another dream.

"Mom? You and Dad used to do tours by train, didn't you?"

"Yes. When Earth's skies were all dark, we could not fly."

"Did you like touring by train?"

"Not particularly. It seemed to be more tiring."

Was there anything you liked about train travel?"

"In the daytime, when it wasn't foggy, we could watch scenery going by."

12.

Richard began the train tour with a solo concert at Oakland's Paramount Theater. The old art-deco theater was a delightful surprise to both. The piano was an excellent Baldwin SD-10, and the acoustics of the hall were very pleasing. Backstage, after the concert, they were thrilled to chat with both Torrie Keys and Samuel Brady. Richard also enjoyed seeing Reggie Chow again.

After the concert and reception, they took the BART under the bay to their suite at San Francisco's St. Regis, compliments of the hotel. Neither of them had ever seen San Francisco, so the next day they did some sightseeing. That night, Richard played Tchaikovsky's *First Piano Concerto* with the San Francisco Symphony at the Davies Symphony Hall. When protestors interrupted the post-concert reception expressing hatred for Char and Richard because of their Christian faith, they excused themselves and quickly went back to their hotel. They prayed for the protestors for over an hour before retiring. After another restful night at the St. Regis, they were taken back to the Amtrak station in Oakland.

In Portland, the weather created difficulties. The train came into the station in the midst of a Yellowstone-effect ice storm, and the temperature was well-below freezing. More than a dozen people met them at the train to take them to the Hotel Monaco, and the hotel staff there moved quickly to make them warm and comfortable. Spending the night there, they could catch up on the news. They saw a video of the protestors coupled with interviews with San Francisco's community leaders, who uniformly said that the protest was out of place and inappropriate.

Schnitzer Concert Hall was a pleasure for Char but a nightmare for Richard. The piano, a very decent

Steinway nine-foot grand, was poorly tuned and needed adjustments. The director, Paul Endo, profusely apologized, saying that the room where the piano was stored had a heating failure. Although Char could tell that the piano was not in decent tune, she told Richard that the Grieg sounded quite good. The staff of the Hotel Monaco was very helpful throughout. They got a good night's sleep, and they were on the train with time to spare to depart for Seattle.

The snow got deeper as they traveled north. Their train plowed through it with ease, but all they could see out their windows was a wall of white. Once they were in their suite at the Four Seasons, however, they relaxed. Richard sat in a large recliner. "As I look back at the concert in Portland, Paul Endo really had my sympathy. Did you know that Raymond Endo, the trumpeter that played with us at the San Diego benefit, is Paul Endo's brother?"

"Really!"

"That Steinway in Portland was quite decent, and I hope they can restore it. A hard freeze really did a number on it. As director, I think Paul Endo's ears hurt as much as mine."

The phone rang, and Char picked it up. "Hello? ... Yes! ... We were just talking about you and that Steinway. Can it be restored? ... Good." Richard shook his head, and she nodded. "Richard can't come to the phone right now, but he likes that Steinway and thinks it is definitely worth restoring. ... Really? That kind of review is good to hear. We appreciate your calling. ... Oh? That's good news. Thank you, and thank you again for calling Mr. Endo. ... Bye." She put down the phone. "He said the review was quite kind. It said the Steinway had been damaged, that it would be restored, and one of the symphony's patrons was so pleased with how you bravely dealt with the difficult situation, he donated the money to double your fee."

Richard laughed. "You're kidding!"

Char smiled. "No. The reviewer went on to say that in his estimation, the Grieg is somewhat forgiving of bad pianos."

Richard bursted out laughing again. "He said that? Who was that guy?"

"Richard Everett Klein, a guest reviewer."

Richard's eyes got big. "Richard Everett Klein? He retired about twelve years or so ago from the concert stage due to degenerative arthritis. He was one of the finest pianists of his generation. He must be in his nineties."

"Did we ever hear him live?"

"No, but when we get home, check our CDs. I've got several of his, including one in which he performed the Grieg with the Philadelphia Orchestra."

They chatted until late, but the next morning they awakened refreshed. At ten, Richard began rehearsing the Beethoven pieces in Benaroya Hall with both the orchestra and the chorus. Once again, the piano was an excellent nine-foot Steinway, only this one was tuned to perfection. They rehearsed most of the day.

On Friday morning after breakfast, both Richard and Char went downstairs to the indoor pool and swam several laps. Afterward, they soaked in the hot tub. For lunch, they both had a fruit salad of canned fruit, and later they had a light dinner.

They arrived at Benaroya Hall about an hour before the concert. Char had a seat in the center of the Founders Tier, in the front row of the first balcony. The program began with Debussy's *La Mer*, followed by Sibelius' *Finlandia*. Char was delighted to discover that no one recognized her. During the intermission, she saw an actor from one of her favorite movies standing nearby, and she greeted him. "Good evening. Did you enjoy the *La Mer*?"

"Yes, but I'm looking forward to the Beethoven. Choral masterworks like the *Choral Fantasy* are so seldom performed due to the cost and logistics. I'm particularly looking forward to this because of Richard Donovan being at the piano for both it and the *Concerto Number Five.*"

"Really? Have you heard him before?"

"Yes. I was at the Hilton in San Diego just before he graduated from high school. I was there for a scene in a movie being shot at the zoo, and I was merely staying at the hotel when I heard that there was going to be a benefit concert. I was able to get a plate at the dinner. That was an evening I will not forget as long as I live."

"Why is that?"

"The classical selections before the intermission were perfection itself, but the jam session was utterly amazing. I don't think I ever heard so much musical talent in one place, and I doubt I ever could again. ... Excuse me, but ... as we've been talking, you are stirring a vague memory. Were you there at that concert in San Diego?"

Char smiled and nodded. "I'm Richard's wife, Char. He and I got married the Saturday morning after that benefit."

"Yes! You were at the electronic keyboard array, weren't you?" The lights went off and back on, signaling the end of intermission.

Char nodded and continued to smile. "You have been in some of my favorite movies. I've enjoyed meeting you."

They started for the doors. "The pleasure has been mine. Where have the two of you settled?"

"We have a home on Signal Hill in Long Beach." She started up the stairs and waved good-bye.

As Char listened to the Beethoven, there were tears running down her cheeks. The experience was easily equal to what they had experienced in Tokyo.

Backstage after the concert, she hugged Richard hard. "Hey, beautiful, be careful – I might break!" She smiled and kissed him.

Char grinned. "I never thought anything of Beethoven's could top his Ninth Symphony, but this easily tops it."

As Richard smiled and responded, people were patting him on the back and thanking him. "I hope that this only the first time in my career that I get to play this with such a fine orchestra and chorus." The director approached them, and Richard stuck out his hand. "Thank you, sir, for the honor of doing this with you. I hope I get to do it again with you someday."

"I hope so, too. You are an amazing young talent. I will be following your career with great interest." He turned and moved away to shake the hands of others.

Slowly but surely, Richard and Char made their way out of the auditorium. As the stage door opened, just outside they recognized a familiar marine, who waved. Richard and Char quickly walked over and got in, where it was much warmer. At the hotel, they went straight to their room. It was well past midnight. They took a shower together and went straight to bed.

Saturday morning was relaxing. They watched a movie on a large flat-screen television. They also went to the pool and swam for a while. After lunch, they dressed casually and warm, and they headed to the new Seattle Dome. Inside, the other musicians were already there, and Richard and Char introduced themselves to everyone. Richard recognized one man who approached them. He was the Chaplain of the United States Senate, Lloyd Black. "Hello, Char! Hello, Richard! It's good to see you both again. You were both in high school when we met a couple of years ago."

Richard nodded. "I remember. I understand that you are the guest preacher tomorrow."

"Yes! I'm looking forward to it. Someone must have had some divine help in getting the two of you to lead this praise team!"

Char nodded. "We did worship and cast lots before we agreed to come."

Rev. Black nodded, and he lowered his voice and became more serious. 'I've not known many people who have cast lots to determine God's will. My parents did. I think it's undoubtedly that practice of theirs that launched my fascination and hunger for the presence of God. I don't do it often, but on occasion, I do. ... Now, I'm going up into the stands to listen to the rehearsal. I'll see you two tomorrow." He waved as he walked away.

Richard went to the piano. "All right, everyone, let's get started with a word of prayer. ... Heavenly father, you've blessed those of us here on this stage with your best measure of talent for each of us. Please use us for your name's sake and for your glory, today, tomorrow, and always, in Jesus' precious name, Amen."

Richard looked around at them. "Let's start with the little cards with the worship order on them. We begin with, 'I believe,' which is simply the Apostles' Creed set to music. Then after the welcome, we do 'Love Ran Red' and 'The Wonderful Cross.' Rev. Black will offer a prayer and read the scripture for his sermon. Then the end of our first set as a praise team is 'Did You Feel the Mountains Tremble.' We will do that last one with a Latin beat and at a tempo of 134." There were nods from the drummer and percussionists.

"At that point you can relax, but don't move around or talk at all. When someone else is center stage, anything we do will distract the audience's eyes." Richard looked around. "A lot of musicians forget that little fact. I'll be accompanying an operatic tenor, Edmund Lanza, as he sings 'Because He Lives.' Then Rev. Black does his sermon. We have to stay up here, motionless, for about thirty minutes. Are there questions, so far?"

A guitar player called out, "Can we sit down?"

Richard grinned. "Of course! Everyone can be seated in a chair after we finish our first set. I'll be getting off this piano bench to sit with my wife during the sermon. Are there other questions?" He looked around. "Okay. We close the worship with a final set of three songs. Look at your list. We start with 'Unstoppable God,' 'Amazing Grace, My Chains Are Gone,' and 'He Arose,' with only a couple of seconds in between each. It's practically non-stop for that set of three. "We're doing 'He Arose' as a jazz piece. After the second verse and chorus, the verse is a jazz clarinet solo, and the chorus is a jazz trumpet solo. For the final chorus, just open up and let loose. We'll stop suddenly, and Rev. Black will offer a benediction. When he says, Amen,' the drummer kicks us off with four beats at 172, and we do 'Victory in Jesus.' Give it everything you've got for God. The style is fast country-rock. Are there any questions?"

The banjo picker called out grinning, "At 172 my fingers might fall off! Praise God it's the last song!" Everyone laughed.

Char used her microphone. "Singers, this is a lot of music requiring a lot of energy. Use your diaphragms for good breath support. Otherwise, your voices will be shot before we're done." The singers nodded.

+ + +

Char and Richard led worship in a packed dome. The singing of the audience easily matched the volume of the musicians on the stage, who were confident that God was pleased. At the end, Lloyd Black approached Richard and Char. "If the two of you come to Washington, I hope you'll let my wife and I buy lunch or dinner for the two of you. When I finished preaching, I sat down, spent. That closing set re-energized me. You can tell how hoarse I am after singing 'Victory in Jesus.'"

Char smiled. "Do you know General Oswald?"

"Absolutely, he and I have talked on a number of occasions. He's a good man."

"Whenever we've been in Washington, he's pretty much taken charge of what we do and where we go. If we're to have lunch with you and your wife, you'll have to arrange it with him, I think."

Rev. Black nodded. "Good enough. I'll talk to him about it when I see him. I have others I have to greet. Have a safe journey!"

They smiled and waved as he walked away. Char recognized a television actress from one of her favorite sitcoms. She approached her, and the actress looked at her. "Aren't you Charlotte Donovan?"

Char nodded and smiled. "I am, and I'm delighted to meet you. We love your show, but on the road, we don't get to watch much television."

She laughed. "I know how that is! I saw a video of you and Richard performing in Tokyo dome. The Blu-ray disks are selling like hot cakes. I was fascinated by Richard's testimony about casting lots. My mother did it when doctors wanted to abort me because it was a toxic pregnancy. As soon as casting lots told her to keep me, she told her decision to the doctor. He was angry, but when they ran a blood test thirty minutes later, the pregnancy was no longer toxic. Here I am."

As Char smiled, Richard approached them. "Hello! I'm so glad to meet you! I'm Richard Donovan."

She hugged him. "I know who you are! I was in London and was in the stadium when you two jammed. That was great fun!"

Richard smiled. "Thank you. You're very kind."

"Kind, sch-mind, you're a fine talent, and when I heard about that protest in San Francisco, I wanted to go up there wring a few necks. That kind of anti-Christian bigotry sticks in my craw!"

Char changed the subject. "We're glad you worshiped with us today."

"I am too. I have to give my Christian faith a higher priority. I know that. I think this worship today may have given me the kick-start I've needed. Bye you two!"

Before they could respond, she walked off.

From the dome, Richard and Char went straight to the Amtrak station and their Pullman car. Their luggage had been transferred from the hotel before they got there. They had a long ride ahead. It took two full days, plowing through heavy snow, passing north of Mount Yellowstone and reaching St. Paul and Minneapolis. Sometimes, when they went to the dining car, Richard would play a digital piano that was in one corner.

After two performances in the twin cities, they went on to Chicago, Cleveland, and Boston. While they were in Chicago, they got a special booking through a call from Bobbi. As a consequence, after Boston, Richard Performed at Carnegie Hall in New York City. He did almost the same program as he had done in Tokyo. Suddenly, Richard and Char were on every party list of the entertainment industry. They had eleven invitations to parties, but they refused them all because of their tighter schedule.

They plunged southward into Philadelphia for concerts there and in Baltimore, before coming to Washington D.C., where they stayed at the Sofitel on Lafayette Square. They were scheduled to be there for three days and two nights with no concerts on their schedule. In their room, they flopped onto the king-size bed. "Whew!" Char sighed. "No concerts until Orlando!"

"Yes!" Richard also sighed. "I think I'll almost be able to do the Tchaikovsky *First Piano Concerto* there practically in my sleep. Not really, of course, but this past month on the rails has been exhausting. I want to get home, don't you?"

Char closed her eyes. "Amen to that!" The phone rang, and she picked up the receiver. "Hello? Okay. ... Richard! Get the other phone! It's the President!"

President Williams was relaxed and spoke gently. "Good evening! I understand that the two of you have been having quite a tour!"

"Yes, sir." They both spoke simultaneously.

"I'm sure that the two of you are tired. My wife, Jane, and I would like you to join us for breakfast tomorrow morning, say, about 8:00."

Richard spoke, "That will be fine, sir. If we take a taxi, how much time will we need?"

"There's no need for you to take a taxi. A car will be at your hotel at 7:45. I'll see you tomorrow." There was a click as the President hung up."

Richard looked at his watch. "It's 6:15. Shall we have dinner here in our room, or go to the Bistro downstairs?"

"When we were here the first time, just as Yellowstone began to become a volcano, do you remember Reginald Curry?"

"Sure, he's the Secretary of the Interior. He's doing a marvelous job supervising our country's changes during these nuclear winter snows."

Char nodded. "He evidently talked to one of the FBI agents who escorted us that day. You didn't hear it, but that taller agent, I don't remember his name. Anyway, he said that Mr. Curry told him to tell me something. We were going to stay here at the Sofitel, and he said the Bistro's food is wonderful, but if we want privacy, the room service is also excellent. Let's take that advice and have dinner in our room, okay?"

Richard stood up. "That's fine. I'm going to take a quick shower and put on one of those plush terry robes they supply. You can order for both of us."

"Okay."

Char took care of it, and then got a shower herself. Richard was relaxed and reading a newspaper when she came out of the bathroom and sat down beside him in the recliner. They barely fit, but Richard put down the paper and gave her the attention she wanted and deserved.

There was a knock on the door, and when Richard opened it, a porter quickly wheeled in a table, set it up for two, left the covers on the food, and departed only when they sat down to begin. After saying a short prayer, Richard lifted the lid off his plate and whistled. "Now *that's* a Porterhouse!"

They ate quietly, and they slept soundly after they worshiped and cast lots.

> "Dad, I was watching the news this morning. Why are some people so nasty about you and Mom?"

> "Some don't like us simply because we're Christians, and some people want to criticize everyone to make themselves feel better about their own lives."

> "You mean, like gossips who want to tell stories about other people's lives, so they don't have to think about problems or sadness in their own lives?"

> "Something like that."

13.

Richard and Char were sitting comfortably with the First Lady, Jane Williams, around a large round table with a white tablecloth. "I'm confident my husband will be with us in a few minutes. Since his day started at 5:00, I'm sure he's hungry by now. I understand you two graduated from high school last year. When did you start dating?"

Char took a sip of orange juice. "Our parents didn't let us actually date until the ninth grade, and even then one of our parents took us to and from the movies or wherever we were going. Before that, we were friends who played together in elementary school."

Richard nodded. "Char started showing the outward signs of puberty about the same time that I began my growth spurt. As we walked together to and from school, we talked about the changes we were experiencing. Now, we discuss everything. We pray about most things, and we cast lots for the important stuff."

Jane Williams sat up straighter. "I've read some about how you do that. In Tokyo, Richard, you referred to your casting lots to determine God's will as a gift. What did you mean by that?"

President Williams came in through a door behind her. "Good morning, everyone. I'm sorry I'm late. In this nuclear winter, we're in a nearly constant state of crisis." He kissed Jane.

Richard stood up to shake his hand. "Good morning, Mr. President. Thank you for inviting us."

"You're welcome." He turned to Char and nodded to her. "It's good to see you again. Did you get some rest last night?"

Char nodded. "Yes, sir, we did. We have stayed at the Sofitel before."

"So I understand." The White House chef approached as the President sat down. He looked up at him. "I'll have whatever you want to fix for me this morning."

"Yes, Mr. President." The chef quietly left.

"Richard, last summer your personal prophecy to me was to repent of my partisan ways. That has not been easy."

He nodded his head. "Repentance is seldom easy, Mr. President. We have seen how hard you have fought to remain neutral in this crisis. Millions of lives have been saved because you have tried to avoid squabbles with our legislature and courts."

Jane spoke quietly. How can my husband remain neutral as he campaigns for re-election?"

Char nodded and looked into the President's eyes. "God has not revealed to us whether or not you will be re-elected. We do know that your only chance for re-election is always to speak the facts truthfully and not be critical of your opponent. That has seldom been done before, and you may not be able to do so."

Richard smiled. "When I was in the seventh grade, my piano teacher asked me to come up with a definition of music that includes all its forms. For days upon days, I thought about rhythm, melody, harmony, form, texture, harmonic tension, and other factors in the music that I had performed. I discussed it with Char and everyone else who was interested."

The President and First Lady had put their forks down, and stared at him. The First Lady asked, "So what's the definition of music that you came up with?"

Char grinned. "Music is an ordered sequence of sounds and silences."

The President shook his head. "What does that have to do with my getting myself re-elected?"

Richard smiled. "Think carefully. 'An ordered sequence' means that music is intentional and structured – it is not random sound. Everything has its place and order. The sounds are intentionally created and planned."

The President nodded. "A campaign has to be intentional and structured. I get that parallel."

Char also nodded. "Richard and I struggled for a long time to come up with that second part of the definition. Music is not just an ordered sequence of sounds. There are silences. The silences are not merely prior to the sounds and after the sequence of sounds, but also in the midst of the sounds."

The First Lady's mouth dropped open, and then she shut it. "In other words, my husband has to know when to keep his mouth shut!"

Richard grinned. "Exactly!" They all laughed. "Mr. President, you don't have to have a public opinion on every subject! You can place emphasis on facts rather than on your opinions. That's hard for a politician, isn't it?"

The President nodded. "That goes against the grain of a politician's instincts." He was thoughtful. "These last few months have prepared me for this campaign in a way."

"Yes." Richard and Char said it together.

The Chief of Staff stepped into the room. "Excuse me, Mr. President, folks, we have a situation."

"Excuse me, please." The President stood up.

Char looked up at him. "Mr. President? Be cautious, and think very carefully about this crisis. It is not what it seems."

Richard nodded. "We only know enough to tell you that what the satellite has picked up is a carefully conceived and prepared deception."

The President blinked. Then he nodded and turned to go out. At the door, he stopped and looked back. "It has been good to see and talk with you two again." After that he was gone. They watched him go, and then they started eating again.

The First Lady was curious. "So you two know what has just happened? Has God spoken to you with an audible voice?"

Richard shook his head. "We told him what we know from prayer and casting lots."

"Okay. You must ask God a lot of questions." She nodded. "Your concert tour is not over, is it?"

Char shook her head and put her fork down. "Tomorrow afternoon we will head south to Orlando. Then it's back up to Jacksonville, followed by Houston, where we do another concert of praise at a big church there. We will also be jamming in the Astrodome. We'll be there for three days."

Richard nodded. "Neither of us has ever been to Houston. From there our train takes us through San Antonio to Fort Worth for four days in the so-called 'Metroplex.' Then we'll go back to San Antonio, where I'll do a solo concert. The next day we head west and do gigs in El Paso and Tucson." He took a sip of coffee.

Char continued. "I wish we could take in the Grand Canyon, but during this weather, there's no point. We might take in Carlsbad Cavern. That's an option. From Tucson, we head home, finally."

The First Lady smiled. "I imagine you'll be glad to get home."

Richard nodded. "We'll definitely be glad to be home, but there's a great deal of spiritual warfare going on in Southern California. We have our work cut out for us."

"I'm glad that the two of you could join us for breakfast here at the White House today. I'm sorry my husband did not have more time to spend with you."

After their farewells, and after thanking the chef, Char and Richard were escorted out, and they were taken back to their hotel. Char snuggled up him in the back of the SUV. "I am surprised that they didn't ask you to do a solo concert in the ballroom this evening."

Richard shook his head. "Actually, they probably tried to arrange it through Bobbi. I told Bobbi when I first hired her agency that it was important that we not do any concert work in Washington until after we're past the nuclear winter."

Char nodded. "I think that was a good call. Still, I hope someday you'll play the White House!"

"Not without you, I won't!" He kissed her.

That evening's worship included an extended time of prayer. They then slept.

> "Mom, have you and Dad ever played the White House?"
>
> "No. We were on good terms with President Williams, but that was some time ago. Since he retired, we have not been invited back."
>
> "Is there somewhere that you and Dad want to do a concert?"
>
> "Yes. Rio de Janeiro."

+ + +

The rest of the tour was just as they had described it to Jane Williams. Their train pulled into Union Station in Los Angeles on a Wednesday afternoon. It took about an hour to get home to Signal Hill from there. Inside, the air seemed a bit stale, but it was warm. Richard took their luggage upstairs while Char started a carafe of tea in the tea-designated coffee maker. She went to the kitchen phone and called Terminal Island. "Hello. This is Charlotte Donovan. Please notify security that Richard and I are home. Thank you." She hung up and opened up the pantry, and it was packed. The freezer and fridge were also full. "Praise God! She murmured.

Richard came into the kitchen. "What was that?"

"I was just praising God again. The pantry, freezer, and fridge are all full. I've noticed that the food in the fridge doesn't get stale or moldy, and the meat in the freezer doesn't get freezer burn. Praise God!"

"Yes! Praise God!"

After getting mugs of tea, both sat down at the counter. Char looked at him. "As we were coming up the hill a few minutes ago, I pictured us sitting in those chairs by the front windows, reading the Bible and praying. I also pictured lots of people here in our great room, studying the Bible, and having soup and sandwiches."

Richard nodded. "While we've been riding the rails, we've talked about being more involved doing church-related things here at the house. Before we have church swim parties here, I think we need to upgrade the lighting in the pool area."

Char smiled. "Those lights do seem awfully cold to me."

He took out his cell phone and touched numbers. "Hey, Charlie, this is Richard Donovan. ... Yeah, we got home just a while ago. ... Thanks. I'm trying to remember something. When you put in our security lights outside and put in the area lights in the kitchen, by any chance did you see our pool area in the basement? ... Good. We want to make the light down there brighter and more welcoming. ... Really? It's that easy? ... HID? ... Good. I'll be practicing all day tomorrow, so come on up when it's convenient. ... Okay. Bye." Richard hung up.

"What did he say?"

"He said he was down in our basement because there are power panels in the utilities room. The fixtures down there are vapor-sealed because of humidity, and they're called HID fixtures. H-I-D1 stands for 'high-intensity discharge.' Anyway, he says that we can change the bulbs to a higher wattage and a different color temperature. He'll come out tomorrow morning."

"Good. On those great room images, when we're casting lots this evening, let's ask about reading our Bibles by the front windows every evening before we have dinner."

"Okay." He stood up, drank the last of his tea, and put his mug in the dishwasher. "I'm going to practice until that Bible study time before dinner. Why don't you call Bobbi from the office and find out the latest from her? If she has some new things for us to consider, we'll add them to our list of stuff to pray about before we go to bed."

As Richard walked towards the Bösendorfer, Char put her mug in the dishwasher. Then she went in and sat across from Richard at the Yamaha. She turned off the digital piano's speakers and plugged in her noise-cancelling headphones. Richard was oblivious to her practicing, and her headphones kept her from hearing him hardly at all as she practiced.

She stayed focused on practicing for a little over three hours, and then she took two stairs at a time going up to the office. She opened the curtains on the window and looked out. It was snowing lightly, and most of the City of Long Beach down the hill was immersed in fog. Sitting down at the desk, she picked up the phone's receiver and pushed buttons. "Hello, Bobbi! This is Char Donovan."

"Hi, Char! When did you get home?"

"We got in a few hours ago. Richard is practicing downstairs."

"Are you glad to be home?"

"Absolutely! What's new in this neck of the woods?"

"Oh, Char, there's so much to tell you. Have you got some time?"

"Sure! That's why I called."

Bobbi began to sound excited. "Okay, I'll fill you in on news for you, and then we'll talk about new things for your schedule. If we run out of time, I'll call you tomorrow morning."

"Right." Char opened her laptop to take notes.

"First, Char, you and Richard are starting to have real money flowing in, not only from your concert fees, but your CD sales." Char started hitting the keys of her laptop. "Royalties from CD sales of your concerts in Europe are really jumping. Even here in the states, distribution is getting you into the top fifty just for the European stuff."

"Great!"

"I'm just getting started. Sony has already sold a couple hundred thousand CDs of Richard's Friday night solo performance. Even better, you and Richard are getting a large chunk of the CD royalties for that performance in Tokyo Dome, and those sales are so far over a half million."

"Wow. That's great, Bobbi."

"There's more. Word from Seattle is that next month they will release a CD of Richard's performance of the Beethoven *Concerto Number Five* and *Choral Fantasy.* Additionally, we've signed a release on Richard's behalf to make a CD of his performance in Carnegie Hall. There's no word yet on when that is to be released."

Char smiled. "This is exciting!"

"That's for sure, Char. I have a question. On this latest tour, did you and Richard make connections with some A-list entertainers?"

"We had some nice conversations. Why do you ask?"

"Well, one connection you made spurred my interest. It was a certain A-list actor you spoke to during intermission in Seattle."

Char thought for a moment. "Yes!!! Even at his age, Ronald Pare is so handsome in person. Why do you ask?"

"He has a lot of influence, Char, and he's been talking the two of you up. As a result, you two have been invited to three parties already, and we're not even into the awards season. I've been holding things off until I talk to you. Some are wanting me to get you to Christmas parties that are months away."

Char laughed. "It sounds like we might be hob-knobbing with the rich and famous."

"You and Richard need to be extremely careful, now, because some of these entertainers are highly seductive. Their lives revolve around money, sex, and power."

"I know, Bobbi. What are the new offerings for our schedule?"

"Your train tour got the attention of a lot of locales in the heart of our country. Because all air traffic is grounded, Amtrak is opening up new schedules. I'm sending you an email before I go home this evening. It will have all the interested venues clamoring for you. You and Richard can pick out what you want to do."

"Okay, Bobbie, is there anything out there in the next few weeks?"

"Well, it's mostly quiet except for the day-after tomorrow. The L. A. Philharmonic is doing a benefit concert this Friday, and there's a party after."

"What kind of party is it?"

"It's mostly for musicians, and it's at the Walt Disney Concert Hall. There'll be a few other entertainers there as well. You and Richard are invited if you want to go. By the way, there's going to be a movie made about the life of Franz Liszt. The director wants Richard to do the sound track for the piano performances."

"That sounds interesting. It's another thing for us to pray about, Bobbi. I'll call you next Monday. We need a chance to chew over all of this."

"I understand, Char. I'll talk to you next week. Bye!"

"Bye." Char hung up. Looking at her watch, she went downstairs to put something in the oven for dinner. As she quietly walked through the great room, Richard was totally immersed in practicing and did not even look up. She silently closed the kitchen door behind her. It did not take her long to put breading on some chops and get them in the oven. She fixed enough for future meals that she could freeze. With the chops, she also put potatoes in the oven to bake, and she prepared some broccoli to microwave later.

Coming into the kitchen, Richard asked, "How soon will dinner be ready?"

"It'll be about an hour."

He nodded. "Let's grab our Bibles and go study by the front windows."

"Okay." Leaving the kitchen, she went to the bookcase, grabbed one, and went and joined Richard at a table near the front of the house. She opened the Bible. "For some reason, I think we should look at First John." They flipped through the pages until they found the book towards the end of the New Testament.

Richard bowed his head. "Heavenly Father, open us to your holy word, and open our neighbor's hearts, that they may study with us. We pray this in Jesus' name. Amen."

"Amen."

14.

There was a knock at the door, and Richard got up to answer. A young couple in their twenties was standing there. Richard nodded. "Hello."

"Hello. I'm Jim McLaughlin, and this is my wife, Rita. We live across the street. We've admired your cross ever since you put it up on your roof. Just now, we saw you sitting down near the window to read."

Richard nodded. "We're doing some Bible study. Would you like to join us?"

Rita smiled. "We don't have Bibles with us."

Richard shook his head. "We've got more. Come in and join us."

As the McLaughlins came in, Char was there to greet them. "Hello! My name is Char Donovan, and you've met my husband, Richard."

Jim's eyes got bigger. "You're Richard Donovan, the pianist? There have been articles about the two of you in the Press Telegram." He shook Richard's hand. They pulled a couple of other chairs up around the table, and Char brought two more Bibles from the bookcase.

They got comfortable, and Richard began. "We had just decided to look at First John this evening. Are you two familiar with it?"

They looked at each other. Rita nodded. "We know it's near the back of the Bible, but neither of us knows the Bible real well."

Char smiled. "That's okay. We're all still pretty young."

They spent about an hour studying, and then they prayed together. Afterward, Rita said, "Whatever you're cooking, Char, it smells good. We'd better be going so you two can have dinner."

Char shook her head. "Nonsense. You're here, and we have plenty. Why don't you join us?"

The McLaughlins agreed, and they got better acquainted as they ate. Jim said, "We tried to start a Bible study group right after Yellowstone blew its stack."

Rita nodded. "None of us knew the Bible correctly enough for us to know what we are doing. You two seem to know the Bible pretty well."

Richard nodded. "We've had some good teachers. If you know others in the neighborhood that would enjoy doing Bible study, all of you can come over tomorrow evening about 6:00, just like tonight."

"Yes!" Char was enthusiastic. "Please do so! I'll fix a pot of stew in my slow cooker, and we'll eat afterward, just like tonight."

Rita shook her head. "We don't want you to go to all that trouble."

Char smiled. "It's no trouble at all. God is blessing us with abundance, so it is up to Richard and me to share."

"Can I bake a cake for dessert?"

"If that's what you really want to do, that's okay, but it's not necessary."

Rita smiled. "I like baking, but I don't do it much for just two."

"If you want to bake, cookies might be simpler."

They all got up and started for the door. Jim shook Richard's hand. "It's been good meeting you two at last. You were gone so long!"

"We were on a tour by Amtrak. Most tours are not that long."

Rita smiled. "Thank you for your hospitality. We'll see you tomorrow evening."

They nodded. "Okay."

Jim and Rita walked down the sidewalk as Richard closed the door. "All that God does, God does well."

"Amen!" Char hugged him. "I've got a lot to tell you. I had quite a conversation with Bobbi." After turning out the lights, they went upstairs. It was three hours before they were ready to go to sleep.

Char awakened the next morning to the faint sounds of piano music. She looked at the clock, which said 7:00, and she jumped out of bed, surprised that she had slept so long, and that she hadn't awakened when Richard got up. After taking a quick shower, she went downstairs into the kitchen to fix breakfast.

Moving fast, she fixed turkey sausage and scrambled eggs, and put them in the oven to keep warm while she fixed pancakes. When she called out, "Breakfast!" it only was twenty minutes.

Richard came in and sat down at the counter with her. "Bless, O Lord, this food to our use, and our lives to your service. In Jesus' name, we pray, Amen."

Char took a forkful of pancake and chewed. "How'd you like the McLaughlins?"

"I think it's the beginning of a nice friendship. Based upon what Jim said, I have a feeling there'll be eight or ten people here tonight."

"Soup won't be enough, so I'm going to fix a pot of beef stew in the large slow cooker. I'll also have sandwiches. Did you notice how thin they looked?"

Richard nodded. "Definitely. The obesity problem of our country is definitely taking a big hit."

"Praise God! I'm glad we have ample food to feed people. Our house could turn into a major feeding center for those who are hungry both for God's word and for food. What are you working on this morning?"

"I'm working on Liszt's Consolation Number Three as a change of pace from Liszt's more challenging pieces. I'm also adding more Brahms to my repertoire."

"I thought I recognized that Liszt piece."

"When Charlie gets here, take him downstairs. Did you know that there's a powered cover for the pool?"

Char's mouth hung open a moment. "Really? Is it solid?"

"Yeah. It's just like a floor sliding out from under the equipment room. I had wondered why we had to step up two steps to go in there. Now we know. When we were down there before we left on our train tour, I noticed a key switch in the far-right corner as you come through the sliding door. I rummaged around through that box of miscellaneous warranties and stuff, and I found the key. I put it on the ledge above the sliding door, but I think we should find a better place for it." He smiled. "Thanks for fixing pancakes this morning. They hit the spot. I'm going back to practicing."

As he went out of the kitchen, Char quickly cleaned up and put things away. Then she went back towards the stairs and went down. In the basement, above the door, Char found the key as Richard had said. She put it in the key switch and turned. With the faint hum of a motor, the pool cover rolled out from under the equipment room and across the pool. When it stopped, the entire room was one continuous floor. She left the pool covered, but she left the key in the key switch.

Going out the sliding door, she started up the stairs, and there was a knock on the front door. She opened it. "Good morning, Charlie. How's the electrical business?"

He grinned. "Oh, it's jumping, what with it being nearly as dark all day as it is at night. With no stars and no moon, people are installing all kinds of additional lighting outside their homes and apartments."

Char tipped her head to the side. "Come on, Charlie, I'll take you downstairs." He followed her.

"At night, when I look out my living room window in the Palos Verdes Hills, I can just faintly see the light of that cross on your roof. The entire top of Signal Hill seems to glow slightly."

"From the Palos Verdes Hills? That's miles away, and the cross is not that bright. That's amazing! Praise God!"

"Amen! You're telling me!" They went in through the sliding door, and Charlie stopped. "Where's the pool?"

"Here." Char turned the key switch, and the floor slid back to expose the pool.

"That's really cool!"

Char nodded. "When we bought the house, our realtor did not tell us about the cover. Richard discovered it recently."

He shook his head in amazement. "If I'm going to change those bulbs above the pool, it'll be easier if you put the cover back on."

"Okay." Char turned the switch, and the cover started back out.

"I've got a ladder and other stuff to bring in. This shouldn't take more than an hour or so with the cover on the pool."

"Okay. I'll be in our office at the top of the stairs if you need me."

"Okay." They both headed up.

Char spent most of the morning talking to Bobbi, marking her calendar, and talking to Bobbi about which concerts they would do and not do. At the end of their conversation, Bobbi asked about the party at the Walt Disney Concert Hall. "So, are you and Richard going to the party on Friday?"

"No, Bobbi, not this time. We've started an evening Bible study here at the house, and since it is just beginning, we don't want to cancel a night for business yet."

"Okay. Tell Richard I said 'hi.' I talk to you next week. Bye."

"Bye, Bobbi."

Hanging up, Char headed downstairs to see how Charlie was doing. He met her at the door. "I'm all done." He called out, "Richard, do you want to see what I've done?"

"Okay." Richard got up and strode across the room.

The three of them went downstairs, and before opening the door, Charlie flipped on the light switch. The door opened, and they went in. Richard nodded. "This is so much improved It's amazingly better. How much of an increase in wattage is there?"

"Changing the ballasts for the increase, there's about a thirty percent change. The new bulbs are a little more efficient, but I also put in some better lenses on the enclosures."

Char nodded. "Yes, Charlie. I like it. How much do we owe you?"

"I'll send you a bill. By the way, I think that if you put a smoother surface on the top of that cover, a few people could dance on it. You'd have to look at the warranty, though, to make sure that the cover can support the weight of a bunch of people. You wouldn't want to crack it or break it." He turned towards the door. "I've got more to do on Signal Hill today, so I'm taking off. Thanks for thinking of me for your business!" He started up the stairs. As Richard followed, Char made sure the cover was on, and she put away the key before turning off the lights.

Upstairs, on her way to the kitchen she stopped by the pianos and waited. When he stopped and looked up, she spoke. "It's getting close to noon. How soon would you like some lunch?"

He shook his head. "Sorry. I ... I was not going to take lunch today, but our marriage is too important for me to skip meals. Can we eat about 1:00?"

"Okay. Sorry I disturbed you."

"It's okay. See you later." He looked down and started playing again.

Instead of going on into the kitchen, she turned and went into their home theater. She closed the soundproof door turned on the computer in the console. As the projector got to full brightness, she did an Internet search of their concerts. For nearly an hour, she watched videos and re-lived some recent memories.

Just before 1:00, she went into the kitchen, and while she heated up some soup, she made a couple of sandwiches. They ate together, and then Richard returned to the piano.

+ + +

At 6:00, they greeted eight adults and five kids. They apologized for bringing the kids, but Char and Richard had planned for them. After worship the night before, they knew. Char took the kids to the home theater, where she had set it up for them to watch a couple of Looney Tunes cartoons, followed by a video story for children about Jesus. With their parents' permission, she gave them each small bowl of popcorn.

The adults went back to the great room. Richard began. "Last week, the McLaughlins and the Donovans did a quick study of 1 John. Char and I will be leaving on a short tour in about six weeks. That will give us just enough time to study the Book of Acts, if we take a chapter or two a week."

Char nodded. "The first chapter of Acts is a good place for us to begin tonight, because in that chapter is the only instance in the New Testament where the followers of Jesus cast lots to determine God's will. Since Richard and I have a decent amount of experience with casting lots, we'll use this chapter for us to get better acquainted."

It took just over an hour for them to get acquainted, study that chapter, and pray together. Then the kids came running in. Char smiled. "Hey, kids! Are you hungry?"

"Yeah!" came a chorus from the kids."

"Okay. Let's thank God together for the food we're going to eat, because God provides us with everything. Will you pray with me? Close your eyes now. ... Our heavenly Father, thank you for these wonderful children, and for their parents. You provide us with all that we need. Thank you for the food we're going to eat together. In Jesus' name, we pray, amen."

Everyone said, "Amen."

Richard pointed. "The kitchen is through there. Your parents will help you get some stew and a sandwich. There's hot chocolate, coffee, and tea to drink. We'll go through there," he pointed again, "into the home theater to have our dinner. There are plenty of places to sit down in there. Let's eat!" In the home theater, Richard turned the television to the Disney Channel for all of them. They agreed to meet three days a week for the study.

Later that night, after Richard and Char had worshiped and cast lots, they sat up in bed and talked. Char was thoughtful. "For these Bible study dinners, it's no problem for adults to hold a plate in their laps, but the kids struggled. Tomorrow, while you're practicing, I'll pick up a couple of folding tables and some chairs. What do you think?"

Richard nodded. "That's a good start. We can always use tables and chairs. I have another idea. Call Terminal Island tomorrow morning and get hold of Captain Severin. He's in command of the Seabees here. Tell him to send someone with engineering background to the house to inspect our pool's sliding lid. Find out how durable it is in terms of people on top of it and having general activities, including eating while sitting at tables on chairs."

"Great idea! I love you!" She kissed him. He kissed her back. "We can also praise God for something special tonight."

"What's that?"

"We did not run out of stew or sandwiches until everyone had their fill. That's fifteen of us eating supposedly two and a half quarts of stew and one platter of a dozen sandwiches. The food did not run out. Praise God!"

"Praise God is right!" They turned off the lights for the night.

The next morning, at 6:00 Richard put on a sweat suit and went downstairs to practice. Char picked up the phone and pushed numbers. "Good morning. This is Charlotte Donovan. I'd like to speak to Captain John Severin of the Seabees please, if he is on duty.

"Yes, Mrs. Donovan, he is on duty. Just a moment."

"This is Captain Severin."

"Captain, this is Charlotte Donovan. A couple of months ago, my husband and I brought a piano here from Tokyo on a sub. Your Seabees unloaded it off the sub to put on a J & J Piano Movers truck in the middle of the afternoon. Do you remember?"

"Yes, I do. We unloaded it from the sub, and J & J took it away. Was there a problem?"

"No, captain, that is not why I am calling. General Oswald of the Joint Chiefs said that anytime we needed something to just to call the base."

"Okay, what can I do for you?"

"We live up on Signal Hill, about twenty minutes away from you. As soon as it is convenient, could you please send someone here with some genuine engineering expertise? We've got an interesting challenge."

"Mrs. Donovan, around here it tends to be feast or famine, today it's famine, and I'm bored. You're in a house at the very top of the hill where the condominiums used to be, isn't that correct?"

"Yes."

"I can be there in about thirty minutes."

"Thank you, Captain. We'll be waiting."

The connection went, and Char quickly got dressed and went to the kitchen. She fixed a couple of breakfast wraps just in time for Richard to walk into the kitchen. He kissed her. "You must have read my mind. That looks like just what I need."

They sat down at the counter and began to eat. "I called Captain Severin, and he will be here in less than a half hour."

"He was already on duty?"

"Yes. I'm really curious about how that sliding floor is constructed and powered."

Richard sipped his coffee. "I am too." They ate in silence. "Thanks for the breakfast wrap. Let's have a nice full lunch together. If you want to go out, let's go to the 'Four Fiddlers,' okay?"

"Good! We've not been there in a long time." The doorbell rang. "I'll get it." She strode rapidly across the great room while Richard went back to the piano.

Char opened the door to a tall, grey-haired Naval Officer. "Hello! You're Captain Severin?"

He nodded. "Yes."

"Please come in." She led him down the stairs. As the door slid open, she turned on the lights. "These are HID lights, so it'll take a couple of minutes to get up to full brightness."

"With those tiled walls, it looks like there used to be a swimming pool down here."

Char grinned. "Past and present, have a look." She turned the key switch, and the floor began to slide away.

"Whoa! That's nice!"

"I'll stop it about half way." In a moment, she released the key.

"This is what you wanted me to examine?"

"Yes, Captain,"

"Call me John."

"Okay. What we need to know is simply this – when the floor is fully in place, with the pool covered, how much can we put on that floor, and what can we do? For instance, could it support the weight of a couple dozen people sitting on chairs at tables and eating? Could it support the weight of fifteen or twenty people dancing on it? How durable is it?"

He nodded. "Those are all good questions." He got down on his knees with a flashlight, and he looked into the groove where there were wheels rolling on tracks. He laid down flat on the deck, putting his face next to the water, and pointed his flashlight up at the bottom side of the floor. Then he examined the flooring. "I need to see one more thing. Where is your machinery room with all the motors and pumps? Through there?" He pointed at the door to the utilities room.

"Yes. This way." They stepped up onto the floor, walked to the utilities room door, and stepped up and in. She turned on the light. "Help yourself, John."

"Thank you." He took a quick look at everything there, and then focused upon a box along the poolside of the room. "When those condos were here, there was an elevator, and this is probably where the pump for it was." Pulling up a ring, he lifted a steel door up and away from the floor. "Here's what I needed to see." He went down a small ladder and turned on a light. He disappeared for less than three minutes. "Okay. I'm coming back up." He came up the ladder.

"Is the whole mechanism down there?"

He shook his head. It's not all of it, but I've seen enough." He closed the steel trap door and sat down on the box. He took out a calculator and made several calculations, making notes in a notebook as he went. It took about five minutes. "The company that made this custom installation is named Lotass, one of the best that there is when it comes to custom installations like this. When I get back to Terminal Island, I'll call them and see if I can get them to email me a copy of the blueprints for it."

"Does that mean that you can't tell us anything yet?"

John grinned. "On the contrary, I can confidently give you an unofficial answer right now. Afterward, I'll write up a full engineering specification for you with a copy of the blueprints and send it to you by messenger for your records. Even if you didn't need them, I want to see the blueprints for this thing just for my own interest. I love these kinds of challenges."

Char smiled. "What's the short version?"

"In once sentence, you can do just about anything you please on this sliding floor. If you like, supply us the materials, and a few of my Seabees can put a hardwood dance floor on this thing so it will look nice when the swimming pool is covered. The work would be good practice for my men."

"How much would it cost in materials?"

"Before I go, I'll measure it and then email you my estimate. Meanwhile, here's the slightly longer version. The moving mechanism is high-quality steel and powered by an electric motor. The floor framing is structural aluminum. Based upon the size of the mechanism and the motor down there, I estimate that the floor weighs somewhere between six and eight tons. It has been built very well, and it can last nearly forever with minimum maintenance. It has some great safety features, but do not let anyone get between the far end of the floor and the wall. They would be crushed and almost certainly would be killed. That's apparently why that key switch is so far off to the side."

They left the equipment room. Outside, they had the floor extend entirely over the pool, and then Char helped him measure it. When they got back to the front door, Richard was there. "John, this is my husband, Richard." They shook hands.

Richard smiled. "Well, is it durable?"

John nodded. "Completely. You'll get my email estimate for hardwood flooring later today or tomorrow. I'll send you a full engineering report as soon as time allows. Meanwhile, you did not mention it, so I have to ask you about something. Did you know that you have a panic room?"

Their eyes grew big. Richard shook his head. "No. How do we access it?"

"I did not see the room, but experience tells me about it. I would be willing to bet that you have an emergency fire exit in back of your home theater, and that there's a twenty-minute fire stairs that comes to it from upstairs." They nodded. At the base of those stairs, on an inside wall of the theater, see if you can find a hidden button. Pushing it opens a trap door to a slide into the panic room. It closes behind you automatically. When the pool is uncovered, the floor becomes an extra ceiling for your panic room. It is ingenious. If you're in the pool area and suddenly need to get into the panic room, it's a bit more difficult." He looked at Char. "You saw me go down that trap door. On the motor for the mechanism, there's a power switch, with a flexible conduit going into the switch box. Hidden under the box next to the conduit, there's a button. If you press it, a panel opens to give you secure access to the panic room."

Char shook her head. "This is all so amazing!"

Richard nodded. "Yeah. The panic room must be under the yard behind the house."

"That's correct. You might have instructions regarding the pool cover with the paperwork that came with the house. Look for an envelope with the company name, Lotass. The only way to learn technically about the features of the panic room is to go to their web site. You have to put in the serial number of the installation to get it. The serial number is on the Lotass label that is on the hand crank mechanism for the floor. I've had experience with Lotass previously. Look for a hidden switch at the top of those fire stairs also. It will turn the stairs into a slide, right into the panic room. When everyone is at the bottom in the room, the stairs will pop back up again, hiding the slide and entrance. This conversation will not be in my records at the base."

They smiled. "Thanks."

During worship that night, they thanked and praised God for his wondrous grace and mercy. In the Bible, they read part of Exodus, where God used Moses to lead the people across the Red Sea. Then they turned off the light.

"Dad, how much do you and Mom have to pay for our security service? Will I have the same service when I get married?"

"Our service started with a presidential executive order, and it was ratified by Congress during the nuclear winter."

"So we're always safe here at home?"

"There's no such thing as perfect safety, except through our Heavenly Father. He's in command, haven't I taught you that?"

15.

Their manager, Bobbi, called the following Monday morning, promptly at 9:00. The phone rang at the desk in their office, and Char picked it up there. "Hello?"

"Good morning Char. How was your weekend?"

"Fine. Is the next train tour solid now?"

"Yeah, it's pretty much as we've already talked about it. Between now and then you have some local stuff, as you know. You have months before that train tour starts. We're continuing to depend upon Amtrak because planes without special filtration equipment can't fly. I checked last Friday. The Air Force says that volcanic ash still makes jet flights impossible. The ash concentration level is slowly starting to drop though."

Char typed notes on her laptop. "You said something last week about a tour into Western Canada and Alaska."

"I'm not ready to recommend that you do that yet. There are only three ways to get from Seattle up to Anchorage. Freighters make it every week, but icebergs are significant hazards. Coastal route trains have no problem getting through, but they're not running at night in the weather soup, and they stop at every single town to take on and let off passengers. It takes forever."

"What's the third way?"

Bobbi laughed. "American ingenuity."

"How's that?"

"Some crazy inventors have created tractor-driven vehicles that will race across the countryside at nearly fifty, not even fifty-five. It typically takes ten days to get from Vancouver to Anchorage that way. Then, there are some even crazier inventors, who have put massive air filters on Korean-War-era rebuilt and modified military transport planes. Would you like your teeth to rattle for many hours of flight?"

Char laughed. "I don't think Richard would go for it, and that would scare me to death! I like jets, thank you," she paused, "but Richard and I will pray about it though."

"You're kidding!"

"No, we pray about everything. We serve a God who is doing impossible things in our lives."

"For instance?"

"I've told you about the little cross that sits up on our roof. It runs on battery packs that power about five watts of led bulbs. A captain from Terminal Island lives in the Palos Verdes Hills. His house is more than ten miles away, but when there's no fog at night, he can see the cross as a pinpoint of light. He says the top of Signal Hill glows."

"No!"

"So, Richard and I will at least pray about going up to Alaska." She opened a file on her computer. "Meanwhile, let me read to you what I've got for our itinerary, okay?"

"Okay."

"Flagstaff, Albuquerque, Kansas City, St. Louis, and Memphis are our eastbound Amtrak stops, right?"

"Right. You'll be in Memphis for three days doing two evenings and a matinee. They're selling it all over that part of the country."

Char smiled. "I'm looking forward to another jam session at that matinee. Next we turn around, heading north, passing through Chicago on our way to Omaha. After that we do two nights in Denver and two in Salt Lake City before heading home by way of Sacramento. Have I got it all straight?"

"That's it. This tour is less than half the length of the last one."

"I'm glad. The last one was exhausting. I'll let you know what we decide about Anchorage. I'll talk to you next week. Bye."

Char hung up and looked at her watch. She was on the phone with Bobbi for less than a half hour.

She saved her notes on the laptop and closed it. She looked out the window, and down the hill, everything was immersed in fog. There were a few snowflakes drifting down in front of the house. The phone rang. "Hello?"

"Hello, is this Charlotte Donovan?"

"Yes, it is."

"Char, this is Akira Eng."

"Maestro Akira! What a pleasant surprise!"

"Thank you, it is good to hear your voice. How is Richard?"

"He's fine. We're leaving on another train tour next week, and he is practicing downstairs."

"I understand. I tried to call your manager, Bobbi Zealand, but I had to leave a message. I'm calling to ask a favor."

"We will if we can, Maestro Eng."

"Please call me Akira. I am in Los Angeles as the guest conductor of the Philharmonic Orchestra here. This weekend, Frederick Klein is scheduled to play the *Grieg Piano Concerto* with us."

Char smiled. "We have heard his rendition of the Grieg on DVD. It is excellent."

"Yes it is. I have just come from Loma Linda Medical Center, where they are prepping him for surgery."

"Really! What is the problem?"

"He went in for chest pain, and he is going to have bypass surgery. I talked to Frederick less than twenty minutes ago, and he reminded me that you live in this area, and that Richard did the Grieg with me in London. He recommended that I ask Richard if he can fill in. Our first rehearsal is tomorrow morning."

"Akira, I will put you on hold for a moment, while I go downstairs and talk to Richard. Please hold the line."

"Of course."

Char put him on hold and sprinted downstairs. "Richard, I'm sorry to interrupt you, but Akira Eng is on the phone and needs to talk to you."

He raised his eyebrows. "I can take it in the kitchen," he said as he got up. "What's it about?"

"It's an artistic emergency with the L.A. Philharmonic."

"Okay. He picked up the receiver in the kitchen. "Hello Akira. It's nice to hear from you. What's the occasion?"

While Richard listened, Char quietly started making a carafe of tea. Char got two mugs from the cupboard, and she put in two teaspoons of sugar in one for Richard, filled the mug with tea, and set it beside him on the counter near the phone. He smiled and nodded at her while he continued to listen. She filled a cup for herself.

Finally, he hung up, smiling. "I'm performing the Grieg this weekend, both Friday and Saturday. Rehearsals start tomorrow morning at ten. How can I *not* do this?" He took a big swallow of tea.

Char nodded, sharing his smile. "I thought you would. Praise God we've nothing else on the schedule this weekend. Will you be brushing up on the Grieg the rest of the day?"

He nodded and walked over and took her in his arms. "I'll only stop for lunch and Bible study. Do me a favor and call Daniel Fitzceri? See if we can get him to tune the Bösendorfer tomorrow while I'm in Los Angeles. I'm being picked up at 9:00, so any time after that." He finished off his tea, and he put the mug on the counter.

"It's not ten yet, so I'll delay lunch a bit and fix us sandwiches around one, okay?"

"Good." He kissed her, and then he headed back to the piano. As she listened, she could not tell that it needed tuning, but Richard knew best for his keen ears.

As she was putting their mugs in the dishwasher, the phone rang. She quickly grabbed it and answered softly, "Hello?" She could not believe her ears, but as soon as she heard the voice, she recognized it.

"Char, this is Taylor Elizabeth Brown. We first met in San Francisco."

She spoke softly. "I've got to change extensions, Taylor. I don't want to disturb Richard while he's practicing. I'll be with you in a moment."

After touching the hold button, Char practically sprinted across the great room, up the stairs, and into the master bedroom. She picked up that extension. "Taylor, your voice is the second nice surprise I've had this morning."

"Whose was the first?"

"Akira Eng is the guest maestro with the L. A. Philharmonic this weekend. Their scheduled pianist is having bypass surgery, and Richard is going to play the *Grieg Piano Concerto* this weekend at the Walt Disney Concert Hall."

"Wonderful! I'll get tickets and be there with bells on. I love listening to Richard play."

"I do too, of course. What's going on with you?"

"I'm putting on a little party at my home in Malibu. It won't be more than a hundred or so. I'd love to have you and Richard come Sunday night."

Char looked up at the ceiling and said a short prayer. "Taylor, we're going to have to take a rain check on that. We have another commitment. I'm very sorry!"

"That's okay. I understand. If you and I see each other Friday night at the Disney, we can do some girl talk during intermission, okay?"

"Okay, Taylor. Talk to you then. Bye."

"Bye, hon."

Char looked up. "Please forgive me Lord. Our first commitment is always to you, and I did not feel right about saying yes to her. If I was wrong, I'm sorry. Please forgive me."

Char went back downstairs. All while she practiced with her headphones at the Yamaha, she thought about that short conversation with Taylor Elizabeth Brown.

+ + +

Although Frederick Klein prefers Steinway pianos, Akira Eng remembered that Richard loves Bösendorfers, so he made other arrangements for Richard. At the center of the stage for the first rehearsal was a Model 20 Imperial. Richard grinned. "Akira! You remembered!"

He bowed a shallow bow. "Yes. Have you played one recently?"

Richard continued to smile. "Sony gave me the one I played in Tokyo as my performance fee."

Akira's eyes got big. "That's quite a fee, young man!"

Richard nodded. "It was a last minute engagement, and they used it as an incentive to entice me to do that jam session in Tokyo Dome."

Akira had a suppressed chuckle. "Amazing! I'm glad you're here doing this with me again. Shall we get started?"

Richard nodded and sat down. Because they had done the Grieg together previously in London, and because the orchestra was totally professional, the rehearsal went smoothly. At the end of the afternoon, they agreed to warm up on Friday afternoon prior to dinner before the evening performance.

Richard got home just in time to join the Bible study group. It had gradually grown to there being eighteen to twenty adults every week, and there were usually ten to twelve children. They went straight to the recreation room in the basement. Only Char and Richard knew that there was a pool underneath the floor.

Near the equipment room, there was a curtain hung from the ceiling and extended almost all the way across the room, so the children could watch Bible study videos playing softly. Char chose that area also because it was next to two large bathrooms. She took off the 'men' and 'women' signs. Near the door at the opposite end, two buffet tables were set up. One was a steam table for the hot food, and the other was refrigerated for salads and beverages.

Rita McLaughlin looked around. "I love this big recreation room. We have a large family room at our house, but this is much bigger. What do you think, Jim? The only way we can have this large of a space is if we open the patio door."

Her husband nodded. "This is great! Shall we get set up, Richard?"

There were racks on the long wall of the room holding tables and padded folding chairs. The men quickly set up enough tables for the group, putting them in a square circle, and the women helped with the chairs. They also set up two tables with chairs for the children to use when they ate.

"Let's begin with prayer." They bowed their heads. "Thank you, heavenly father, for the fine friendships that we are forming as neighbors. Thank you for their children, and for graciously watching over them and over us. Please have your spirit move among us as we study your word once again tonight. In Jesus' name, we pray. Amen."

Alice, an African-American woman with graying hair spoke out. "Before we start, my husband and I want to express our appreciation, not only for your hospitality with our Bible studies, but for the cross on your roof. If we could see the moon or stars at night, or if the streetlights were on after eleven, we probably wouldn't notice. In the total darkness, however, we can easily see the cross, and it puts a subtle glow over the neighborhood. We live almost two blocks away, and we enjoy your having it up there." There were murmurs of agreement throughout the group.

Richard nodded. "Thank you. We don't know where it comes from or who gave it to us, because it was in a small box in the piano crate when it was delivered. We enjoy it too."

Char smiled again. "As we finish the book of Acts tonight, I think you should notice two things. First, the story is left hanging with regard to what happens to the Apostle Paul. Church tradition says that he was martyred, but it does not say so in the Bible. Additionally, we have talked about churches evidently planted by the Apostle Paul that are not mentioned in the Book of Acts. Be thinking about these things as we complete our study of this book."

Richard smiled. "If you remember our discussion last week, Paul and everyone he had sailed with were shipwrecked....." He taught with intensity because enjoyed teaching, and he really looked forward to the evening Bible study sessions. Those evenings could be exhausting, and on the nights they had Bible study, they always slept soundly.

"Mom, in school today, we learned about people dying of starvation during the nuclear winter. Were you and Dad affected?"

"We've always had plenty of food, and we've shared it with others. Our neighbors invariably look out for you when we're on tour. We provided for them during the dark time."

"Was our church affected?"

"We all shared with each other and with our neighbors. Some people got started going to our church because they got a meal on Sunday. Some joined because they were part of our Bible study here at the house. Then they discovered Jesus'

presence in their lives, and they've
been active ever since."

"Do you and Dad give a tithe of
your income to the church?

"We give a double tithe to God's
work, and we distribute it among
several churches."

16.

The media reviews on Sunday were universally positive. After Friday's concert, Richard was said to have performed the Grieg "flawlessly" and "with amazing flair and confidence." On Saturday night, when the standing ovation went on and on, Richard surprised everyone, including Akira Eng, when he sat down to do an encore. According to several reports, he tipped his head back and closed his eyes for almost a minute of total silence in the concert hall.

As Richard explained to Char later that night, he knew that the hall was packed with the best of the best in the entertainment industry, including some of the finest musicians in the world. He told her, "I was scared more than I ever had been in my life. I knew I had to have a measure of God's peace, or my encore would be a flop, because it was transcribed specifically for that model of piano. God gave me everything I needed and more."

Richard played the Bach-Busoni *Chromatic Fantasy and Fugue.* The critics all agreed that no one could have imagined such a beautiful rendering of Bach's masterpiece on such an incredible instrument as that Bösendorfer. One journalist wrote a detailed sidebar article about the history of that model of special piano, about the transcriptions designed for the piano, about music written for that piano, and about Richard.

In Church on Sunday morning, Char and Richard sang God's praises with fervor and listened to the sermon intently. In the foyer of the church, several people spoke of his weekend performances. Char and Richard felt humbled. They went back into the worship area and knelt on the steps of the stage to pray.

They stopped on their way home for pizza. Because meat was so expensive, it was three times the price they had paid a year earlier. A rancher's cooperative formed between ranches all over North America. Those in the cooperative shared profits and losses based on the size of the acreage owned by the rancher. Ranches in the north were abandoned to minimum maintenance personnel, while the rest headed south. The atmosphere for all of Latin America became primitive but effective. Frontier justice was more common than a courtroom. The cartels decided it was good business not to raise the ire of the armies and law enforcement, so they stayed away from food distribution.

Expensive or not, Richard and Char enjoyed their pizza. Some of their friends from church followed them to the pizzeria, and Richard and Char bought pizza for anyone who came through the door for more than two hours. As they were leaving, Char took out their checkbook and called the manager over to their table. "John, you're selling a lot of products today, aren't you?"

"Yes, Char, we appreciate your business. You and Richard have been good customers."

"How late are you staying open?"

"We have to obey the 'power for heat' ordinance, so we have to close by ten because the street lights are turned off at eleven. Why, what are you thinking?"

She looked at Richard, and he nodded. She started writing the check as she spoke. "You're an honest man, and Richard and I trust you to do the right thing. There're many hungry people, and Richard and I are going to make a small dent in that hunger. I'm writing you a check for ..." Richard mouthed 'ten.' ... "Ten thousand dollars. We want you to keep serving pizza until time runs out, food runs out, or money runs out – whichever comes first. If there's any money left over, please donate to Long Beach Community Christian Church, and take the donation off your taxes. Okay?"

He nodded. "It will be a pleasure. Thank you! God bless you! I'll have to make a call and have the police help control the crowd. They'll eat free anyway."

When Richard and Char got back home, they flopped on their bed and slept for over an hour, then Richard went downstairs to practice.

Later, Char fixed chef's salads for dinner, but neither of them was really hungry. After starting the dishwasher, Richard took the compacted trash out to their dumpster while Char finished the cleanup.

Their worship that night was like an extension of the praise they had begun that morning. They read Richard's reviews in the *Press-Telegram* again, and offered prayers for several people in the news. They went to bed early because both were exhausted.

+ + +

The weeks flew by, as their lives became somewhat routine. The Bible study group met Mondays, Wednesdays, and Fridays, and they completed their study just before the train tour was to start. The night before they left, Char unpacked and repacked their suitcases, trying to make access to whatever they needed more convenient while Richard continued to practice downstairs. She also added a couple of things to surprise him.

The next morning, as they rode in the SUV it was total darkness because there were no streetlights on. Richard noticed a display in the middle of the dashboard, showing the freeway as though it was bright daylight. He pointed. "What's that display, Ensign?"

"That's a J-Scope, sir. We have ultra-sensitive receivers, front and rear, equipped with a combination of infrared camera, sonar, and radar, processed by a computer, and fed to the display. They're showing up all over, sir, not just with the military."

"What does the 'J' in 'J-Scope stand for, Ensign?"

"You can call me Bob, sir. I don't know, but I can find out. Sam?"

Sam took a microphone off a dashboard clip and spoke. "Dispatch, this is the Donovan escort. Mr. Donovan wants to know what the 'J' in 'J-Scope' stands for. Over."

A voice said, "Just a moment." There was about twenty seconds of silence. "Tell Mr. Donovan that the 'J' refers to his brother, Joshua Donovan at the CIA."

Char and Richard both burst out laughing. He nodded. "Thank you! ... Char, that sounds like Josh, doesn't it?"

Char was still smiling. "He's going to be rich!"

Richard shook his head. "No, the government will hold all the patents. I imagine he's gotten a promotion, though."

When they arrived at Union Station, the two ensigns made quick and easy work of getting their luggage into the Pullman compartment on the train. Char gave each of the ensigns twenty dollars.

As they settled into their compartment, Richard turned on the television.

Char smiled. "That gives me an idea!" She went to her suitcase and pulled out a sound bar about a foot long. Finding the outlet for earphones, she plugged it in. The sound from the TV filled the room.

Richard stared at it. "Where did you get that thing?"

"It's from Sony. It's not yet in production because they want to add a few more features, and they're not releasing many new products until after the long winter."

"I like it! The bass response is amazing for something so small." The television kept them entertained for hours.

If it were not for the long winter, that first segment of their trip would have taken just over ten hours. It took twelve. Their suite at the Flagstaff Courtyard was very comfortable. It had two king-size beds and a comfy lounging area. Richard hooked up their sound bar to the television and turned on the news. There was a three-minute segment on his solo concert, which he was to give that evening in the ballroom downstairs. "Richard, your piano down there is supposed to be a 1940s-vintage restored Steinway. Bobbi made a big deal with someone here to make sure it is in good shape. We can only hope, of course."

He nodded. "Right. I'm not really concerned. I hope people will enjoy it. I'm going to a mix of Bach, Brahms, and Broadway."

There was a surprise. The manager was a friend of Captain Steven Lyman, from their submarine voyage. It was learned Char played a Yamaha Avant-Grand at home, so on the stage, nestled into the Steinway, was a Yamaha. After Richard played Bach and Brahms on the Steinway for about an hour, they took an intermission. Afterward, Char joined him on stage to jam Broadway show tunes and Christian praise music. The evening was a hit. They were still too young for the champagne, so they enjoyed sparkling cider instead.

The next morning they got on the train, and seven hours later, they were in Albuquerque. Richard thought the New Mexico Philharmonic was an amazing surprise. In the first half of the evening, they played Tchaikovsky's *Pathetique Symphony*. It was a magnificent performance. Both of them were moved to tears. In the second half, Richard played Tchaikovsky's *First Piano Concerto* with them, and he found it a totally enjoyable experience.

After solo concerts in Kansas City and St. Louis, they went on to their next destination, a full day away. Memphis Central Station's enclosed waiting area was partially filled with musicians, who offered them a musical welcome with both country and rock music. While others took care of their luggage, Char and

Richard were escorted closer to the band, and rack of electronic keyboards was standing there. With Char standing in front of him, Richard started playing the top keyboard, while Char played the other two. They jammed with the band for about fifteen minutes for a very appreciative audience.

The van from the Peabody Memphis was waiting for them when they left the station. As they got in, both were smiling. At the hotel, they were told that a table was reserved for them in the dining room. Tired after the long train ride, however, they took a shower and changed clothes. After a leisurely lunch, they went to the Cannon Center for the Performing Arts, where Richard sat down at the piano. Playing his favorite Mozart Sonata, he found that it was a very nicely tuned and adjusted Steinway. He went on to try portions of his intended selections of Bach, Beethoven, Brahms, Debussy, Ravel, and Gershwin. After telling the stage manager that he would return at 7:30 for the 8:00 performance, they went back to the hotel and relaxed. After dinner, Richard's evening performance had no problems. His conclusion with the Chopin Scherzo No.2 brought him a standing ovation, but he was restless.

Going back to the hotel, Richard could not put his finger on what was bothering him. He had performed admirably. They read the Bible and prayed, but he was still restless, walking around and around their room. Finally, he said, "Let's cast lots and see if God wants us to go to Anchorage."

"Really? Is that what has been stirring you up?" Char was puzzled. "I've been thinking about Anchorage, too, mainly because we haven't fully discussed it, let alone made a decision. I'm up in the air. Are you?"

He nodded and took her in his arms. "Mostly, I'm reluctant to go. I've never been there, but I cannot imagine them having a decent piano in good tune up there. Also, I cannot imagine there being an audience there for classical music, and I'm not sure about what kind of music they actually would like. Would you and I jam?" Char silently listened, and he started pacing the room again. "I can't see any good purpose in our going up there, with so many people evidently dying of starvation." He stopped and looked at her. "The flip side of all of that, Char, is that I've got this strange feeling that God really wants us to go there." They worshiped again, and they cast lots.

The next morning at the FedEx Forum, some of the biggest names in country music were there on the stage with them. They rehearsed all morning, broke for lunch, and rehearsed for three hours in the afternoon. Richard and Char were star-struck with all of them, but they focused on the concert they were to perform. Char and Richard managed to remain professional.

That evening, they had a wildly appreciative audience, and at their first of two intermissions, Richard was at the microphone. "It's time for our intermission, so if you need to go, we'll be back after about ten minutes. Since we're in Memphis, and Char and I are Christians, we sort of assume that here in this amazing southern city that most of you are Christians too."

There were thunderous applause, whistles, and foot stomping. Char stepped up to her microphone. "That's really good, because we want to share something with you that we would not share otherwise. If you don't want to listen, just go get your nachos." There was laughter, and then the audience became very quiet. "After Richard's performance last evening at the Cannon Center, when we got back to the hotel, Richard was restless. I must admit that I was a little restless too. After reading the Bible and praying, he was still restless. We have talked off and on for weeks, about whether or not we should go to Alaska and put on a performance in Anchorage. Travel to and from Alaska is risky at best, and the same is true for Hawaii. We've not even started talking about Hawaii yet."

Richard continued. "Most of you know that Char and I are considered by many to be a strange couple because we are open about the fact that we cast lots to determine God's will. Last night, after a lot of prayer, as well as after an extended session of casting lots, we came to a decision."

"Just try to imagine, Christian friends, an experience like the one we had last night." Char's voice was soft but intense. "We cast lots using three quarters. The routine is simple. Humbly ask God a question, and cast lots. Consider the answer. If at *any* time you get a mix of heads and tails, God is not talking, and you stop. Period. That's it, at least for casting lots at that time. You then simply thank God and say amen. If you get all heads, meaning yes or blessings, or all tails, meaning no or curses, you can go on to another question. Let me assure you. It can be truly scary, because we serve a God who is the very definition of awesome. That kind of fear requires humble courage from us. When Richard first told me on our wedding day that he was doing this, I was skeptical. We are now past our first anniversary, and we have been casting lots for four to five days a week. Usually, we cast lots just five or six times in a session of worship. We have seldom gotten a mix of heads and tails at the beginning of worship. Think about it: How many times could you toss three coins without getting a mix? How many?"

Richard's voice, was now stronger. "We ask for your prayers for the days ahead. Last evening, for the first time, we cast lots twenty-three times, asking twenty-three questions, and each time we got the same answer: Heads-heads-heads. We made many phone calls this morning. After our last concert in Salt Lake City, we are flying in a specially modified military transport plane to Anchorage Alaska, and we're going to make all kinds of music – classical, folk, rock, country, Christian praise, ... or you name it. The trip will be dangerous. We will be in unimaginable cold for at least a week. It will be difficult. We trust God to deliver us to and from Anchorage. ... We're going. ... Please pray for us."

Scattered applause began, and then it began to spread. Soon people were rising to their feet and stamping their feet and cheering. Richard called out loudly on the mike, "We're taking ten."

For the remainder of the performance, both those on stage and those in the audience were energized. After doing two encores, they concluded.

At the hotel, they went to the restaurant and had a relaxing dinner. Richard was thoughtful. "I was relieved this afternoon."

"Me too. It seemed as though most of the audience was Christian, and we had their spiritual support for what we told them we are going to do."

He nodded. "Tomorrow we will go back north to Chicago, where our Pullman is going to be connected to a train going west to Omaha. It will be like old times."

"Yes, like going home," Char smiled, "going to another Hilton. Bobbi says that the Grand Central Ballroom where you'll be performing is very nice. It has two video screens, so those in the back will see you up close and personal on the screens."

"It'll be a long ride getting there."

"Yes," she nodded, "Eleven hours or so to Chicago, then at least nine to Omaha. Shall we worship and get some sleep?"

He nodded.

+ + +

Richard was shocked, truly dumbfounded. In the Grand Central Ballroom, the piano was identical to his piano at home. Why would this hotel have such an expensive and special piano? He sat down and adjusted the bench. Since the Hilton Omaha manager requested Debussy's *La cathédrale engloutie* ('engulfed cathedral'). He tried it, and he was doubly amazed. The piano was every bit as well adjusted as his, and in perfect tune. In addition, the center *sostenuto* pedal, which is essential to appropriately playing the piece, was properly adjusted. The Debussy flowed perfectly for him. Following the order of his planned program, he tried Debussy's *L'isle joyeuse* ('joyous isle'). Impressed, Richard adjusted his program. "This is going to be fun!" he said to himself.

That evening, after the two opening Debussy pieces, he did some other pieces that had been requested through various sources in the area. Richard was not particularly impressed with them, but it was their show. After doing the Chopin Scherzo that Char loved so much, he ended with the always impressive Bach's *Passacaglia* and the Bach-Busoni *Chromatic Fantasy and Fugue.*

After they went back up to their suite, Char gave him a lingering hug. "Thank you for doing the *Scherzo*. I know it is a workout, but I love hearing you do it. Is it as difficult as it sounds?"

Richard nodded. "Definitely.' They got into bed. "Do you remember Mr. Fitzer, that jazz piano teacher that helped me to improve my Gershwin work?"

"He smoked a pipe, didn't he?" They snuggled closer together.

"Yes. I was shocked when he assigned that scherzo to me. He said that I needed that Chopin piece to improve my musical discipline. It did, but I would not even perform it for my parents or you. The only reason you heard it is because you snuck into our living room while I was practicing, and I didn't see you."

Char smiled and kissed him. "That's been one of my favorites ever since." She paused. "If we could, I would love for us to move to our Pullman car tonight, so that we wouldn't have to get up early in the morning. We could just snuggle up together in the lower bunk."

Richard let go of her and reached for the phone on the nightstand. He pressed zero. "Hello? ... Yes, our Amtrak train is leaving early tomorrow morning. If we could transfer our belongings and move to our Pullman car this evening, we would not have to get up so early. Could you find out if that is possible with Amtrak? ... Thank you."

He went back to snuggle with Char. "We need to talk about when we want to start a family. Do you still want to wait until this nuclear winter is over?"

Char snuggled closer. "A gloomy world cannot be good for the disposition of babies growing up."

The phone rang, and he picked it up. "Hello? ... We can? We'll be ready in ten minutes!"

The transfer to the train was easy, and their Pullman attendant was one that they knew before. Richard hooked up the sound bar, and they watched the news. They got ready for bed, worshiped, got into the lower bunk together, and turned out the light.

"Dad, you and Mom were once in Alaska, weren't you?"

"Yes."

"Was it beautiful?"

"We didn't see any of it. It was always snowing and cold, and we were either inside buildings on the base or on transports."

"So you didn't see any of Alaska?"

"No. That's why we've planned this family vacation for all of us."

17.

It was dusk when they pulled into Denver, and it was much colder due to the altitude. They liked the Four Seasons hotel, but both were beginning to be apprehensive about the flight to Alaska that they would take from Salt Lake City. While signing in at the front desk, they were given slips for eight messages. Rick stuffed them in his shirt pocket as they followed the bellhop to their room.

In the elevator, Char looked up at him. "Who are the messages from?"

He took them out of his pocket and looked at the top one, and then shuffled them. "Let's see ... Tom Dobbins, Lou Mendez, Lori Simpson, Angel Madison, Bob Presley, Jim Gehringer, Rick Stevens, and Bill Jones."

The elevator doors opened, and they followed the luggage cart. "Those are all world-class musicians, Richard. I think all of them were in Memphis when we were."

Richard nodded as they went through the door into their room. He tipped the Bellhop. "Why don't you call Bobbi, and tell her we've got these un-returned messages. Ask her what she thinks. This room has a whirlpool. I'll fill it while you call Bobbi, and then why don't you come and join me?"

"Okay."

Richard filled the tub, and then he added some of the Char's favorite bath salts. He got in.

Less than thirty seconds later, Char got in with him. "Bobbi says she'll return the calls and get back to us. She said we did the right thing by letting her return the calls. If they want to go to Anchorage with us, General Oswald is going to have to get involved. We're going to be performing on base, so all of them will have to have security checks. I would think that at least some of them have already been cleared since they have done USO tours."

Richard was ready to get out of the whirlpool to answer the phone, but Bobbi did not call back that evening. Their first night in Denver they slept peacefully, at least until 5:00 A.M. The message light on their phone began flashing, and Richard's eyes opened and saw it.

He picked up the phone and pushed zero. "This is Richard Donovan. Our message light is flashing."

"Yes, Mr. Donovan, we have a voice-mail message for you. Would you like to hear it now?"

"Yes, please."

"Good morning, this is Bobbi. I've been working on those eight people who left messages that they want to go to Alaska with you. Seven of the eight are going. Jim Gehringer had a family crisis develop after his call, so he's the one not going. You know the instrumental capabilities of the other seven. All have good singing voices, in case you didn't know it. Tom will be bringing his banjo and twelve-string as well as his regular guitar. Lou Mendez said that Char could do some singing, and he wants to do a couple of duets with her. He also says that he's bringing some stuff that can be done a capella. Finally, and most importantly, the modified military transport plane is already in Salt Lake City, and as instrumentalists arrive, their gear will be loaded. Ground support will keep the plane warm until you take off. Good luck you two – good luck to all of you." The message ended.

"If you need to hear the message again, Mr. Donovan, we will hold it until your departure tomorrow."

"Thank you." He hung up and looked across the bed. Char's eyes were open. "Good morning, beautiful! Seven of the eight will be going with us to Anchorage. Jim Gehringer is out. The plane is already in Salt Lake City. It'll be warm at least until we take off."

Char rubbed her eyes. "Are you going to do the same music today both at the matinee and this evening?"

"Unless the piano downstairs is as good a Bösendorfer as that instrument in Omaha, I'll not do the same program as I did there. I can't. I'll have the room to myself until 10:00 AM, as planned, so I'll adjust my program to the instrument and the room." He slid over to kiss her, and they enjoyed a few moments together.

Char was content. "You can get up, shower, and dress first, while I order breakfast. After we eat, I'll call Bobbi to get any updates and check the paper for reviews. I'll also see if there is any news on the Internet. Do you want to have lunch here in our room or go to the restaurant?"

"Our neighbor, Jim, told me that the Edge Restaurant here at this hotel is outstanding."

She nodded. "Why don't we plan on having our main meal at noon, and then after the matinee we can have a light supper before you play in the evening?"

"That sounds good." Richard got up to get started with his practicing, while Char picked up the phone to order breakfast.

The morning went quickly for both. The reviews from Omaha were excellent, but Char expected no less. She talked with Tom Dobbins, Lou Mendez, and Angel Madison on the phone, and each of them gave her some program ideas for Anchorage.

Meanwhile, the hotel manager talked to his counterpart at the Hilton in San Diego. The San Diego manager suggested that there in Denver he should try to get a Baldwin SD-10 or a Bösendorfer. He couldn't find either at first, but after many calls, he got what he wanted for Richard.

That morning, shortly before 9:00, Richard sat down to another Bösendorfer Imperial. Silently praising God repeatedly, he practiced parts of every piece he had used in Omaha. He knew from experience that each time he performed that repertoire, it became more highly polished.

Both the matinee and the evening performances were sold out, and Richard felt particularly energized at the evening performance. Although the audience at the matinee was supportive and applauded enthusiastically, the people attending the evening performance gave him an extended standing ovation. Char was thrilled, and during their worship that night, they felt particularly close to God.

The seventeen-hour ride from Denver to Salt Lake City included high winds as well as heavy snow. Twice, the conductor apologized to them for their slow progress. In their compartment, everything was quiet, unless they had their television turned on and hooked up to the sound bar.

After they awakened from their naps in the afternoon, Char went to her suitcase. "I've got a toy for you to play with."

"A toy? You bought a toy for me in Denver? When did you go shopping?"

She shook her head. "I brought this with us since we left home, but I've kept it hidden in my larger suitcase, waiting for the right time. It's late in our tour, and we're a little bored, so here it is." She unfolded a full-size plastic keyboard with the usual eighty-eight keys, but it was less than an inch thick. She put it onto the lower bunk. "Here, Richard, plug this into the sound bar, and put it behind the keyboard." She moved two chairs over next to the middle of the bunk, and then she pushed a slide switch on the right-hand end. The keyboard lit up.

Richard grinned. "Are you kidding me? This is terrific! I wonder how it sounds." He played a couple of chords. "Not bad. There're no pedals and no accelerated action, so something written for organ or harpsichord will work best." For the next hour or so, he played pieces of music from the Baroque era by Bach, Buxtehude, Vivaldi, and

Scarlatti. Both enjoyed themselves and played some things together.

Char pointed at the end of the keyboard. "There's another little slide switch, but it's longer, and with three positions. Let's try it," She pushed it to the middle, and he played some chords. It was the sound of a string orchestra.

"Cool!" He smiled and tried a little Handel piece. "This sounds good, but I don't think Handel intended it that way. Try putting the switch in the third position."

Char nodded and slid it all the way over. "This is fun!" When Richard started playing a Bach Prelude, she sat back. "Pipe Organ? That's amazing for that little sound bar and this instrument!" She listened. "I just had an idea. Do you remember the Beethoven Sonata for four hands we did when we were juniors in La Jolla?"

Richard smiled. "We haven't done that in ages! Do you still remember the first movement?"

"I think so. Let's try it." They did. Then, for the next hour, Richard played more Bach, and they both thoroughly enjoyed themselves.

+ + +

It was late when they arrived at Salt Lake City's Intermodal Hub. They were definitely tired of traveling on trains. A large SUV from the Grand America Hotel drove them quickly to their five-star facility, After checking in, going to their room, they had a short time of worship. They left a call for 7:00 and turned off their lights at 1:00 A.M.

Rehearsal with the Utah Symphony started late, but by mid-afternoon, Richard could go back to the hotel confident that the performance would go well. That evening's performance on a very decent Steinway was satisfying. Back at their hotel, they went to the spa for an hour, and then the worshiped and cast lots.

After turning off the light, Richard kissed Char. "I hope I don't have to perform the Grieg again for a while.

I've played it so often in the past sixteen months or so, and I don't want it to get sloppy or stale."

"It doesn't sound like its getting close to either being stale or sloppy."

"No, and I don't want it to. Good night, my love."

"Good night."

Their wake-up call seemed earlier than usual, even though they were still on Mountain Standard Time. A second lieutenant and his team took their belongings to the airport, while Richard and Char went to the Garden Café and had breakfast.

It was a relatively short drive to the waiting plane. Inside, most of the other musicians were drinking hot chocolate. They went down the aisle to great all of them. Richard grinned. "Good morning, Tom, Lou. Have you been here long?"

They shook their heads. Tom gestured toward the others. "None of us have been here more than fifteen minutes. I understand that this plane and others like it were officially out of service for better than forty years. A lieutenant told me that the Air Force had spent the last six months refurbishing them and refitting them for transport through this volcanic muck. He said there are less than a dozen planes that are flight worthy."

Richard nodded and turned to the two women across the aisle. "Good morning, Lori and Angel. It is good to meet you at last. Char and I have many of your CDs, as well as CDs from everyone on this junket."

Char nodded. "This may be rough, unless we can get above the clouds." She and Richard went to the second row. "Good morning, Bob, Rick. Are you all set for this roller coaster?"

They both grinned and nodded. Richard also smiled. "When we get to Anchorage, we'll have a full day to get our act more or less together. We'll be rehearsing and performing in what used to be a large hanger. The Seabees have double-insulated it. A friend of ours stationed at Terminal Island told us one day that it's insulated to roughly R-100 in the walls, and R-200 in the ceiling. With snow and ice banked all around the building, it is supposed to be fairly comfortable. They've made bedrooms out of what used to be offices along the sides of the hanger, so we'll be living in that one building as well as performing in it."

Bill Jones was sitting across the aisle. "What do you think the acoustics will be like?"

Richard shook his head. "The acoustics will probably be pretty bad. I've never been in a military venue where acoustics were truly good." He grinned. "On the other hand, echoes can cover a multitude of sins." They all laughed, a little nervously.

"Excuse me!"

They turned, and a lieutenant was standing in the aisle near the flight deck.

"For those to whom I've not spoken, I'm Lieutenant Charles Cash. You can call me Chuck. We'll be getting underway in a couple of minutes. It's a good idea to loosen your shoes. Before we start, the Captain wants to say a few words." He turned, and a man in fatigues and a heavy jacket came from just beyond the bulkhead. His black hair had grey streaks.

"Good morning, everyone. I'm John Scott. I've flown prop planes exactly like this one in air shows for the last ten years, and I've flown almost every type of aircraft that the Air Force currently uses. I've been flying one of these specially modified planes for about two weeks now. The air that comes inside, both for us and for the engines, goes through innovative filtration that removes 99% of the pollutants. You won't be coughing, and the engines won't either. Don't worry when we're bouncing around up there. These birds are tough. During the Korean conflict, they flew through anti-aircraft fire. We will first refuel at Seattle-Tacoma. Next, we'll refuel at Juneau. Finally, we'll land at your destination, Elmendorf

Air Force Base in Anchorage. I'll taxi as up close to the building as I can, but the temperature will be around fifty below zero."

As the Lieutenant secured the doors, the Captain continued. "This is going to be a rough ride, and it will tend to get rougher as we go further north until we close to Juneau. Since this is at least theoretically summer up there, storms tend to track farther south. North of Juneau, we may well be capable of getting above the clouds, where you'll be able to see some hazy sunshine through the windows. Are there any questions?"

Lou was concerned about their instruments. "Will the cargo be in heated air?"

"Yes. It should remain in the high 60s in the cargo hold. Our passenger air goes on through that hold before it goes out. Anyone else?" They all shook their heads. "Okay, we're headed to Seattle-Tacoma. Buckle up!"

At one point in the first leg of their journey, Char glanced over at Richard and asked, "I wonder if this is what it is like to ride a bronco in a rodeo?" Richard grimly smiled.

Two hours later, when they landed to refuel, everyone zipped up their jackets and dashed for the terminal to go to the restrooms. When they got back on the plane, Chuck had put covered cups of hot chocolate at every seat. They drank it eagerly.

The flight to Juneau was longer, but it was not quite as rough. It was the same routine at the terminal. After using the rest rooms, some of them ran in place to get their blood circulating.

Taking off from Juneau was as rough as a typical flight through a storm, but in less than thirty minutes, they saw hazy sunshine coming through the windows as the turbulence quieted down. Still buckled up, they smiled and murmured to one another. That leg of their journey was almost enjoyable. For everyone but the crew, they were seeing sunshine for the first time since Yellowstone erupted.

In Anchorage, as they taxied up to the hanger, Chuck spoke to them for the first time since they left Juneau. "We're going to get as close to the hanger as we safely can, but right now it is fifty-six degrees below zero. Bundle up and move as fast as you safely can."

Those were instructions easy to obey. Once inside, they lowered their hoods and looked around. What they saw appeared to be the size of two football fields side by side, and the ceiling appeared to be fifty feet or more. When they unzipped their jackets, they found that the temperature seemed cool but comfortable. All of them headed for the doors that had restroom symbols on them.

Looking to his side, Richard saw that Chuck was standing next to him in the restroom. "What's the local time here?"

"Locally, it's 0100. In Salt Lake, it is 0300."

"Could you please pass the word on that, so everyone can adjust their watches?"

"I can, but there is a large 24-hour digital clock above the door where we came in. I'll point it out to them."

"Thank you. Can you arrange for a buzzer or something to go off at 0800?"

Chuck nodded. "There's a door out there with a big 'B' over it. That opens to a tunnel that leads to the mess hall. I'll tell the cook that you and your team will have breakfast at 0815. How's that?"

"Excellent. Thank you." They both left.

Char met Richard outside the restroom door, and together they explored the building until they found a door with "Donovan" on the door. Inside, they found all of their luggage and a queen-size bed. Richard smiled. "This will do."

Char smiled, and they hugged for some time.

Since all of them were living on one side of the building, Richard knocked on their doors and gathered them immediately outside their rooms for a quick meeting. "If you'll look at that clock," he pointed, "it is 0116, which means that in Salt Lake, it is 0316. A buzzer or something will blare at 0800, and at 0815, we'll go through that door over there," he pointed, "that has a 'B' over it. That door opens into a tunnel leading to the mess hall. The cook will expect us at 0815. Let's get some sleep." Goodnight everyone!"

"Mom, why don't you and Dad do more concerts close to home?"

"We've done a few here in this area, but it is a big world, isn't it?"

"Yeah, Mom, but then you and Dad could come home after the concerts more often."

"That's true. Maybe Bobbi can set one up in San Diego so that we can all go to the zoo."

"Yeah!"

18.

When a loud buzzer went off, both Richard and Char sat bolt upright on their bed. Char stretched. "That was definitely not enough sleep!"

"I agree, but let's get dressed. We can get showers later."

Moving fast, they got into the mess hall almost on time. Char got to the window first and glanced at the list of foods. "I'm famished. I'll have a pancake sandwich, bacon, and sausage."

The cook nodded. "Got it. ...and you sir?"

Richard paused. "I'll have eggs over easy, country potatoes, wheat toast, preserves, and bacon."

As other ordered their food, they went to a drink area and got juice and coffee.

They all sat down at one big table. Between bites, Richard talked. "While we were riding that bucking bronco yesterday I couldn't talk with each of you, so this morning we'll wing it, so to speak." He disposed of another forkful. "I've got cue sheets for all of us, both in concert and B♭ setups. We have the hanger to ourselves until 1600 hours. I don't think we'll have to rehearse the whole time – we're all pros." He had another forkful. "My manager, Bobbi, told the Base Commander, that it would be great if we had some kind of video display so people could sing along for some of the songs, but I don't know if that will happen." He picked up some toast and added preserves.

Bill Jones waved his fork. "After talking with Bobbi, I decided to bring along electronic drums, which I don't prefer, but she pointed out that we could control the sound better that way despite bad acoustics. What kind of amplification are we going to have?"

Richard swallowed. "This place is supposed to have a decent-sized sound board, with a snake that will take twenty-four inputs. We've got plenty of mikes, though you won't need them for your electronic trap set."

Lori put her fork down. "Are the singers' mikes going to be wired or wireless?"

"We'll soon find out, I guess." They were all about done, and Richard stood up. "While we've been eating, a stage crew has begun to set things up for us. Let's go see what we have." They all moved.

Angel approached them as they walked through the tunnel. "All seven us who volunteered to join you on this trip are amazed that you two feel just as comfortable with mainstream music as you do with classical."

Char put her arm around her. "When musicians put out good music, Richard and I don't care what style it is or how old it is. We love excellence."

Getting everything set up to everyone's satisfaction took just over an hour. They warmed up with "This Land Is Your Land," had a few laughs, and then settled down to work. The piano was an excellent Baldwin. At 1500 hours, they stopped to take naps, take showers, and get into fresh clothes.

As expected, the concert was a hit. When people in the audience called out requests, they would look at each other, and those who nodded in unison would fake it. The commandant asked Richard to play something classical by himself. Surprised, he thought a moment, and then played the Chopin Scherzo that Char loved, telling them that it was one of her favorites. Dinner started very late, but no one cared. All the musicians scattered to sit with whoever else was in the mess hall, and the majority was civilians. After dinner, there was a call for more music, and without hesitation, they went back to the stage and played for another hour. Richard and Char went to their room at about the same time as the previous night. After worship, they turned off the light and went immediately to sleep. They hardly stirred until the buzzer went off.

At breakfast the next morning, the atmosphere was quiet and thoughtful. Char was very appreciative. "Richard and I cannot thank all of you enough for joining us to do this. It's been difficult in many ways, but we're both happy we did it, and we're pleased all of you did it with us."

Tom was curious. "Richard, how long have you been playing that Chopin piece?"

"About four years, why do you ask?"

"I've been pickin' banjo and guitar just about all of my life, and most people say my fingers are fast, but I'll be darned if I've ever witnessed anything like that before in my life!"

Richard grinned. "My jazz piano teacher asked me to learn that to teach me musical discipline."

Tom and a couple of the others burst out laughing. "That's a jazz piano lesson?"

"Yeah, kind of. I was working on some Gershwin pieces, and he told me that my efforts sucked."

They all laughed. Char kissed him on the cheek. "No way, my love!"

Tom nodded. "I think I've now got a story for a friend of mine, a pianist who's pretty wrapped up in himself. There's a CD out with you playing that, I think, right?" Richard shook his head. "Not yet. That Memphis performance was the first time I'd ever done it in public. It will be out in a few months, maybe. I honestly don't know." He looked further down the table. "Is there something on your mind, Lori?"

"Yeah, I think so. Just before you and Char got on the plane in Salt Lake, we were talking about letting Anchorage be the beginning of a tour of military bases. Does that interest the two of you?"

Char shook her head. "Knowing the demands of our schedule, I don't think it can be done right now, and probably not these next eighteen months to two years."

"Really! You're booked that far ahead?" Lori's mouth hung open.

"We're not solidly booked, but because of our being in the media with prophecies and other things, we keep getting last minute engagements. That trip to Tokyo was on less than two months' notice. Sony was the sponsor, and I guess they really wanted us to do that jam session in Tokyo Dome. To sweeten the deal, they delivered a brand new Bösendorfer Imperial 290 piano to the concert hall for him to play the classical music on. They gave us the piano as his fee, and shipped it to Southern California for us."

Angel's eyes got big. "Holy Toledo! Isn't that a terribly expensive instrument?"

Char grinned. "To say the least, yes."

An airman approached. "Excuse me, sir. There's a phone call for you. We're patching it through to that phone over there on the wall." The airman turned and left.

Richard went to the wall and picked up the phone. "Hello? ... Steve! It's good to hear from you. ... Wow, that's great! ... No, they have other plans. ... How soon? ... Okay. ... Okay. ... Okay, see you then." He hung up and stared at the wall. Then he came back to the table.

Char put her arm around him. "Who was it?"

He was thoughtful. "It's a small world, Char. That was Steve Lyman."

He eyes got big. "Do you mean the captain who..."

He interrupted. "Yes." He turned to the others. "We were talking a few minutes ago about the concert we did in Tokyo. Just as we were about to get on a plane to fly home, all commercial air traffic was grounded. The U.S. Navy put us on a sub that took us back to Terminal Island, south of Los Angeles. That call was from the Captain of that sub. The Secretary of State is going to be here tomorrow morning to talk to us about something, and then Captain Lyman is standing by to take us to where we need to go, but we may be here a few more days. The seven of you will take off to go back to the lower forty-eight tonight or tomorrow morning, as soon as you are ready." He turned to Char. You and I have a lot to pray about tonight." He sat down and gave Char a kiss. "Tom, you'll be getting a call from the USO before noon today."

Tom nodded. "Good. I wonder if they're still planning on us doing a train tour. Our managers have freed us up for the next month or so. The seven of us can practice for a while we wait to hear from them."

They all got up and left the mess hall. The seven went to the stage still set up from the previous night. Richard and Char went to their room.

She sat with her legs crossed on the bed. "It wasn't a long call, but I have a feeling you did not tell us everything there in the mess hall."

He nodded. "That's true. He spoke in military shorthand, but here's what I think he said. ... The U.S. and Australia are cutting an agriculture cargo deal. The Secretary of State will be here to talk with us about it because the President sweetened the deal with the possibility of you and I doing a concert tour down under. We'll know later tonight or tomorrow morning, when the Secretary gets here."

"So we have a lot to pray about, and we need to cast lots for this, don't we?"

"Yes. ... My internal clock is all screwed up. I want to take a nap before we worship and pray."

She nodded. "Me, too."

They slept.

Several hours later, there was a knock on their door, and Richard answered. "Yes?"

"Mr. & Mrs. Donovan, Secretary of State Gloria House is here. If you'll come with me, I'll take you to a conference room." The messenger paused.

"Give us just a moment, please." As Richard ran a comb through his hair, Char put on her shoes.

It seemed as though they walked at least a quarter of a mile before they were led down a hallway.

In a conference room, the base commander and an Asian-American woman stood up to greet them. "I'm Admiral Shultz, and this is Secretary of State Gloria House. Madam secretary, Char and Richard Donovan."

Char greeted her. "Mrs. House, I believe we met in Washington at a Cabinet meeting."

She smiled. "Yes. I remember that meeting." She shook hands with both. "You are quite an artist, Mr. Donovan – actually both of you. I was in Omaha to hear you. Please sit down, both of you." They sat down.

"The two of you, and your friends, flew up here in a plane that was both a classic workhorse and a successful experiment. Pratt and Whitney anticipated that success, and they began manufacturing an engine they initially designed towards the end of World War II. An Air Force C5A has been fitted with new piston engines designed a half-century ago, and yesterday was a completely successful test flight. Early this morning," she looked at her watch, "actually, yesterday morning, our President was talking with the Prime Minister of Australia. They have a tentative agreement to exchange the abundance of our hydroponics vegetables for their beef, pork, and mutton. To sweeten and advertise the deal, the President said he would ask the two of you to do a two-week concert tour of Australia. Now, I am asking you: Are the two of you willing to do a two-week concert tour in Australia?"

Richard responded cautiously. "Char and I knew you were going to ask, and we have prayed about it and cast lots for it. If we do this, we have stipulations."

"Stipulations?"

Char nodded. "Our stipulations are not negotiable."

"Go ahead."

"Neither government can tell us what music we can and cannot play. Both governments are to see to it that any advertising or promotion of our concerts does not mention politics, a political connection, or any aspect of this deal whatsoever."

The secretary scowled. "I cannot speak for Australia, but I will tell them of your stipulation, and I will ask them to confirm their response to you directly. Is there anything else?"

Richard nodded. "Yes, one more thing for each government. Our government is to provide submarine transportation, both to Australia and back to Terminal Island. In Australia, our concert fees and expenses are to come from private funds without any kind of government subsidy."

Gloria House smiled. "Again, I cannot speak for Australia, but I understand that we do not have a deal, unless they agree to your terms. Am I correct?"

Char nodded. "That is correct, Secretary House."

The Secretary of State relaxed and sat back in her chair. "I like the way the two of you negotiate. Your parents did a great job raising you."

Richard smiled. "Praise God."

"Indeed." She nodded and turned to Base Commander Schultz. "Will you please make arrangements for us to be aboard that submarine within the hour?"

He nodded. "I will inform Captain Lyman, and I will arrange for base personnel to escort the three of you on board and transfer your belongings."

She nodded. "Thank you, Admiral."

They moved quickly. As Richard and Char went into the hanger, the practicing stopped while they said their good-byes. Less than a half-hour later, they were on board the sub, which got underway.

Char and Richard enjoyed being reacquainted with several members of the crew, including Shorty, their favorite cook and friend. For the next nine and a half days, sometimes they chatted with Secretary House, and often with the Captain or members of the crew. Twice, Richard and Char led worship services for those Christians who were interested, using the toy keyboard and soundbar. They prayed with Captain Lyman on three different occasions, and they also prayed with other members of the crew. Shorty went out of his way to cook things he thought they would enjoy.

When they surfaced in Sydney, the temperature was much warmer than it had been in Alaska, but the skies were cloudy. At the dock, there was a large SUV there to whisk the special passengers to the Prime Minister's residence, Kirribilli House. Malcolm Rudd greeted them warmly.

Richard shook the Prime Minister's hand. Sir, I have a suggestion, if you don't mind."

"What is that, Mr. Donovan?"

"It is my understanding that you and Secretary House have political business to discuss that does not involve my wife and me. Since it is not raining, may we walk around and explore your beautiful property? Perhaps someone can point out its features to us?"

Mr. Rudd grinned. "Mr. Donovan, I do believe that if you were not a musician, you would make a fine diplomat." He turned to a woman standing nearby. "Sydney, would you please help the Donovans explore the official residence?"

Sydney smiled. "I would be happy to." She looked at Char and Richard "Please, come with me. I can point out some of the lovely features of our Prime Minister's official residence." She took the better part of an hour pointing out the bay windows, the steeply pitched roofs, the fretwork, and the bargeboards. Later, she pointed out some of the plants and trees native to Australia. Her beeper went off, and she looked at it. "We are being summoned back to where we began."

As they approached the entrance, the Prime Minister came down the steps to greet them again. "Did you enjoy your little tour?"

Char smiled. "Yes, we did, sir. It is beautiful here."

He nodded. "Thank you. When the two of you were on the dock earlier today, you and your husband were recognized by someone from one of our largest cattle stations. I have had a telephone call tell me that several of the cattle station owners will sponsor the two of you if you wish to put on some concerts here while Secretary House is visiting. Is that agreeable to you?"

Richard smiled. "Yes, sir, that is agreeable if you affirm the other restrictions regarding our visit."

The Prime Minister beamed. "Certainly! I can easily enforce those restrictions. This is splendid." He turned to Sydney. "Sydney, the Donovans will be staying at the Park Hyatt. Will you please help them? A first concert is desired on Friday evening at the Opera House."

"Yes, sir, I will take care of their needs." Sydney turned to Richard and Char. "If you will come with me, I will take you to the Park Hyatt." She took out her cell phone. "Paul, the Donovans will be staying at the Park Hyatt. Please see to their luggage. ... Thank you."

Soon they were on their way to the hotel. As they drove, Sydney continued to chatter. "When we learned that the two of you might be coming to visit, many telephone calls were made, and many emails have been exchanged. You may know our guest conductor that we have with us for the Sydney Symphony Orchestra. He is from Rome. His name is Luca Ricci."

Richard smiled. "Yes. During our first European Tour, he and I did the Grieg Piano Concerto together."

"Good. After we get your luggage to your room at the hotel, I will take you to the Opera House. Mr. Ricci will see you there, and the two of you can plan the weekend."

Their two weeks in Australia passed quickly. They often traveled at night, doing thirteen concerts in fifteen days. At the end of their tour, they went back to Sydney Harbor at 2300 hours. They were welcomed aboard by Steve Lyman again, and quickly and silently they got underway.

Char and Richard were exhausted. In their cabin, they softly sang some praise music as part of their worship. They had a time of prayer. That led to talking about what was lying ahead for them back in the United States. It was 1:00 AM local time when they turned out the light.

"Mom, Dad, we want to go to church camp this summer. There's one on the road to Big Bear every year. Can we go to that one this summer?"

"No, that one got taken out by a flash flood." Char's voice was sad.

Richard was upbeat. "How about Sea Scout camp on Catalina?"

"Yea!"

19.

Late, but home at last, they put their clothes in the laundry, changed into swimsuits, and went to the basement. They rolled back the floor, and after swimming a few laps, they soaked in the hot tub.

Char murmured. "This is good. We'll be able to sleep for a week after we soak here for a few minutes."

Richard stretched into the water. "That so-called 'shorter' concert tour lasted longer than the previous one by the time we did Anchorage and Australia. We'll get our energy back in a few days, but I know that you're just as tired as I am."

"It's a good thing we agreed to take a break after Australia. Barring last-minute calls to fill in for someone, you've got several months before your next performance."

"What's next?"

"You'll be doing Brahms' *Second Piano Concerto* at the end of September."

"At least I've got plenty of time to learn the rest of it."

"You don't know all of it? I thought you liked it."

"Actually, I like it a lot, and I started working on it in our senior year in La Jolla, but you know how other things got in the way as we were getting ready to graduate."

Char sunk down into the water over her head and came out, sputtering. "Oooh that felt good. ... While you're learning the Brahms and polishing it, I'm starting a book."

"Really!"

"Yeah. I've decided to write a kind of memoir on our lives together, reflecting on what we've learned and experienced as musicians and prophets. Bobbi suggested it because a publisher has inquired. I've been meaning to ask you something about our last American train tour."

"What?"

"You did a couple of Debussy pieces that I'd not heard in a long time, and that surprised me. Do you know any more of his Etudes?"

"I can resurrect two or three, I suppose. Do you think I should have a Debussy segment in my longer solo performances?"

"I think you should consider it. I'm turning into a prune. After we slide the cover back over the pools, let's go upstairs, and we'll finish off our day."

"Good. I'm so relaxed in this hot tub right now I could almost fall asleep."

They headed upstairs.

The next morning, after they awakened, Char turned on the flat-screen television, which was on the wall across from the foot of their bed. Still on the same channel as before they went on tour, an infotainment show was on, and they were talking about national politics.

The phone rang, and Char muted the TV as Richard pushed the speakerphone button. "Hello?"

"Mr. Donovan? This is John Faber from UBS News. I understand that you and your wife have returned from your concert tour in Australia."

"That's right."

"You have talked with President Williams on more than one occasion."

"That is correct, and any conversations we have with government officials are kept confidential."

"Can you tell us anything about those conversations?"

"Mr. Faber, my wife and I have just returned from several weeks of hard work. We are taking some time off. This conversation is a waste of your time and ours."

"Can you tell me anything about your tour in Australia?"

"Good bye, Mr. Faber." Richard punched the speakerphone button. Then he picked up the receiver and pushed a familiar number. "Cindy? I'm glad you're on duty."

"Good morning, Richard."

"Char and I are tired, and we want you to screen our calls until further notice. Let calls go through from those on our friends and family list, and allow official government calls and those from Bobbi. For everyone else, take messages – not voice mails. We'll call in after lunch every day to check on messages. Okay?"

"I'll take care of it. Tell Char hello for me." She disconnected.

"Cindy said to say 'hi.' What do you think? Do I need a shave?"

"Let me see." She gave him a lingering kiss. "You had better shave this evening before we get frisky."

He grinned. "That I can do." He gave her another kiss, and then hopped out of bed and got dressed.

As Richard went downstairs, Char got out of bed, put on some sweats and headed to the kitchen to fix breakfast. Through the closed kitchen door she could hear him working on the Brahms. She started by fixing some bacon. Finding some chopped dates in the pantry, she added some to her pancake batter, and she heated up some homemade maple syrup. It was one of her better breakfast efforts. When Richard could no longer resist the aromas that Char was creating, he stopped practicing and joined her in the kitchen to eat.

Later, as they were finishing their last sips of English Breakfast tea, Richard put his cup down. "I'm pretty rusty on the Brahms. I'm going to relax in the recliner and memorize the whole thing before I attempt any further efforts at working out fingering. It'll take me at least a week, possibly ten days. This afternoon, when I take a break, maybe you and I can do some jamming."

Char smiled. "I'll keep as quiet as I can. I'm going to check in with Rita, now that we're home. She may want to go shopping with me or something. Shall I leave a sandwich for you in the fridge?"

"No, that won't be necessary. I can fix myself something if I'm hungry for more than finger food and snacks." He got up from the counter, kissed her on the cheek, and went back into the great room.

Char put the dishes in the dishwasher and headed upstairs to the office. As she passed by, Richard was listening with headphones while following the musical score. When she got in the office, she closed the door behind her so as not to disturb him.

Sitting at the desk, she picked up the receiver and pushed a number. "Good morning, Bobbi. This is Char."

"Welcome home! I guess you got in last night, didn't you? How was it? We haven't talked since you and Richard left Salt Lake City!"

For about ten minutes, Char reviewed the events of the previous three weeks. Then she told Bobbi the real reason for the call. "Bobbi, as you know, we're taking a kind of break from the pressure of the tours. Right now, Richard is simply memorizing the Brahms concerto that he is doing in September and November. We're screening our calls because we're exhausted."

"I understand, Char."

"We're letting calls from you go through, but don't call us unless it is something really important. I'll call you periodically to update you on his progress with the Brahms."

"Okay, I'll pass the word to the others in the office, not to bother you. Would you like to hear about the *Magnificent Seven*?"

"Do you mean the classic movie?"

"No, the Magnificent Seven includes Tom Dobbins, Lou Mendez, Lori Simpson, Angel Madison, Bob Presley, Bill Jones, and Rick Stevens."

"That's our Anchorage team! Is that what they call themselves?"

"Yep. That plane that the nine of you flew to Anchorage has become their transportation ever since, and it is continuing. They have done concerts at nearly twenty military bases on their USO tour, and now their engagements for the next month as individuals have been canceled. Tomorrow, they are getting aboard an Air Force C5A that has been fitted with piston engines. They're sharing space with tons of vegetables. They'll drop off vegetables and do concerts at military bases on their way to Australia. There, the same ranchers who sponsored you and Richard are sponsoring the Magnificent Seven. As the seven leave Australia, they'll supply both produce and beef to American military bases and do concerts on their way back north. Every performance is being recorded on high-definition video. Those guys and gals are performing gratis, but they'll rake in the dough on DVDs and Blu-rays."

"Wow! That's incredible."

"You're telling me! By the way, your performances in Memphis, Omaha, and Anchorage were all recorded. As it happens, the security cameras in Anchorage are 4D, and there was a direct feed from your soundboard into the video system. The next day, your performance was uploaded via military satellite to bases all over the world. General Oswald got Sony to push disks into production. You and the other seven musicians are going to get royalties for a long time."

"This is such good news, Bobbi. I'll pass it on to Richard this evening. I have to go. I will probably call you late next week, but I can't guarantee it. Good-bye, my friend."

"Bye, Char."

She hung up and pushed another number. "Hey, Rita, this is Char."

"Hey, Char! Welcome home, neighbor! We've missed you at Bible study. I guess you must have arrived last night. We can see the glow of lights in your house."

"Yeah, it was pretty late. How's the Bible study been doing?"

"It's kind of crowded with a couple dozen people in our living room, but we make do. Our dinners have been potluck. We met last evening. Will you and Richard join us on Wednesday?"

"We could, Rita, but why don't you pass the word to everybody that it's less crowded in our basement. We'll supply the dinner. What have you got planned today?"

"Not much. With you and Richard gone, the neighborhood has been quiet except for our Bible study sessions and snow removal equipment. Why do you ask?"

"I'm thinking that you and I can have some girl time together. We can go to the mall and look at things we don't want – or at least not need – and have lunch while we're out. How about it?"

"What about Richard?"

"He's learning some music for concerts next fall. If Jim wants to come along and doesn't mind shopping with a couple of gabbing women, that's fine."

"Actually, we're babysitting a couple of nieces and a nephew, as well as our own kids."

"Well then, maybe those kids might like a change of scenery and be in the recreation area of the mall, while you and I walk around and talk. Ask Jim."

Char could hear voices in the background for a couple of minutes before Rita came back to the phone. "Jim says this sounds great. He wants to call our other neighbors in the Bible study group, and maybe make it a neighborhood mall day. Can we meet you by the entrance to Bobbo's in about an hour?"

Char looked at her watch. "That'll be perfect. I'll see you then." After she hung up, she went to the bedroom to put on some better clothes for shopping, and to do something with her hair. She grabbed the keys to their SUV.

When she reached the bottom of the stairs, Richard saw her and took off his headphones. "Are you going to meet Rita?"

Char grinned. "I think we've come up with something far better."

"What's that?"

"Instead of Jim babysitting some nieces and a nephew as well as their own kids, he's calling our other neighbors in our Bible study group. We're going to have a neighborhood mall day."

"Great! What time to we need to be there?"

"We???"

"You and I have been on the road forever. Learning this can be delayed one day with no harm. What time?"

"We're meeting there in," she looked at her watch, "about forty minutes."

"Great! I'll go change my clothes. At the mall, I'll keep the men together, while you keep the women together."

"Okay. We'll leave the kids at the recreation area. I'll call security and tell them we need some people to watch the kids."

+ + +

In Los Angeles, John Faber was in his producer's office at UBS News. He played back a recording he had made of his conversation with Richard that morning.

The producer was thoughtful. "We can use this."

John Faber was suddenly more alert. "How?"

"Talk to our copy editors. In a segment this evening, we can say something like this: 'We called Richard and Char Donovan this morning to talk to them about how President Williams' has handled the problems posed by

Mount Yellowstone and the resulting nuclear winter. They had no comment for us.'"

John shook his head. "I don't like it. It is true that they had no comment, but I was not able to get to the question."

The producer was firm. "Let's make it low-key, as a passing comment within the larger story that is impacting the upcoming election. If asked, we will have nothing further to say about the Donovans."

John Faber continued to shake his head. "I still don't like it. It's a half-truth, and it will definitely come back to bite us. I don't want any part of it."

The producer nodded. "Have it your way, John. I'll have one of our less-experienced correspondents deliver the line."

John shook his head. "You'll be sorry for this, Bob."

At noon, while Richard, Char, and their neighbors were having their neighborhood mall day, the line was delivered on the air. Less than ten minutes later, Richard's cell phone rang. "Hello?"

"Hello, Richard, this is General Oswald."

"Yes, sir. How are you?"

"I'm fine. Did you talk to John Faber from UBS this morning?"

"Yeah, he called early and wanted to pump me regarding conversations that Char and I have had with the President. I told him that we were tired because of being on the road, and that conversations with the President are confidential. When he tried to press further, I hung up."

"Okay. UBS is evidently trying to generate debate between the candidates for the upcoming Presidential election, and they're drawing you and Char into the middle of it. They're saying that when they asked you that you had no comment. I'm not even going to suggest what you should say, but if you make any public statements, I assume you'll continue to make it clear that you're not interested in political gamesmanship."

"You've got that right, sir. Char and I will pray about it and do something this evening or tomorrow morning."

"Very good. I hope you and Char and the others are having fun there at the mall."

"It's relaxing, thank you, sir." The call ended.

At lunch, while he and Char were doing their best with a couple of huge Emperor Burgers with fries, he quietly told Char. "General Oswald called a while ago. A situation is developing after that phone call from John Faber." She nodded. "UBS is saying that they called us to talk about our conversations with President Williams, and that we had no comment. They're trying to draw us into the center of political debate over actions taken during the nuclear winter."

Char nodded. We'll need to pray and maybe cast lots over this. My initial reaction is to keep our response out of the broadcast media where UBS has so much influence. Why don't we use the Internet?"

Richard nodded. "I think that's probably the way we should do it, but let's not decide now. We've still got the afternoon ahead of us with our friends." He spoke up louder. "Char and I would like to treat all of you to a movie, but our little home theater is too small for all of us. We can call the new multiplex on Ocean Avenue and try to reserve one of the theaters to ourselves. Kids, tell your parents what you want to see, and see if all of you can agree."

The parents all thought it was a great idea, and in just a couple of minutes it was clear that the kids wanted to see a new animated feature film from Disney. Richard winked at Char, and he got up and stepped aside to stand by a tree. He took out his cell phone and called security. "Hi. It's Richard. Can you secure one of the theaters in the multiplex on Ocean Avenue, so we can see the new Disney flick?"

"Just a moment." It took about three minutes. "Since this is a weekday afternoon, it's no problem, as you probably imagined. It'll be theater number six. They will show the movie just as soon as all of you are there and you wave at the projectionist."

"Thanks." He closed his phone.

He went back to the table, nodding at Char. She spoke loudly. "Okay, everyone, it's all set up. That Disney movie is staring in about ten minutes. Are you ready?"

There was an answering chorus of "Yea!"

As they started walking to their SUVs, Char took Rita aside. "Everything's all paid for. We're going to go in, and then after about ten minutes, Richard and I will leave quietly. Richard got a call earlier, before lunch. There are some things we must do. We'll see everyone at 6:00 on Wednesday at our house, okay?"

"Okay. Is it serious?"

"If we take care of it right away, I don't think it will be a problem at all. If I get a chance, I'll tell you about it on Wednesday."

"Good. You've got me curious, Char."

When they got to the theater, Richard and Char led the group like pied pipers into theater number six. It took a few minutes for the parents to get their kids to be quiet, and then Richard waved at the projectionist. Except for Rita and Jim, nobody noticed when Char and Richard left.

Until they turned north, they were silent, but as they were driving up Cherry Street towards Signal Hill, Char was emphatic. "We cannot let ourselves get dragged into the political arena."

"I agree. Have you been praying about it?"

"Ever since you told me, I've been praying silently."

"You've been the one maintaining our web page. How many followers do we have right now?"

"Just over nine million."

"Dear Lord! I had no idea!"

"I've got our page up to date until just before we left Australia. I'll summarize that trip and our arrival back home, saying 'home at last.' Then, I'll say something simple, like this: 'Throughout our marriage and our lives as musicians and prophets, we have taken great care to stay out of the political arena. We are continuing to do so. Although we have met and talked with political leaders both in our own country and elsewhere, our conversations with them have not been political. We have simply shared our lives with them, and we have asked them to keep our personal lives out of their public rhetoric. So far, every one of those leaders has honored our wishes in that respect. Anyone who indicates otherwise is a liar.' How do you like that?"

Richard grinned. "I like it. It's short and concise. I hope the story now becomes the lies told about us rather than our personal lives." He turned east, steeper up the hill, and their garage door opened as they approached. Inside, he touched a button, and the drapes for the front windows closed. "I'll get back to work. After dinner, you and I can watch a movie in our own theater, okay?"

"Okay. 6:30 for dinner?"

He nodded and went to the recliner. He studied the score for the rest of the afternoon. That evening they ate dinner in the theater and made out. A little after 11:00 they went to sleep. Richard dreamed.

"Dad, the doctor said that I was not born in Long Beach."

"That's right. You were born on a submarine."

"Why was I born on a submarine?"

"Your mother and I were trying to get home before you were born, but you were born prematurely. The captain is a friend of ours."

20.

General Oswald called the next morning, telling Char that her post on their web page had been effective. He thanked her for taking care of it.

For several days, UBS was almost universally raked over the coals, even after John Faber issued a sincere *mea culpa* on the air on behalf of the network. Their ratings plummeted, and John Faber got a new producer when his previous one was fired. In addition, after that posting on their web page, they got fewer invitations to parties in Hollywood.

It took just over a week for Richard to memorize completely the first two movements of the Brahms, but he had previously known those two movements pretty well. The last two movements were harder. It took him nearly three weeks to commit them to memory. As always, he was memorizing the orchestral parts overall, as well as his own part.

Each day, after lunch they would jam for an hour or so. When he had the Brahms fully memorized, he began working on the fingering, moving slowly. During all this time, they met with their neighbors three days a week for Bible study and dinner in the basement. Char loved doing it and looked forward to those days because Rita worked with her to plan and prepare the meals. Rita and Jim had become close friends with them, and they all knew that they could count on each other.

In August, the Air Force announced that it would be safe for commercial air travel again within a few months. Planes with modified piston engines were being seen more frequently. The November election's approach became a secondary story for about two weeks, as the airlines once again were getting planes ready for going into the sky, and airports were being prepared to re-open to full commercial traffic.

They flew to New York to begin rehearsing with the Philharmonic Orchestra to prepare for his first performance of the Brahms. He ended up performing it three times, to two sold-out evening concerts along with a nearly sold-out matinee.

Richard also recorded three solo performances for the public television stations to use when raising money from their patrons. He and Char agreed to donate half of their royalties from the audio and video disks to the city's local public television station.

They were signing autographs at the Los Angeles airport when someone asked if he was going to vote in November's election. Richard answered. "Of course, I'll vote. I vote in the privacy of the voting booth, and even my beloved wife does not know how I actually vote." He turned and winked at Char. That wink was seen all over the country and on the Internet the next day. Inside, at the airline counter, John Faber was waiting for them, but without a camera or microphone. Richard recognized him. "Hello, Mr. Faber."

"Hello, Mr. & Mrs. Donovan. I am here to make peace without cameras or microphone." Someone pointed their cell phone at them, and he said, "Please, no," but they didn't stop. Quietly, he asked, "May we talk in the lounge, far from the crowds?" Richard nodded, and John walked off, to go to the lounge while Richard and Char continued to check their luggage.

Afterward, they went to the lounge. John Faber stood up. "Thank you for meeting with me." They sat down in a conversation pit.

"You're welcome. Char and I don't carry grudges. Failing to forgive someone is like taking poison and waiting for the other person to die."

John was thoughtful and nodded. "I like that. I may use it sometime. ... First, whether you believe me or not, I was against that tactic that my UBS producer used. I told him it would come back to bite him, and it did. He was fired, thank God."

Char nodded. "You're a brilliant and honest journalist, Mr. Faber. I'm not surprised that you were against it."

"No one knows it except my wife, but I'll be leaving UBS soon, and next spring I'll be with another network. Meanwhile, my wife and I are going to take a second honeymoon. We've been married nearly twenty-five years."

Richard smiled. "Congratulations. When you make the change, will you be remaining in New York?"

"No. I'll continue to do network broadcasting, but from Los Angeles. I know you live out there. I don't want to do a formal interview of you two at this point, but maybe next spring, my wife and I can take you two to dinner."

Char smiled. "You've already talked to our manager, Bobbi, before you called us that fateful morning. If you still want to get together for dinner next spring, let Bobbi know. I'll tell her that we'll try to work it in."

"Thank you." He stood up. "I'll be going, and the two of you need to get your flight. Thanks again."

Richard nodded. "God bless you."

"Thanks, yet again." He walked off.

While they were in the air, a cell phone video of them talking with John Faber went viral, but it was without sound. Many assumed that John Faber had not learned his lesson and was trying to get an interview. As far as Char and Richard were concerned, it didn't matter. That incident was settled.

As the final days of the political campaigns heated up, President Williams did not talk about Richard and Char. The candidates mentioned prophecies, but did not use the names of the "Signal Hill prophets." Late in October, General Oswald called just before they were going to sleep on a Friday night. Richard answered. "Hello?"

"Richard, this is General Osmond."

"Good evening, General. What's up?"

"Did you know that President Williams and the First Lady have a ranch near Gorman, California?"

"Yes. I understand that they have built a rather large home there."

"Yes. The First Lady wants the two of you to be their guests for a visit at their ranch next spring. She likes both of you, and so does the President. There will be no pressure for either of you to perform. Bobbi tells me that you are scheduled to lead a praise team for an Easter service at Staples Center in Los Angeles. The President and First Lady would like you to be their guests for the week following. Is that idea agreeable, if Bobbi can arrange it?"

"General, Char and I pray over just about everything, particularly important things. We'll call you with our answer for the First Lady tomorrow morning."

"That'll be fine." The connection ended.

Richard slid over and put his arm around Char's shoulders. "The President and First Lady will go out of office in January, and they would like us to spend a week with them at their ranch near Gorman for the week after Easter, if Bobbi can fit it into our schedule. We're at the Staples Center for Easter Sunday, if we decide to accept their invitation. That is the first I've heard about the Easter event."

Char snuggled up to him. "Me too. It's so far in the future, Bobbi evidently knows about it, but we didn't until now. We'd better worship and then get some sleep."

"Right."

Saturday morning, after calling General Oswald to confirm their stay at the Williams ranch, Char posted a notice on their web page.

> For those of you who follow our web page for news regarding the nuclear winter, here's what we know at this point. In the Southern Hemisphere, the nuclear winter clouds will begin to disburse in January south of the Tropic of Capricorn. By the fourth week of March, the clouds will begin disbursing closer to the equator. By mid-June, all weather patterns will appear nearly normal except North of the Tropic of Cancer, but heavy rain and flooding will continue through September in the Northern Hemisphere. By the seventh anniversary of Mount Yellowstone, there will be no further measurable evidence of its ash in our atmosphere. Praise God!

After dinner, Char called their answering service and put it on the speakerphone in the kitchen. "Hi, Cindy, I would imagine we've got a few messages."

Cindy laughed. "You've got hundreds. All of them are regarding what you posted on your web page this morning."

Richard was smiling. "Cindy, can you email them to us?"

"Sure! It's just a couple of keystrokes. ... There! It's in your inbox. Good luck!"

"Thanks, Cindy." The connection ended. Char was also smiling. "We both know that this is generating controversy without looking at the news or going to the Internet."

He nodded. "Tomorrow morning our street will be packed with media vehicles." He thought for a moment. "Admiral Schultz is now on Terminal Island. We met him in Anchorage, remember?"

Char grinned. "If he's willing, he can interview us on Armed Forces Television, and other media can pick it up. He'll have to get permission from the General, but that should not be a problem. Then we'll call the police on the non-emergency number to tell them what we're going to do, so they can control traffic tomorrow."

Richard nodded. "That's a plan. Let's pray about it first."

+ + +

At 0630 hours, a Naval Police vehicle pulled into their driveway, as Signal Hill and Long Beach police controlled the crowd of media people. They drove quickly to Terminal Island. Once their vehicle was inside the main gate, the media had to wait outside the base.

In the lounge of the Officers' Club, the Admiral discussed everything with them conversationally, but not as a formal interview. It lasted just over forty-five minutes. At the close, Richard and Char made it clear that they would not be talking to anyone in the media about it. They acknowledged that this decision would not sit well with the fifth estate. They also acknowledged that Internet bloggers would probably not be kind in their criticisms. They explained that they were discussing it at a military installation because they wanted to avoid any political implications due to the closeness of the election.

Back at their home on Signal Hill, Char set up an informal survey on their web page, simply asking how many people were willing to wait until the clouds disbursed before passing judgment. The response the day after was ninety-four percent supportive.

That evening, Char and Richard prepared a video for their web page. They simply talked to each other and to the camera. For a little over thirty minutes, they talked about things that they had not discussed with the Admiral. Then Richard looked at the camera. "Friends, Char and I are entertainers. We are also open about the fact that we are unashamedly Christians. We have done and said things that have attracted the attention of people associated with politics. We are *not*, however, political activists. We do not seek publicity."

Char nodded. "We are not interested in partisan politics, but there are those who have tried to use what we say for political gain or profit. That is both their responsibility and their risk. God will deal with them as He chooses." The posted the video, and then they stayed in the house and out of sight.

Except for their neighbors coming for Bible study, Char and Richard remained alone in their house until Election Day. Gradually, people in the media went on to other stories. They kept their sheer curtains closed throughout the house, even when their drapes were open.

Then came Election Day. They got into their SUV in the garage. Richard backed out, and a few media reporters scrambled for their vehicles as the young couple went down the hill to vote. In their polling place, they were friendly with everyone inside because all were neighbors. As they left after voting, some reporters tried to approach, but a few neighbors ran interference. They got back to their SUV without having to ask any probing questions. As they drove away, they praised God.

The next morning, an SUV picked them up. Char recognized their driver. "Good morning, Malcolm. Has your wife recovered from her surgery?"

"Yes, thank you, Carol is at home and almost back to normal. The doctor says they got it all, but she'll do some chemo just to be sure. Thank you for praying for us and with us these past few months."

They rode the rest of the way to the L.A. Airport in silence. At the terminal, a few reporters tried to get close, but the military security was as good as usual. Their five and a half hour flight was turbulent, but they arrived on time. In Philadelphia, a shuttle from the Rittenhouse Hotel quickly got them to their hotel, and into their complimentary room. After lunch, they went to the Kimmel Center so that Richard could see the piano and try it out.

Neither Richard nor Char had requested it, but sitting on the center of the stage was a Bösendorfer Imperial. Richard smiled and hugged Char. "All that God does, God does well!"

After playing a few chords and running a chromatic scale, Richard stopped. "Excellent!" He launched into the Bach-Busoni fantasy. As he played, the conductor for the Philadelphia quietly approached from behind Richard. At the end, he applauded. Startled, Richard turned around. "Herr Schmitt! I did not hear you come on stage. It is good to see you!"

He beamed. "It is good to see you as well." He nodded towards the piano. "It is my hope, if you do an encore after we do the Brahms, you will do that Bach-Busoni fantasy to take advantage of the instrument."

Richard shook his head. "I don't plan on doing an encore. What time do you wish to have me here tomorrow?"

"0900 will be sufficient. After we break for lunch, the orchestra will be rehearsing Tchaikovsky's *Sixth Symphony*, which opens the program. I do have a request for you, which you may refuse with no hard feelings."

"What is it?"

"My first violinist was in Omaha when you played Chopin's *Scherzo #2*. Several in this orchestra have purchased recordings of your performances. They have asked me to prevail upon you to perform the Chopin. If you do it, I would program it after the Tchaikovsky and before the intermission."

Richard closed his eyes and tipped his head back for about thirty seconds. "Okay. I will do it. I will need to sit down and rest during the intermission. The Brahms is very demanding of a pianist's strength, as is the Chopin."

"I understand."

"We will go back to our hotel." They all left. Char and Richard enjoyed a relaxing evening at the hotel. After their evening worship, they slept soundly but dreamed.

In a shared dream, brilliant light surrounded them, and a thunderous voice penetrated their sleep.

"I am the LORD, your God. Be in Cheyenne when seven years of winter have passed. The clouds will part for a short time over Mount Yellowstone at mid-day. Make an image of yourselves with the mountain seen behind you and put it on your web page. I am the LORD. I promise. I deliver. I am using you for my name's sake, and I am faithful."

21.

When Char and Richard awakened in the morning, they talked and realized that they had both had the same prophetic dream. After breakfast, as Richard practiced, Char called Bobbi. "Good morning, Bobbi."

"Good morning Char. I wasn't expecting you to call until next Monday."

"Right. Richard and I need to have you make arrangements for us to be in Cheyenne, Wyoming, on the volcano's seventh anniversary, and we need the hotel room to be one that faces northwest, on a floor that is as high as possible."

"May I ask why?"

"You will know why, at least partly, after the anniversary."

"Okay. ... "I'm making notes. Have you gotten an invitation to perform?"

"No. You can set up something if you want to, but we need the anniversary day to be free in Cheyenne. The evening would be okay, but we would rather not."

"I've got it. You're asking me to set this up, the better part of a year in advance. Do you want me to schedule anything else between now and then?"

"Bobbi, between now and then, things will be business as usual. We trust you to do whatever you think is best. I'll call you next Monday to check in."

"Okay. Bye!"

Hanging up, Char picked up her laptop and took it to a comfortable overstuffed chair. Opening it, she launched her web browser and started shopping. After downloading some scores that she and Richard had talked about, she paused, thoughtful. She put her computer in hibernation and closed the lid. Taking out her cell phone, she called her close friend and neighbor. "Good morning, Rita."

"Hey, Char, how's it going?"

"So far, so good, my friend, I just did some music shopping, and now I need some advice."

"Shoot."

"I know that you and Jim share photography as a hobby, and you shoot both stills and videos."

"Right! We met at a camera club two years before we got married, while we were still in high school. We graduated eight years before you and Richard did, I think."

"Right. I'm still using the camera that my Dad gave me for Christmas before I graduated. I think I want something that will shoot both video and stills, like your camera. It looks like it's compact and pretty light, but I noticed that you had a weird-looking device on top of it when you shot video of your kids one day. What was that, Rita?"

"That was a super-directional microphone or 'shotgun mike.' The built-in mike is good when we're backpacking and there's not a lot of noise around, but I use that directional mike a lot."

"Is it easy to switch back and forth between making videos and stills?"

"It's simple, Char. I have mine programmed so that if I'm shooting a video, and I press the shutter release, it stops the video and takes a picture. When I push the video button, it resumes shooting video. I can even do it with my wireless remote, when I have it on a tripod."

"I don't have a tripod, Rita."

"If you're going to get serious about photography, Char, you'll need a good tripod and a remote release."

"Where did you get yours?"

"I order most of my stuff online because the nearest camera store suitable for serious amateurs and professionals is on the North side of Los Angeles. I only go to them when I want to try out a new camera body or a different kind of equipment. If you and Richard want to come over and join Jim and me for lunch, we can do Internet shopping. It's Jim's day off."

"Great! Richard likes to get out of the house once in a while for lunch."

"Good. Come on over about noon. I'll see you later."

"Okay, bye, Rita." As Char put her cell phone away, the phone on the desk rang. She quickly got up and went back to the desk. "Hello?" She sat down.

"Good morning again, Char."

"Bobbi! What's up?"

"I just got off the phone with tourism's head honcho in the city of Brasilia."

"That's the capital of Brazil, isn't it?"

"Exactly. She wants you and Richard to do a concert and jamming tour next spring in Southeastern Brazil. I know that you and Richard have wanted to do some work in South America, but I also know that you'll have to pray about it. I hope you can give me your answer in your call this coming Monday."

"What about the Easter service and the visit to the Williams ranch, Bobbi?"

"There's no conflict. Easter is the last weekend in March next year, and you wouldn't leave for Brazil until late April. The tour will last at least two weeks, but not more than a month."

"Okay. Richard and I will discuss it. Is anything else coming up?"

"I have Richard blocked out in June in a recording studio to make a two-disk set of CDs. Moreover, I'm putting a Northern Europe tour together for the late summer, but I've got your Cheyenne thing locked in, so there's no interference. The following summer you have tentative dates set up for Scandinavia, with the possible addition of Moscow and St. Petersburg."

Char smiled. "It sounds like we're getting a steady stream of bookings."

Bobbi laughed. "Are you kidding? Ever since those CDs from Tokyo became available here, the two of you are being touted as prodigies. That means you can work as much or as little as you want to."

"Are you building in vacation breaks?"

"Of course! I don't want burn outs!"

"There's one more thing to keep in mind, Bobbi."

"What's that?"

"After Cheyenne, Richard and I are planning to start a family."

"Really! I've wondered about that."

"Richard says that whenever I'm pregnant, he does not want any concert obligations for three to four months either side of our due date."

"That's six to eight months!"

"Your math is as good as mine."

"So, when you get pregnant, some of the things on your schedule will have to be postponed."

"That's absolutely true. Anything else?"

"There's nothing firm, so far. I'll talk to you Monday."

"Bye, Bobbi." Char looked at her watch, and then she started filling in the dates on her calendar that Bobbi had given her. With time left over before lunch, she printed out the music manuscripts that she had downloaded earlier.

With most of the morning gone, she headed downstairs. For a while, she stood in the doorway, just listening to Richard's practicing.

Finally, he looked up. "Is it time for lunch already?"

Char smiled, walked over to stand next to him, and kissed his cheek. "Not quite yet, but we're going over to Rita and Jim's for lunch. We should probably change clothes before we go." He stood up, and as they went up stairs, she continued. "I'll tell you all about a couple of conversations I've had with Bobbi this morning while we're eating lunch. I think Jim and Rita may like to hear it too. It will make for a little longer lunch, but we're not pressed for time, are we?"

"Nope."

As they ate soup, salad, and sandwiches with Rita and Jim, it turned out they were very interested in the latest developments. As Richard and Jim started talking about their possibly going together on the tour to South America, Char went with Rita to their den to look at their camera equipment. Char found a web site on Rita's computer where she could order what she and Richard needed. She sent an email to herself with her shopping list.

By the time Richard and Char got back from lunch it was mid-afternoon. They decided to have dinner a little later, and Richard returned to practicing.

+ + +

The headlines on New Year's Eve revolved around the mix of scattered sunshine and thundershowers in the Southern Hemisphere. As the southern half of the world was celebrating their first real summer in seven years, the Northern Half of the Earth had heavy snows and rain. Winter seemed to pass quickly for Char and Richard as they prepared both for Easter and for their journey to South America.

Richard and Char rehearsed new praise music for the Easter worship service at Staples Center. They emailed copies of the music to all the other musicians who would be there that day, and they also emailed them recordings of the music that they played on the two pianos in their great room as previews of what they would be doing. Jim and Rita decided that he could not take so much time off his job to go with their neighbors to South America. They put it off to go on a future tour.

The day before Easter, all the musicians for the Easter worship service met at Staples Center. Richard sat on the bench of a Yamaha digital piano and began the rehearsal. "Let's get started. I know everyone has had the music since January, but doing it is bound to be different. The service will start with a three-minute video, and next we will launch into the first set. Reginald Curry, the Secretary of the Interior that managed so much of our country's response to the nuclear winter, will offer a prayer. We'll do the second set of music, and then there'll be the sermon by Archbishop Gonzales. We will all be seated while he is speaking. As he begins his closing prayer, we will resume our places on stage for the final song. Are there any questions?"

He looked around because he and Char were on the center of the stage with the singers, while the other instrumentalists were on both stage left and stage right. "Okay. Let's go straight through once, only stopping if we have to." They made three false starts due to sound system difficulties, but then they succeeded in going straight through. For three hours, they went back over each song, taking care of the rough edges."

Since they were already packed for their week at the Williams ranch, Richard and Char spent the night at a Four Seasons Hotel that was close by. Sunday morning, when the video was supposed to begin, nothing happened. On his headset, Richard was told that there was a glitch. Richard muted his mike and called out in a stage whisper, "The video has a problem. Does anyone know, 'I Walked Today Where Jesus Walked' well enough to do it from memory?"

One of the men waved. "I can do it. How about the key of C?"

Richard nodded. He started a Bach prelude for several measures, and then he nodded again. As the song began, the rest of the musicians almost immediately knew what was happening and what Richard was doing. Char came in with orchestral strings on the electronic keyboard at the beginning of the second phrase. As the singer got to the end of the first verse, he nodded to the woman who played the clarinet, and she repeated the melody that the singer had done thus far. The singer sang another verse, and Richard worked in variations of the Bach, while Char picked up on it with the strings. Just before the final section of the song, the trumpeter did a blues variation. As the song ended, Richard did a variation of the Bach as a tag line.

They paused for about ten seconds, and then Richard looked at the drummer, and on his mike, Richard said, "He is risen!" He pointed at the drummer. "Go!" Not half way through the first song of the set, eighteen thousand people were standing and singing, following the words of the praise music on giant displays.

By the end of Easter's worship, both Char and Richard were exhausted by happy. Later, over Easter dinner with Everett and Jane Williams, Richard and Char learned that the former president and his family had watched the entire morning on a satellite hookup. A high-definition recording had been made, and when they went back to Signal Hill a week afterward, Richard and Char had a Blu-ray disk of the event.

Fully rested, Richard and Char left for South America four days later. Both were amazed at how different it was from the train tours they had taken since they had gotten married. When they got there, two portable full-size Yamaha keyboards were loaned to them for practicing, for the duration of their time down there. The pace was slow and laid back. Built into their schedule was time for being tourists, and they always had both an escort to smooth their way and a translator. Char made videos and took pictures as they went along.

At the end of their first day, Char mentioned that they would worship before they went to sleep. Their escort modified their schedule, so that the two of them had at least thirty additional minutes at the close of each day for worship, while still getting enough sleep.

It was a valuable lesson, and Char made sure that Bobbi knew all the details. Richard, as well as Char, hoped that, in the future, there would not be as much pressure on them as there had been while they were on their honeymoon.

Bobbi arranged for a sound crew to come to their home on Signal Hill to record music that had been written or arranged for the Bösendorfer Imperial. Since the house was not soundproof, they recorded at night for an entire night. The recording company would release the CD in time for Christmas.

+ + +

They need not have worried about pressure on second their European tour. In Great Britain, France, and Italy, they stayed at the same hotels and were treated like long-lost relatives. Richard and Char were no longer unknown and new. Robin and her husband met with them in Rome, and they gave them a tour of the vineyard owned by the family for generations. Robin's husband, Sal, was a gracious host.

People throughout the European musical community treated them with great courtesy and respect. The media were not necessarily so kind, writing articles about their "questionable" Christian faith, which was not popular or respected. That did not seem to matter when it came to their music. As they played in Germany for the first time, they found themselves making a number of new friends. They found the same to be true in Austria and Poland.

They flew home from Amsterdam. Richard and Char found themselves returning to Signal Hill for just five days, before going to Cheyenne. Rita and Jim went with them to Wyoming, and they had adjoining suites in the Little America Hotel and Resort. The four of them planned the anniversary pictures and video very carefully.

The anniversary of Mount Yellowstone began with torrential rain, and with lightning and thunder. They had breakfast together in Jim and Rita's room. Jim glanced outside. "I'm glad you two are certain about getting pictures and video at noon, because the forecast is for nasty."

Richard nodded and smiled. "We have learned to trust the Lord with everything, no matter what."

Char nodded. "I think that everyone can feel the quakes. A swarm of quakes began three days ago, and many people are leaving the area because of what happened seven years ago."

Bright lightning flashed nearby, and all four of them cringed simultaneously with the clap of thunder that shook the room. Rita shook her head. "I can never get used to lightning and thunder. Your house's roof is higher than ours, so I figure if lightning is going to strike on Signal Hill, your house will get hit before ours."

Char laughed. "So far, God has delivered us from that danger, thank the Lord. Thanks for saying that, Rita, because now I'll think about what you just said every time we have a thunderstorm."

Richard stood up. "Let's leave the dishes to room service and start setting up. Jim, I think that the first thing we need to do is move the dresser, so that we can set up the tripods next to the wall."

All of them walked through the connecting door. Char pointed. "Rita, let's put our hoods up and move the balcony furniture to that side." She pointed. "Then the cameras will have a clear shot without too much furniture in view from across the room."

Rita nodded. "We want the lens zoomed to moderate telephoto and stopped down so that everything will be in focus from you on the balcony to the mountain we can't yet see in the distance. That'll also make for a clear path for you and Richard to get in and out off the balcony when it is time."

It took most of the morning to get things set up exactly as they wanted it. It was 11:45, and they all sat on a space on the bed that was out of their work area. At 11:50, the lightning and thunder stopped. At 11:55, the rain suddenly stopped. Richard and Char stepped out onto the balcony, and they stood next to the rail with their backs towards the northwest, where the mountain should be. The ground became quiet, without the slightest tremor. Jim and Rita double checked the aim of each camera.

Looking at his watch, at 11:58, Richard spoke. "Okay, go video."

Char smiled. "Hello friends, we are standing on a hotel balcony in Cheyenne, Wyoming, because Richard and I shared a dream one night several months ago, when God spoke to us in that dream."

Richard nodded. "In a moment, according to the dream, the clouds behind us will part for forty seconds, and Mount Yellowstone will be bathed in sunlight. Then the clouds will close again for a week."

Char looked at her watch, and then at Richard. "Okay, my love, let's turn and look." As they turned, Char glanced down at the parking lot to see other hotel guests gathered there, and then she joined Richard in seeing the mountain.

Faithfully, as God had promised, the clouds in the distance parted, and bright sunshine washed over twenty-one thousand four hundred-foot Mount Yellowstone. Then they turned back to the cameras.

Char smiled. "See! God is faithful. All that God does, God does well." The clouds closed. "Last evening, we told people in this hotel that the mountain would appear at noon. Hundreds left the lobby to see what we saw just now. We hope that this video, as well as the pictures that have been taken, will renew and refresh the faith of Christians all over. We also hope that some people will invite Jesus into their hearts for the first time."

Richard nodded. "God bless us all!"

The cameras were turned off, and Jim and Rita cheered. "Praise God!"

Rita went over to the cameras. "We were taking five frames per second on the still camera, so you'll have plenty to choose from to find one for your web page that looks good for the mountain, as well as for both of you."

Char nodded. "Let's look at the stills."

The two women quickly played the stills and video on the flat-screen television in their room, while Richard and Jim moved the furniture back in place. Char saved them all to the hard disk on her laptop. "Richard, come look. Tell me which one you want to use." She scrolled through dozens of stills that clearly showed the two of them with the mountain unmistakably seen in the background.

Richard nodded. "Let's go through them again, more slowly this time." After a few seconds, he pointed. "There! See how the mountain glistens. Both of us look good too. Our eyes are open for both of us."

For their web page, the headline read, "A Picture Can Be Worth a Million Words." Char gave the story a subtitle. "Praise God! This is an unaltered picture." The high-definition video was positioned just below the picture. It took several minutes to upload all of it to their web page.

The four of them quickly packed up all of their belongings and went downstairs. The manager met Richard at the front desk. "Mr. Donovan, both rooms are complimentary. You have provided us with great publicity for the future."

"Thank you. Can your shuttle take us to the airport right away?"

"Certainly, Mr. Donovan."

As it turned out, Char did not need the second half of the subtitle. People in the parking lot took cell phone videos and stills, and the picture picked out by Char and Richard went viral on the Internet. It went to the front page of newspapers, and a frequent headline read, "God Promised; God Delivered." The video also went viral, and it was the lead story in newscasts."

+ + +

Jim and Rita went back to Signal Hill. When journalists asked them where Richard and Char were, they said they honestly didn't know. They did an interview regarding their part of the trip to Cheyenne.

Richard and Char disappeared. There were rumors of course. Supposedly they had been seen in several different places. No one had any pictures or videos to back up those rumors, however, because they took care to remain hidden. They talked with Bobbi and General Oswald every week, but they stayed out of sight. For weeks, when their pastor was asked where they were, his simple statement was always the same. "They are taking a much-delayed vacation."

On December 23, Rita and Jim called all the Bible study neighbors. They told them that Richard had sent them a key to their front door, so that the group could have a Christmas Eve Bible study and party. They also told them that they were decorating the house for Christmas that day using money Richard had sent them, and that they were welcome to help.

With nearly fifty people working, the house was decorated inside and out within a few hours. When a television crew showed up to ask about what was going on, Rita told them that Richard and Char had invited them to use their house for a Christmas party.

On Christmas Eve, there were no cars on the streets at the top of Signal Hill. All the snow had melted. A hot Santa Ana wind was blowing in from the desert, making it a warm December evening for the first time since the nuclear winter had finally ended. Some went to the beach to celebrate Christmas Eve.

A van from the Long Beach Airport dropped off Richard's parents, Debby and Bob, at a little after five. Char's parents, Joseph and Marie, arrived a few minutes later. Shortly thereafter, Richard's older brother, Josh, arrived with his fiancé in the same van as Char's older sister, her husband, James, and their kids. Rita and Jim fixed dinner for Char & Richard's relatives, and the neighbors began walking up the street and into the house at a little after seven. The media, seeing no news to report, all left.

Everyone went to the basement, which had been decorated as much as the rest of the house. All of them talked about how they hoped that Richard and Char were doing well. The kids were given some snacks, and Christmas programming was started at the far end of the basement on a flat-screen television on the wall. Everything was warm and festive.

At seven thirty, everyone suddenly got quiet. They could hear music coming from upstairs. Jim called out in a stage whisper. "Everybody be quiet and listen!"

Some of the kids giggled. Rita put her finger to her lips. "Shhhhhh!" Quietly, they gathered at the end of the basement near the stairs, and they listened. Rita and Jim started up the stairs, and everyone else followed. As they came into the great room, the curtains were still closed. Char was playing orchestral strings on the Yamaha, and Richard was playing the Bösendorfer.

Rita began passing around little booklets of Christmas carols and other holiday songs. Jim put his hand on Richard's shoulder as he played "Silent Night," and Rita gave Char a hug while she was playing.

After singing several carols, they stopped. Char smiled. "Merry Christmas, everyone!"

Everyone responded with the same.

Char looked across the pianos. "Come and sit beside me here, Richard."

He got up, sat down beside on the bench, and kissed her. "Merry Christmas, again!"

Char grinned. "I have an announcement for you and for everyone here. Merry Christmas, Richard. You're going to be a father in about seven months."

He grinned. "This definitely will be a Christmas to remember!"